THE
DAY
SHE
DIED

THE
DAY
SHE
DIED

S.M. FREEDMAN

DUNDURN
PRESS

Publisher: Scott Fraser | Acquiring Editor: Rachel Spence | Editor: Shannon Whibbs
Cover designer: Laura Boyle
Cover image: Composite image: rain: istock.com/1001slide Landscape: shutterstock.com/OksanaGoskova
Printer: Marquis Book Printing Inc.

Library and Archives Canada Cataloguing in Publication

Title: The day she died / S.M. Freedman.
Names: Freedman, S. M., author.
Identifiers: Canadiana (print) 20200319655 | Canadiana (ebook) 20200319671 | ISBN 9781459747401 (softcover) | ISBN 9781459747418 (PDF) | ISBN 9781459747425 (EPUB)
Classification: LCC PS8611.R4355 D39 2021 | DDC C813/.6—dc23

We acknowledge the support of the Canada Council for the Arts and the Ontario Arts Council for our publishing program. We also acknowledge the financial support of the Government of Ontario, through the Ontario Book Publishing Tax Credit and Ontario Creates, and the Government of Canada.

Care has been taken to trace the ownership of copyright material used in this book. The author and the publisher welcome any information enabling them to rectify any references or credits in subsequent editions.

The publisher is not responsible for websites or their content unless they are owned by the publisher.

Printed and bound in Canada.

Dundurn Press
1382 Queen Street East
Toronto, Ontario, Canada M4L 1C9
dundurn.com, @dundurnpress

For Hannah
Who walks beside me from afar

Everything you can imagine is real.
— Pablo Picasso

ONE

EVE GOLD WASN'T SURPRISED to die on her twenty-seven birthday. The Angel of Death's greasy fingers had been pressing against her spine for ten years — maybe longer — and in the underground of her mind where truth squirmed away from the light, she knew that it was just a matter of time before press turned to shove. No, death wasn't much of a shock. The real surprise was everything that followed.

She left the gallery early, hoping to get home before the storm hit. Six of her paintings about life on Vancouver's Downtown Eastside were set to debut the next day, as part of *The Other Side* exhibit. After years spent hiding behind her role as an event coordinator, her artistic debut was causing Eve heartburn and night sweats. Her birthday was a perfect excuse to leave work early.

The rain hit as she left the bakery, and it meant business. It pummelled her blind and deaf, and by the time she ducked under the Starbucks awning to wait for the southbound bus, she was soaked to the skin. Her feet squished inside her boots and her hair dripped into her eyes. Even worse, the cake box sagged from her fingers by a twist of string, waterlogged and threatening collapse. Button would be ticked.

Over the years, her grandmother had worked hard to perfect, and then weaponize, THE LOOK. Her lips would pull downward and her eyes would deepen into pits of sorrow. THE LOOK could penetrate Eve's walls like nothing else, and there was nothing else needed to keep her in line.

Which was why she still lived at home, why she had no social life, and why she kept up the illusion that all was well. That *she* was well. On every one of her birthdays, she'd sit next to her grandmother, choking back coconut cake and watching *The Golden Girls* on their flat-screen TV, smiling and laughing and pretending she was glad she'd been born. She did it for Button, who cried less often but still roamed the house at night in search of some lost object she would never find. Wherever Donna had gone, she wasn't stashed behind the linens in the sideboard.

Lightning cracked, and across the street the courthouse's glass atrium mirrored the blinding flash. Her mother had died in that building, and Eve wondered if Donna still haunted those darkened courtrooms, unable to sleep until justice had been served.

Shaking off a fresh surge of apprehension, she turned away from the damp wind whipping around the corner. She pulled her scarf over her nose and mouth and breathed deeply of the woollen fabric, hoping to mask the acrid smell of coffee. The scarf still held the clean scent of her moisturizer, which didn't remind her of her mother in any way.

From the corner of her eye, she watched a man step through the sheets of rain pouring from the awning. He wore a long overcoat and fedora. His shoes were square-toed and highly polished. He paused at the door to the coffee shop, turning to her with a friendly smile.

"Eve?"

He looked familiar, and her first thought was that he was one of the art gallery's trustees. She could never keep them straight. Hector had once made her a chart of all the old farts she shouldn't offend. He'd typed their names under their pictures in a screaming red font, as though trying to burn the information into her brain. It hadn't worked.

The man cocked his head to the side, as though waiting for her to recognize him.

"You look just like your mom. Like Button, too."

Was he one of Donna's old colleagues? But no, he knew her grandmother, as well. Seconds stacked up, and Eve was still drawing a blank.

"I'm sorry, where do I know you from?"

His smile widened to reveal stained teeth and pale gums. "Just take my hand. I'll stay with you."

She stepped back, pressing against the glass display window. It felt cold and slick against her back, even through the fabric of her coat.

He moved closer, reached for her hand. His ring finger was gone from knuckle to tip, which sparked a jolt of recognition she didn't have time to process. His eyes were the colour of dark amber. She wondered if they'd spark

3

in the sunlight, like hers did. Donna used to say she had eyes like fool's gold.

"Take my hand," he said with more urgency.

"No," she wanted to say, but never got the chance.

Tires screeched, followed by a loud popping noise. Her body lifted from the ground and slammed through the display window, which exploded in a spray of glass sharp enough to pierce even her lie-toughened skin.

Eve flew over people and chairs and tables like a broken missile. The cake box soared from her grip. People scattered for cover. A Rorschach of blood droplets splattered the glass display case. She was above it all, seeing everything but comprehending nothing. She smelled bitter coffee and sweet coconut, tasted the salt of her own blood — all reminders of who she was and the things she'd done.

She slammed to the floor and the air whooshed from her lungs. Her eyes fixed on a brown stain on the ceiling, where a teardrop of water formed. It grew fat-fatter-fattest, wobbled with anticipation, and dropped. It splashed into her right eye and slid toward her temple.

Strangers surrounded her, spoke words she couldn't understand. They had worried faces and sad faces, moon faces and balloon faces.

"It's okay," she tried to say. "I'm not hurt."

To her left, a woman screamed. It was like an electric shock that jolted Eve's body to life. She tried to look, and the bones in her neck ground together with a protesting creak. Her head felt soft on that side. Mushy.

The front end of a silver Lexus wedged through the Starbucks window like a ship run aground. The hood was crumpled, dripping, one headlight smashed. And of course it was silver. Silver like moonlight on a pond, or secrets kept.

"Take my hand now. It's time. Let me help you." The old man bent toward her. He'd lost his fedora and his hair was a gossamer cloud around his head.

She opened her mouth and felt a gush of something hot and wet spill over her lips. She remembered the trail of vomit on Donna's cheek, and the dead man in the forest, and how quiet the river had seemed once the screaming stopped.

"Take my hand."

At the touch of his fingers, the top of her skull popped open. The inside of her head became a wind tunnel spiralling toward a blinding, horrifying white light.

Like the last pea in a can, she shook loose from the centre of her brain, spun in nauseating circles, and was sucked up into the whirlwind. She whipped to the opening, toward light that screamed — and somewhere beyond, she felt certain she would find her reckoning. No way was she ready for that.

She skidded along the curved bone of her skull, moving faster and faster. Desperate to burrow back into herself, she kicked backward and dug into the meat of her. She slowed to a stop and the light flickered and went out. A tidal wave of pain slammed her back and down, flooding her with inky silence. Like a spider swept toward the bathtub drain, all she could do was curl into a ball and hang on. When she tried to scream, her mouth filled with salt water. Or maybe it was blood.

TWO

Eve's Sixth Birthday

"IT'S A DOLL!" Sara said before Eve had even finished tearing off the pink wrapping paper. Her new friend bounced on the couch, full of cake and soda.

"Do you like it? I wanted to get you an American Girl doll, but Mom said we couldn't spend that much money so we got you a cheap knock-off instead."

"Sara!" Mrs. Adler said.

"What's a knock-off?" Eve asked. "Is that like when you play Scat?"

The adults laughed and she felt her face grow hot. "You know, like how you have to knock when you get thirty-one?"

"It's not like that." Mr. Adler's voice was kind. "It means that your doll isn't actually an American Girl doll."

"Oh. I like her, anyway. She's got curly hair like me."

"I knew you'd like her! Wanna play dolls? I'll go get Fiona." Sara jumped up and ran from the room.

Donna leaned forward. "What do you say to the Adlers?"

"Thank you," she said, trying to free her doll from the box.

"Leigh!" Mrs. Adler said. "Bring the scissors from the kitchen, would you?"

"It's so kind of you to have us over like this." Button placed her empty cake plate on top of the pile of boxes they used as a coffee table. "And that was delicious. I hope you didn't go to too much trouble."

"It's just a mix." Mrs. Adler waved a long-fingered hand in dismissal.

"Well, it's a treat. And I think the girls are getting along nicely."

"Yes," Mrs. Adler said. "We were worried Sara would have trouble making friends. New school, new neighbourhood. She can be shy, so it's been a hard transition for her."

"For all of them," Mr. Adler said.

"I can't find them!" a boy shouted from the back of the house.

"Check the junk drawer!" Mrs. Adler turned to Button and Donna. "Moving is the worst, isn't it? On Sara's first day at the new school, Eve ran right over and invited her to play."

"How nice," Button said.

"They're not here!" the boy shouted.

"Oh for heaven's sake. Dear, would you mind?"

Dutifully, Mr. Adler got up and left the room.

"Sara was so thrilled to make a friend so quickly."

"Eve usually isn't very good at making friends," Donna said. "She's so awkward."

Eve's head snapped up from the box she was having no luck opening in time to see Mrs. Adler's eyelids flutter.

"She's just choosy," Button said quickly. "Some of the girls in their class aren't very kind."

"How do you know? She's never invited anyone over for us to meet."

"I know because I listen to your daughter," Button said.

"And you believe everything she says."

"Du fangst shoyn on?" Button said in Yiddish, and Donna's jaw tightened. Turning to Mrs. Adler, Button asked, "How many children do you have?"

Mrs. Adler let out a breath. "We have three girls — Sara's the youngest, Margie is eight, and Danielle is ten — and one boy, Leigh, who's eleven."

"You certainly have your hands full," Donna said.

"Yes." Mrs. Adler turned in her seat. "Have you found those scissors yet, dear?"

"Here, Mom," a boy said, loping into the room. "Catch!" He pretended to throw and grinned when the adults ducked. "Just kidding."

"Leigh!" Mrs. Adler barked, clutching her chest. "That's not funny."

The boy looked down at his feet. "Sorry, Mom."

"I thought it was funny," Eve said, feeling bad for him. Being yelled at in front of strangers was no fun, she knew.

Turning toward her, he smiled. "You must be Sara's new friend."

"Yeah."

"Yes," Donna said.

"Happy birthday." He sat on the carpet beside her, turning his back on the adults in a way that made them seem suddenly less there. He tucked his long legs to the side and hunched down so he was on her level. "Do you want some help with that?"

She handed him the box and watched as he cut her doll free. He had to keep pushing his hair out of his eyes and his arms were long and skinny, his knuckles covered in healing scrapes.

Handing her the doll, he asked, "What are you going to name her?"

"I don't know." Eve rubbed a finger over the doll's hair. It felt coarse, and she touched her own curls for comparison. She was glad her hair felt much softer. "What do you think?"

"Hmm." He scrunched his brow in concentration. "Gertrude?"

She shook her head, stifling a giggle.

"Henrietta?"

She slapped a hand over her mouth and shook her head emphatically.

"I know. Persephone!"

She laughed. "That's not a name!"

"Sure it is. She's the queen of the underworld."

"Really?" Eve rolled the name around in her head. She kind of liked it. "What does that mean?"

"Don't frighten her, Leigh," Mrs. Adler said. "He did a school project last year, and now he's obsessed with Greek mythology. Would you like more coffee?"

As the adults turned back to their conversation, he leaned close enough that she could smell his bubblegum.

"When she was just a young innocent girl, she was playing in a valley with all her friends. She saw the most beautiful flower. But when she bent down to pick it, the earth under her feet broke open and this chariot burst out, pulled by giant black horses. It was Hades, the god of the underworld. He wanted to marry Persephone, but her mom had said no. So, he grabbed her and dragged her down to the underworld."

She blinked at him, feeling a thrill of fear. "What's that?"

"It's the kingdom of the dead."

"Is it scary?"

"It's really dark and there's all kinds of beasts. Like centaurs and Gorgons."

She didn't know what those were, and decided she didn't want to know. "What happened to her? Did she die?"

"Hades made her his wife. Kind of romantic, right?"

She didn't know what the word *romantic* meant, but sensed he was testing her. Maybe he was waiting to see if she'd burst into tears or tell her mother that he was scaring her. But she wasn't a baby. Straightening her shoulders, she looked him square in the eyes. "Persephone. I like it."

He smiled at her, nodding his approval. "You're cool, Eve."

Her cheeks heated with pleasure. "I know," she said, and then flushed even more when he laughed. But his laugh was like an invitation into a private joke, so after a moment she joined in.

"Eve!" Sara bounced into the room, clutching a doll with yellow hair to her chest. "This is Fiona. Wanna come play in my room?"

Jumping up, she looked to her mom for permission.

"Ten minutes," Donna said.

Turning to Leigh, who sat on the carpet with the empty box in his lap, she held up her doll. "Persephone says thank you."

He gave her a grin and a little salute.

She bounced out of the room on Sara's heels.

"It's my birthday in a week," Sara said as they climbed the stairs, moving around boxes and toppling piles of clothes still attached to their hangers. "I asked for another doll. And I want a bunk bed for them to sleep in. I saw one at Walmart that has pillows and blankets and everything. This is my room. It's green right now but Daddy said we can paint it any colour I want."

"It's big."

"Yeah," Sara said. "Hey, it's cool our birthdays are so close. It's like we're princesses and this whole week is about us."

"We should get cake every day for the whole week."

"Yeah! And presents." Sara jumped onto her bed and started bouncing. "We need secret princess names."

Eve climbed onto the bed and bounced beside her. "My name is Princess Doodlebug. My superpower is that everything I draw comes to life!"

"You're a superhero and a princess? Cool! Um, my name is Princess Gumdrop, and my superpower is that everything I touch turns to candy!"

"All right!"

"Eve, it's time to go," Donna called from below.

"Aw, so soon?" Sara said.

Eve knew better than to argue, so she jumped off the bed. "Coming, Donna!"

"Why don't you call her Mom?" Sara asked.

11

She grinned up at her new friend. "Because she's not really my mom, she's an evil queen who wants to keep me locked in a dungeon."

"Cool," Sara said. "Is your dad an ogre?"

Button and Donna argued a lot when Eve was supposed to be sleeping. Once she'd heard an argument about her dad where they called him the Donor. She didn't know if that was his name or if it meant something else, but whatever it was, it didn't sound good. She liked Sara's idea of an ogre better. "Yeah, he's a big green one with black teeth."

"Woah," Sara said.

"Eve!" Donna called again.

"Coming!"

Sara jumped down from the bed. "Can you come play some other time?"

"For sure."

"Sorry you got stuck with my brother for so long. I couldn't find Fiona. Maybe we can play dolls next time?"

"Yeah! And it's okay. He's really cool."

Sara rolled her eyes. "He smells like socks."

THREE

"EVE, CAN YOU HEAR ME?" The man's voice warbled somewhere in the distance, and she moved toward it.

For either hours or decades, she'd been lost in a field of quicksilver plants just like the one she'd avoided for most of her childhood. It was foggy, icy water dripping onto her head and the back of her neck. It hurt her lungs to breathe and made it impossible to see more than a few feet ahead.

A woman walked nearby, calling out to her from time to time, trying to get her attention. Eve wanted nothing to do with her. All she wanted was to find a way out.

As she moved, silver leaves left slug-trails across her skin. Branches loomed out of the fog to snag her clothing. She yanked herself free and kept going, not caring if her clothes tore. If she continued downhill, she should come out near the pond.

"Eve, squeeze my hand if you can hear me." His voice was a soft rumble, which brought to mind the St. Bernard in those cold-medicine commercials, the one who braved snowy nights just to help someone battle the sniffles.

At the sound of his voice, tendrils of fog drifted up toward the sky.

"Urrrrrr ..."

"Don't try to speak. Your jaw is wired shut."

The world around her came to life, like those slick moments just before dawn.

"Do you know where you are? Squeeze my hand once for yes and twice for no."

Did she have hands? She felt like her body was a balloon. It swelled with panic, and the fragile shell bulged with explosive threat. What would happen if the pressure mounted? Would she burst right out of existence?

"Ouch! No need to break my hand." He chuckled, and she felt a pinprick of relief. If she'd hurt him, she must still be real.

"You're in the ICU at St. Vincent's," he continued. "You've been in a medically induced coma for almost three weeks."

His voice was familiar. It was like the kiss of cool water on sunburned skin, and mud between her toes. It was the taste of strawberry milkshakes and tears.

"Don't try to move! You've still got casts on, well, just about everything. Do you remember the accident?"

Accident? Eve remembered the smell of bitter coffee and coconut cake. And was there something about a man in a fedora?

"That's okay, some things are worth forgetting. There was a storm, and this guy was driving while on drugs. But what's important is you survived. It was touch and go there for a while. They're doing everything they can to put you back together."

A chair squeaked and she sensed he'd moved closer. "I'm doing everything I can, too. We're going to get through this."

His voice. Recognition seared her skin, awakening her from fingertips to heart and spreading like brushfire down her broken body. It also awoke the pain, which ripped down the fault lines of her mending bones. For the moment it didn't matter. She knew the man behind that voice, could taste his name on her tongue, could feel the thrill it had given her to let it escape her lips — so quick and breathless the syllables blurred together: Leigh Adler, after all this time.

He must have felt her jolt of recognition, for he squeezed her fingers in acknowledgement. Her hand still felt so small within his grip. She could picture him standing before her, not as he must have looked now, but as she'd known him years ago. Before what happened to the man in the forest fused them together. Before Sara's death tore them apart.

"You remember," he said.

Instead of squeezing his hand, she opened her eyes.

FOUR

Sara's Twentieth Birthday

"YOU'RE DRUNK." Button's arms were crossed over her bony chest, her lips pressed together so tightly they'd turned white.

"My art history teacher's a sexist ass," Eve said as she took off her coat. It took several tries to snag the hook on which to hang it. She leaned against the wall to kick off her boots, picked them up, and dumped them on the shoe rack.

"Hmph," Button said.

Avoiding her grandmother's piercing gaze, she walked with slow deliberation to the kitchen. She pulled a beer from the fridge and slid onto the bench at the Formica table.

"You're not supposed to mix alcohol with your medications."

Button stood in the doorway to the kitchen, her silver curls glowing in the overhead light and her face twisted into THE LOOK. It was usually enough to keep Eve pretending that all was well, but not tonight.

Twisting the cap off the bottle, she said, "It's just one beer."

"And how many before that?"

"I'm celebrating Sara's birthday." Her voice echoed back to her from the mouth of the bottle, rounded and warped. A laugh gurgled up her throat and escaped on a bubble of beer, leaving fire in its wake.

"Eve." Button placed a hand on her shoulder. "It's a hard day for both of us. But we're all we've got left. We need to stick together."

She ran a finger over the ring of rust where Donna's tin of maple syrup had sat for the first seventeen years of her life. It had never occurred to her before this moment that the rust was the same colour as Donna's eyes. She yanked back her hand and wrapped it around the bottle of beer, as though trying to soothe a burn.

"Are you listening? I'm tired of watching you turn your back on everything you have."

"I have nothing except you."

"You think so? Come here." Button grabbed her hand and pulled.

She slid along the bench and allowed her grandmother to lead her into the hallway.

"*Kuk arop, vest du visn vi hoykh du shteyst.* You forget how far you've climbed. How much you've overcome, even in this past year."

Button had hung Eve's paintings along the hallway. Over the years, she'd filled every inch of available wall space.

"Look at this." Button stabbed her finger at a painting. "Really look. What do you see?"

"A better life." A time before Donna bounced her tuition cheque and Eve had to spend her first year at community college instead of Emily Carr.

Button let out a breath. "But what did you paint?"

"Paris. The cobbled street of the Rue Crémieux after a rain shower."

"One of my favourites. I love how the light from the street lamp bleeds into the shadows. It's very fluid, very dreamlike."

Button pulled her along the hallway. "And this one?"

"A café on the Rue Saint-Honoré. I'd paint it differently now. Tighten the focus to that scatter of bread crumbs, and where the coffee splashed into the saucer. Highlight the imperfections."

"Yes," Button said. "You should try that. And what's this one?"

"All right. I get it."

"What is it?"

"It's the field of quicksilver plants in the Crook, where Sara and I used to play. The leaves look like tinfoil."

"They do," Button said. "And see how the tiny yellow flowers seem to glow, as though lit from inside?"

"They look that way at dusk, in the spring. The flowers smell like honey."

Button nodded. "You really captured something. It's haunting and whimsical. Sad, too."

"I painted it the year after Sara died."

"Yes," Button said.

"I wish you'd take it down."

"That won't change the past. It won't hide you from the truth."

"I'm not hiding."

Pulling her down the hall, Button pointed out each painting, highlighting the parts she thought were particularly good, and reminiscing on the story behind each. When they reached the end of the hallway, they stopped in front of Donna's bedroom door. It hadn't been opened in three years.

The painting was of the Adlers' backyard in early summer. Leigh stood in the driveway with a basketball tucked under his arm while Sara picked flowers that looked like daisies. Button touched Sara's painted cheek, traced the flowers clutched against her chest, and ran her finger over the blood-red soil at Sara's feet.

"Button, don't."

"You still miss her, don't you?"

"She was my only friend."

"It wasn't your fault. You understand that, don't you? No matter what people might have said."

Eve didn't bother arguing.

Button sighed, turned back to the painting. "My Frida. My beautiful artist. Since you were very small, you always dreamed so vividly. With so much colour and detail. To have the talent to paint those dreams, to share them with others, that's a gift from God."

"You don't believe in God."

"Who said that?"

"You did. You said you didn't care how you were raised, you had trouble believing in a God that would let children die before their parents." Button was born in the Warsaw Ghetto. She'd seen more atrocities in her childhood than Eve could ever imagine.

19

Button waved a hand, looking flustered. "Ignore what I said. Atheism is a luxury afforded the young. At my age, I'd be foolish not to hedge my bets."

"Don't talk like that. You're going to live a long time."

"I've already lived too long. My point is, don't use your heartache as an excuse to give up."

"And my guilt?" Eve asked before she could stop herself. "What should I do with that?"

"What do you have to feel guilty about?" Button turned away before hearing the answer, as she always did.

For a moment Eve paused on the cliff's edge, staring down into the abyss. She imagined unburdening herself, speaking of everything Button pretended not to know. But her grandmother looked so small and fragile in her threadbare bathrobe, and the lines etched around her eyes looked like cracks in an old foundation.

And despite all the evidence to the contrary, Button believed she was a good person. She needed that.

Stepping back from the edge, she said, "Nothing. Let's eat. I'm starving."

She pulled her grandmother away from the painting of the Adlers' yard, and led her back to the kitchen.

FIVE

"YOU KNOW IT'S A LIE."

The woman had been speaking to her for a long time, but her voice was muted and warbling in the thick air, as though she spoke from a great distance. Eve kept losing track of the words.

"Are you listening?"

Out of the corner of her eye, she could see a dark splotch somewhere to her right. It kept pace with her as she moved downhill. She knew that if she turned her head she'd be able to see it more clearly, or at least the shape of it, but she didn't want to know what it was. She needed to get to the pond, where there was sunlight.

"Eve? You need to listen to me."

She saw a faint brightening ahead of her, and moved faster. Wet leaves slapped her face while branches tore at her skin and snagged in her hair. The fog lifted, steaming up toward a lightening sky. The sun rose ahead of her, a delicate lemon yellow.

From somewhere in the glow, a woman said, "How long will you be staying?" Her voice was clear and familiar.

"Button." Eve started to run.

"I've put in to transfer my medical licence."

Leigh?

She slipped and slid over wet leaves, through fog and tinfoil, and into a light so bright it blinded her. She fell backward, landed on something soft, and her body stopped working.

"What does that mean?" Button said from somewhere to her right. She could hear the tension in her grandmother's voice.

Where were they? It was so bright. Had she gone blind? She'd always thought that blindness was like being lost in the dark, but she felt like her eyeballs were cooking. And she couldn't move. Did the rest of her body still exist?

"It means I'm staying."

"Is that a good idea?"

"Eve needs me."

Her grandmother didn't answer, but Eve knew that silence well. She imagined Button's lips tightening like purse strings.

What had happened to her? Had there been an accident? Maybe she was paralyzed. She focused on her neck, picturing the muscles than ran up the sides of her spine. She willed them to life, and with enormous effort managed to turn her head a fraction of an inch in their direction.

"Eve?" Leigh's face emerged like a black spot on the sun. "Welcome back."

Button's face appeared next. Her eyes drooped with exhaustion, red and raw. Her skin hung like that of an emaciated Shar-Pei. She looked older, and no wonder if she did. Whatever had happened was clearly very bad.

"Hello, *bubbalah*," Button said, and promptly burst into tears.

She tried to reach for her grandmother to pat her hand or give her some kind of comfort, but it was no good. She was no more than a floating head, disembodied and useless. And her eyes were on fire.

"Liiights."

Her voice shredded her throat. Her jaw hinges throbbed and ached. Her face felt swollen, her tongue like a rotting plum cramped behind the jail of her teeth.

"Liiights." Her voice was clearer this time.

"Is it too bright?" Leigh said, and a chair scraped. The lights flicked off, and she blinked in relief.

"Waaater."

Button brought a straw to her lips, and she sipped gratefully at the tepid liquid. It soothed her throat and seemed to bring every cell of her body to life.

When the cup was empty, she eased back against the pillow. The back of her head felt numb and tingly, as though cushioned in tight wrapping. She could feel her body now. It hurt in a million different ways, but every part of it felt present and accounted for. She filled her lungs and thought how glorious it was to be able to breathe, even if there was an elephant sitting on her chest.

But her grandmother's face was pinched with worry.

"Button," she paused to pull in a breath, "are you ready?"

Button furrowed her brow. "Ready for what?"

"To go dancing." It was a poor joke, but all she could manage. And it had the desired effect.

Button smiled and some of the tension left her shoulders. "Rain check?"

"You bet."

Her grandmother bent to stroke the hair off her forehead. *"Mir zol zayn far dir, mayn kind." I wish I could take your pain for myself.*

Button's hand felt feverishly hot against the chill of her skin. It was soothing, and Eve's eyelids grew heavy.

"Button?"

"Mmm?"

"Where's Donna?"

"What?"

"Why isn't she here? Is she still mad at me?"

"Oh, Eve."

As she drifted away, she wondered why her grandmother looked so sad.

SIX

Eve's Seventeenth Birthday

EVE HAD SPENT her whole life trying to understand her mother.

Publicly, Donna Gold was a saint. She was the founder and CEO of a charity organization called Under Our Wing. It was a coalition of lawyers, therapists, and medical experts, dedicated to helping abused and exploited children. When it came to her cases, Donna had endless time and passion. She made regular appearances on news stations, at schools, and in the courtroom. She fought the good fight, determined to save children from abuse everywhere except under her own roof.

On Eve's seventeenth birthday, Donna was presenting closing arguments in a molestation case at the downtown courthouse. Eve waited in the gallery, sucking icing off her fingers. Court was supposed to break at noon, but her mom wasn't working at her usual hair-trigger pace. Sweat dampened the back of Donna's silk blouse. She could practically hear the nausea in Donna's voice, and doubted her mom would feel up for lunch.

She wedged a finger through an opening in the cake box and scooped out a mouthful of icing, hoping the sugar would ease her anxiety. Her mother did not look well at all.

On court days, Donna always wore a crisp suit and styled her hair into a perfect black helmet. But now she looked rather wilted. Though her high heels cracked like gunfire against the tile floor as she paced, she clutched the table for support.

Watching her mom caused Eve's chest to tighten with unease. She turned her focus to the reflection of rain droplets sliding down the crimson locks of Donna's client's hair. It made her curls a living thing, like snakes coiling around her shoulders.

Eve itched for her coloured pencils, imagining the swift, bold lines she would draw. She'd make that hair coil from her head like Medusa, hissing and biting, and play up the contrast of red to black in the coils.

Mentally setting aside the drawing, she turned her focus to the judge sitting at the head of the room. His face was heavily lined, with the sagging jowls and drooping eyes of a basset hound.

In her mind, Eve began once again to draw. She deepened his sad brown eyes, weighted the sides of his face with heavy black strokes, softened the tufts of hair into velvety ears … and yes, a tinge of yellow along the cheeks, and a sturdy red collar around his neck, blending into the black of his robe.

Perhaps she would call it *Dog Justice*, Eve mused, filling in the desk below him, imagining watercolour splashes of red and white and then blue and yellow to signify the flags behind his head. Her mind was lost to her surroundings while the scene came to life before her.

At the age of six, she'd used Donna's expensive makeup in their hallway, smearing eyeshadow and lipstick into the blank wall to create a lush meadow where fairies lived with pet unicorns, and rainbows danced across a velvet sky. She'd sprinkled the whole scene with Donna's gold eyeshadow, to create fairy dust.

Donna had been furious.

"She's an artist," Button had said in her most matter-of-fact voice, the one Donna dubbed "Button knows best." "Buy her some real art supplies and you'll see."

But it was Button who bought Eve her first art kit, perhaps so she could be proved right. There was nothing Button loved better than being right.

On canvas or paper or even on the sidewalk in front of their home, Eve gave birth to the things that lived behind her eyes. Button plastered the hall with her artwork, praising each one as masterful.

Donna had a different reaction. Her eyes wouldn't rest for more than a second on a piece of Eve's artwork, as though afraid her retinas would burn. Moving away, she'd shake her head and mutter, "Well, she didn't get it from me."

Of course not, Eve had wanted to say once she was old enough to understand the circumstances of her becoming. She must have gotten it from file #7543, the thirty-two-year-old anonymous sperm donor. Button accused Donna of doing it that way so she could create a mini version of herself, without any of the complications an actual father would bring to the picture. Her grandma was usually right.

Eve had buried herself in her studies and managed to escape high school a year early, happy as a convict released from prison. She'd spent that summer painting in Paris — much to Donna's consternation and Button's delight — and returned ready to start the fall semester at Emily Carr, only to discover that her seat had been filled because Donna had bounced the tuition check. By accident, she'd said.

Trying to salvage the year, Eve had enrolled in art classes at the community college. And she hadn't spoken to her mother since, unless it was to yell. That morning, Button had made a teary plea for a truce. So she'd agreed to meet Donna for their customary birthday lunch. There were two people she couldn't refuse, and one of them was her grandmother.

After stopping at La Dolce Vita Bakery, she'd headed to the courthouse instead of going home to her art studio. The Gold family tradition was coconut cake, homemade birthday cards, and reruns of *The Golden Girls*. Button related to Sophia, the sly old mother, while Donna pretended to relate to Blanche.

Lost in her own thoughts, she didn't know something had happened until the woman on the next seat stood and pushed past her to the centre aisle, knocking a hip into the cake box and stomping on her foot.

"Hey!" Eve grasped the box before it toppled from her lap. All around her, people stood to get a better view. Some pushed into the centre aisle, crowding near the gate that led to the front of the courtroom.

"What?"

The word clogged her throat. Her skin prickled with heat. Pushing herself up onto legs that felt suddenly wooden, she turned in the opposite direction and squeezed past the other people in her row, tripping on bags and stepping on feet as she went.

The outside aisle was unoccupied, and she moved to the front of the courtroom. Every step revealed more of the scene before her. The judge's desk was empty. So was the court clerk's.

A couple more steps revealed Donna's client, whom Eve had previously seen only from behind. Her face was a pale moon, marked with the healing scabs of a drug user. Her mouth gaped open to reveal blackened teeth and a shockingly pink tongue. Another step, and there was the judge. He issued orders to the court clerk, his arms waving so the black sleeves of his robe looked like the wings of a giant bat taking flight.

The clerk nodded and pushed toward the crowd forming at the gate, her meaty hands raised above her head with fingers splayed. In response, they surged forward, excitedly vying for the best view of the action. They clearly weren't going anywhere.

Dreamlike, Eve moved forward until she met the resistance of the railing separating the gallery from the front. It hit her at hip height. Clutching the cake box to her chest, she lifted her leg over the railing, straddled it for an awkward moment, and then swung across. She moved past the empty defendant's table and around the bellowing clerk.

"Everybody back!" the clerk said. "Everybody back!"

Eve slipped past her, shoved through the wall of lawyers huddled like crows on a line, and came suddenly into open space.

The smell assaulted her nose and sent her reeling back a step. Mixed in with the scent of hot bile she caught the bitterness of half-digested coffee and the sweet tang of maple syrup.

That damned maple syrup, Donna's weakness. She ordered it by the case from a supplier on the east coast and slathered it on everything. Perhaps in reaction, neither Button nor Eve could stand the stuff. At home, the tin of syrup sat in its appointed spot on their kitchen table. Over the years, a ring of rust had formed on the yellow Formica, marking its home.

There was another smell, one that was horribly out of place inside the dignified walls of a courtroom. It was a septic kind of smell, acidic and feral.

The first thing she saw, or that her brain was able to process, was a shoe. It was a shiny black high-heel with a scuffed red sole. It lay on the grey tile as though casually tossed aside, the gel insole hanging out like a strange blue tongue.

Her mind fixated on the shoe, familiar and yet so out of place, to avoid looking at the foot just inches away, at the red polish on the toenails, at the pale ankle visible through a ladderlike rip in the stocking. She wouldn't have to see the blue suit skirt pushed up to expose the bruise on Donna's thigh, evidence of yet another encounter with the corner of the kitchen cart. Or how Donna's body twisted at an odd angle, her right leg curled under and her arms flung wide. And most of all she wouldn't have to see how

Donna's mouth gaped open to spill a trail of vomit from rosy lips down powdered cheek.

"Oh my God," she wheezed. "Mom …"

The shock swept through her, exposing memories like bones.

She'd crawled right over him, not knowing he was there. A tuft of black hair was still attached to his skull.

The room tilted sideways and she went with it, head hitting the floor just feet from where her mother lay. The tile felt cool and slick against her cheek.

She'd clung to the log, fighting the pull of the icy current. Splinters pricked her skin, and Sara's tears were salty on her lips.

The bakery box hit the floor and split open in a splatter of cake and icing. It sprayed Donna's blouse, her cheek, and her hair. A large chunk hit her perfect black eyebrow, paused for a moment, and then slid off. And her eyes …

When she looked up, the stars were bleeding.

"You have the eyes of a cat hunting in the moonlight."

The women in Eve's family all had the same distinctive amber-coloured eyes, wide-set with a downward tilt at the outer edge, so they looked perpetually sad. It was the only trait she'd inherited from her mother, or so she believed. Donna's pupils were dilated, the amber swallowed by black holes. They fixed on her with blank accusation, as though everything Donna had merely suspected was at last confirmed.

There was blood in the ground, if you knew where to dig.

"I'm sorry," Eve whispered. But it was too late to ask for forgiveness.

SEVEN

"IT'S A BRAIN INJURY."

Leigh's voice pulled Eve from the quicksilver. She blinked away the fog, and the sterile walls of a hospital room came into focus.

The first thing she recognized was Leigh's right hand. It was rough-knuckled, the fingers long and lean and currently drumming a nervous beat against his thigh.

"What?"

Eve was wrapped in a fleece blanket in an armchair by a window. The pale light from outside didn't warm her at all. When she turned her head she could see a parking lot below. People moved to and fro, and near the exit cars lined up for the pay booth. The yellow arm went up and down with regularity, releasing one car at a time.

"I said it's a brain injury. The blacking-out that you're experiencing. And the memory loss."

"What happened to me?"

"There was an accident." He said it as though they'd had this conversation before — perhaps many times. "You were hit by a car. It shoved you through the window of a Starbucks."

"Starbucks?"

"It's a coffee shop."

"I'm not a moron." She turned her narrowed gaze in his direction. "I know what Starbucks is."

"Of course." He seemed uncomfortable with her scrutiny, and she wondered why. He wore faded jeans and a fitted button-down shirt. His hair had thinned a bit at the top; his sideburns had dimmed from dark blond to grey. He'd grown a beard. No ring on his finger, she noted.

All in all, he didn't look much different from the last time she'd seen him. Was that after Donna's funeral? A flash of memory, yet another jagged piece of bone unearthed from an old grave — something about rain and maple syrup, and that detective. What was his name? He'd had a big, booming voice. The memory slithered away, leaving her empty and confused.

"There's one last major surgery to go, and then you'll be transferred to a rehab facility," he said, bringing her back.

"What surgery?"

"To repair your craniectomy. They've stored the bone flap in a freezer until your brain swelling has —"

"Fuck, stop talking. I don't want to know."

"You asked," he said, and then more contritely he added, "Sorry."

"Hopefully my brain will hit delete on this memory, too."

"Hopefully not on all of it." He reached for her hand.

33

She pulled away. "Why are you here, Leigh?"

He hesitated, his eyes flicking to the side before coming back to meet her gaze head on. "Where else would I be?"

"Anywhere else but here with me."

"No. That's where I've *been*." He gave her a look that was dangerously earnest. "But I'm tired of living that lie."

"It's not a good idea." Truer words she'd never spoken. Yet hope bubbled within her like cream soda.

"Have you told anyone?" Leigh asked.

Her heart jumped inside her chest, causing her to let out a short, barking cough. He handed her a cup with a plastic straw. She sipped, watching him as she did.

His eyes were the blue of a winter sky, impossibly innocent. They made her feel the way Alice must have felt falling down the rabbit hole. But instead of Wonderland, she would land back in her own childhood. Would Leigh still be as good at getting to the secret places inside her? At being the only one who could cross her barricade of insecurity and willfulness? That, at least, she remembered.

"Does your grandma know?" he prompted.

"Does she know what?"

He didn't answer, and after a time she wandered back to tinfoil leaves and the woman who waited for her in the shadows.

EIGHT

Eve's Ninth Birthday

IN LATER YEARS, Eve could pinpoint the afternoon of her ninth birthday as the moment her life made a seismic shift. Standing on the before side of the fissure was a girl who had once peed herself when Annabeth O'Neill and Myra Knottsworth — Snottsworth, the kids had called her behind her back — challenged her to a fight after school. On the after side, someone very different began to grow. Someone better, or so she believed for a long time.

She awoke before dawn, eager to plow through her Sunday chores so she'd be free to go to Sara's house once her mom gave her the green light. Sara lived on the other side of Fraser's Arm, a small neighbourhood on Vancouver's southeastern edge that had been named for the way the land jutted into the Fraser River. The Arm was five blocks wide and ten blocks deep, and four half circles of newer houses filled in the hand.

Sara lived in an old three-level house near the wrist joint. It had peeling green paint, a giant front porch, and, according to Sara, had been built before the invention of straight lines. She'd helped Sara and her dad wallpaper Sara's bedroom last summer and learned that Mr. Adler, usually the calm eye of the family storm, could cuss in five different languages. She'd enjoyed the education.

She and Donna had moved into Grandma Button's home after Grandpa Max died. Their house was where the base of the thumb would have been if the hand had been complete. Built in the fifties, it was a one-level pale pink leftover with Formica counters and exposed brick. The best thing about it was the yard, which rolled to the river unimpeded, save the train tracks. Trains carried drums of oil past their home three times a day, rattling the windows and causing the lights to flicker.

Waiting for her toast to pop, she opened the curtain above the kitchen sink and was relieved to see the day looked fine. The sky was grey, but not heavy with impending rain. Sara had planned a picnic in the Crook to celebrate Eve's birthday, and though neither girl minded wet weather, rain would make it harder to convince Donna that Eve should spend the day out of the house.

The Crook jutted into the river a block east of Eve's home, like an angry green finger accusing the industry on the south bank of destroying the previous century's farmland.

A boggy mess at most times of the year, it was a place where rain boots got sucked into mud swamps and spiders grew fat off mosquitoes and other winged creatures. This made it an undesirable place for adults and a sanctuary for local kids.

Dotted with blackberry bushes and tangles of vegetation, the Crook slowed tugboats roaring up and down the river and trapped log booms against its marshy beaches. A small pond nestled into the fattest part, surrounded by marsh grasses around the curve of the river, and an explosion of evergreens and blackberry bushes on the opposite side.

On the west side of the Crook, a giant army of quicksilver plants marched to the pond's edge in a fabric-tearing tangle. Everyone called this area the Foil, because the leaves looked like strips of tinfoil. When the wind picked up, the Foil rattled and hissed like an angry snake. It was pretty creepy.

Though she wasn't usually much of an adventurer, Sara was the only one who would go into the massive silver mess. She liked to hide there during games of Seekers, mainly so she could snicker about how she was foiling everyone by hiding in the Foil. Eve didn't get the joke, but there was a lot about her friend that she didn't get. Sara read at an adult level and finished the crossword puzzle every Sunday *without* help. According to Donna she was too smart for her own good, whatever that meant.

When Donna shuffled into the kitchen that morning, Eve was munching toast with chunky peanut butter and sliced banana, enjoying the mixture of salty crunch and soft sweetness on her tongue. In anticipation of her imminent release, she'd leaned her backpack by the kitchen door. It was stuffed with her sketchbook, coloured pencils, a bottle of water, and a bag of pretzels. Sara had promised to bring everything else.

"Coffee?" Donna said.

Her mouth was full, and Donna had already reached the counter and could see for herself that there was a fresh pot, so she didn't answer. Watching her mother grab a mug and pour coffee, she searched for signs of Donna's mood.

Donna sipped, then grimaced. "How many scoops did you use?"

"Two. Like you showed me."

"It's weak."

She took another bite of toast rather than answer.

Donna scooped a blob of cottage cheese into a bowl and sprinkled almonds on top. "Where are the bananas?"

Her scalp prickled with heat. "This is the last one. Sorry."

Donna muttered something unintelligible, in which Eve only caught the word *potassium*, and plucked a package of dates from the cupboard. She chopped them into her bowl and slid onto the bench across from Eve, grabbing the tin of maple syrup from its accustomed spot. She poured about a gallon of it over her breakfast, and Eve stifled the urge to wrinkle her nose in disgust.

"So, you're nine."

"Uh-huh."

"It's hard to believe."

It didn't seem like a difficult concept, so Eve shrugged.

"So, who are you?" Donna asked.

"What?"

"At nine." Her mother looked like a cat calmly stalking its prey. "Who are you?"

"Um. I'm Eve?"

"But who is *Eve*? What does she stand for? What does she believe in?" Donna leaned forward, trapping her with the intensity of her amber gaze.

"I don't know."

"By the time I was your age, I was volunteering at the soup kitchen twice a week and reading to the elderly at the Louis Brier."

"I know." She dropped her toast back onto her plate. There wasn't enough room in her throat to cram in both food and air.

"So, you should believe in something." Donna spooned cottage cheese into her mouth.

In desperation, Eve said, "Equal rights?"

"Hmm."

"Global warming," she said more firmly.

"What about it?"

"Well. It's bad? And people should do something about it."

"*Who* should do something about it?"

"Um. Me?"

Donna shrugged. "Is it important to you? Or would you rather go around all the time with your head in the clouds? All you seem to care about is scribbling in your notebooks and playing with your friends. And how is *that* helping anybody?"

She was spared from answering by the creak and slam of the front door. Moments later, Button squelched into the kitchen. She wore her pink tracksuit and two-pound ankle weights. Her salt-and-pepper curls glistened with dampness.

"My Frida!"

Donna's mouth pursed at the nickname.

Button swooped down and wrapped her in a damp hug. "Happy birthday. *Biz hundert un tsvantsik*, you should live to one-hundred and twenty."

39

"Danken," she said, and kissed her grandmother on the cheek.

"You're nine, can you believe it?"

What was it about her age that was so hard for adults to grasp? "Well, yeah. I've spent my whole life getting here."

"Eve," Donna said, but one corner of her mouth curled into a smile. Seeing it eased the pressure that had been building in Eve's chest.

Button pinched her cheek affectionately. "That you have, clever girl."

Putting on the kettle for tea, Button asked what her plans were for the day.

Taking her chance to get out of the house unimpeded, she said, "Sara's planned a picnic. And other surprises. She's expecting me in fifteen minutes."

"Chores," Donna said.

"They're already done. And I even cleaned the bathroom, so tomorrow's are done, too."

Donna scooped more cottage cheese into her mouth. Score one for Eve.

"Do you have time for a present before you go?" Button asked.

"Yes!"

"Not until after dinner," Donna said at the same time.

"Nonsense." Button barely looked in Donna's direction. She poured steaming water into the teapot, gave the tea a quick stir, and set it to steep. "Do what you want with your gifts, and I'll do what I want with mine."

"Mom, I told you —"

"Yes, yes. But this is a little something extra."

Donna looked suspiciously at her mother. "What is it?"

"You'll have to come see." She opened the kitchen door and stepped outside.

Donna and Eve slipped on shoes and followed her into the yard. They crossed to the storage shed at the back of the property. The ankles of Eve's jeans were soaked by the time they reached it.

At the door, Button turned to her and held out a key. "This is yours, my Frida."

She took the key and, at Button's nod of encouragement, slipped it into the lock. The door opened inward, and she paused nervously on the threshold.

Button reached around her and flicked on the light. "Go on, dear."

The space had been cleared of boxes and junk, and the walls had been painted a matte grey and lined with the same kind of rolling shelving she'd admired at a funky art gallery downtown. Already on display were a dozen pieces she'd painted in the backyard. There was a giant pile of blank canvases stacked under the window, and a large easel sat in the corner next to a wooden stand filled with tubes of paint, both oils and acrylics, a set of new brushes, and a mixing palette.

"I had them put in those natural light bulbs, since you won't get any north light in here," Button said. "I hear they're the next best thing."

"Mom, this must have cost a fortune."

Button smiled at Eve. "Do you like it?"

She flew into her grandmother's arms, knocking her backward. Button crowed with laughter, stroking her curls away from her forehead.

"Is that a yes?"

"This is the best birthday present *ever*!" She rained kisses on her grandmother's cheeks. "Thank you, thank you, thank you!"

"Eve doesn't need to be wasting more of her time —"

"We'll discuss it later." Button's tone of voice brooked no argument, but Donna wasn't about to let it go.

"Stop encouraging this obsession of hers. She's never going to do anything with her life if she stays locked up in here all day."

"What nonsense," Button said. "Who raised you to be so foolish?"

"*I* did, thank you very much, since you were never around —"

"Well, I'm sorry I had to start working after your father's first heart attack. I suppose you would have preferred to starve."

"Please stop," Eve said, but neither listened. They never did.

"You're always doing things like this! Trying to make up for my shitty childhood by spoiling my daughter."

"She's my granddaughter, and someone should do something nice for her once in awhile."

"What's that supposed to mean? You think I don't take care of her? She wants for nothing."

"She wants for a father," Button said.

Donna threw her hands up in the air. "Not this again."

"A child needs a father, not a number picked out of a catalogue. In my day —"

"Oh, yes. Do tell me how much better things were when women couldn't make choices about their own bodies."

"Please, please stop," Eve said.

"Choices!" Button tsked. "Everyone should do whatever they want, whatever makes them *feel good*. No need to worry about repercussions. Want a baby? Sure! Just pop on over to the sperm bank —"

"You're oversimplifying again —"

"Who needs a man around, anyway?"

"I take care of *everything* around here," Donna said. "All the bills, food, everything. And need I remind you, without me here you'd be in a government-assistance program, dying by inches in some old folks' home."

"Oh, yes. Don't ever let me forget! *Ikh bin an alter shkrab*, I'm no better than a worn-out old shoe. Thank you, Donna, for not throwing me in the trash." Button's face crumpled, and tears ran down her cheeks.

Eve flew to her grandmother's side and wrapped her arms around Button's slender waist. "Stop it! Just stop it!" she said to her mom.

Donna threw her hands up in the air. Her face was almost purple. "It's an act! This is what she does. She knows I'm right, so she brings on the waterworks."

She squeezed her grandmother's waist even tighter, pressing her face against Button's chest.

Voice trembling, Button said, "I wanted to do something nice for her birthday."

"Nice. Sure," Donna said. "Where'd all the stuff go?"

Button sniffed. "To donation, much of it."

"Mom, a lot of it was *my* stuff. I didn't give you permission to get rid of it. And my *files* were in here. You better not have thrown them out."

"What do you take me for?" Button said.

43

"Oh, gee, where should I start?"

Eve pulled away from her grandmother and stomped her foot. "Stop it!"

Donna spun on her. "Go on, defend her like you always do. Enjoy your little club of two, and roll your eyes at me behind my back. You think I don't know? Let me tell you, you have no idea what it was like for me growing up in this house. The woman you call Grandma is very different than the one I call Mom."

"That's enough, Donna," Button said. Her bottom lip trembled.

"Yeah, it is. I'm just wasting my breath. As usual." Without another word, Donna left.

They stood in silence for several moments, and then Button gave her hand a squeeze. "Sara will be waiting for you."

"Right." Eve wiped her eyes with a sleeve.

"Go ahead, dear."

"But will you be okay?"

Button sighed and said under her breath, *"Besser oyf der velt nit tsu lebn, eyder onkumen tsu kinder." Better to die than become dependent on your children.* Eve heard that one a lot.

"I'm sorry."

"Now, what do you have to be sorry for?" She curled Eve's fingers around the key and gave her a watery smile. "This place is yours now. It will still be here when you get back. Go enjoy your birthday."

She gave her grandmother a hug and another kiss on the cheek. "Thank you. It really is the best present I've ever gotten."

Button waited while she turned off the lights and locked the door, and they crossed the yard side by side.

"She's really mad, isn't she?"

"*Mah Nishtana*. Don't let it ruin your day." Button pulled open the kitchen door and went to pour her tea.

"Button," she said, hoisting her backpack onto one shoulder.

"I love you, too," Button said without turning. "Now go run around with Sara like a couple of *forts in roosl*."

Eve giggled as she always did at the idea of farts rolling around in a pickle barrel. She blew a raspberry into the palm of her hand in farewell, and headed out the door.

"What a witch. I wish she'd take a long walk off a short pier."

Sara leaned back on her elbows, blond hair hanging behind her. They'd spread their picnic blanket near the edge of the Foil, where there was a good view of the pond and the river beyond.

She giggled. "Sara."

"I'm sorry, but she is. I don't know how you can stand it." Sara pulled her ponytail over the top of her head and used the ends to cover her forehead in a decent imitation of Donna's severe bangs. Her lips curled down in disapproval. In a raspy voice she said, "When are you going to stop fiddling with those stupid paintbrushes and do something useful with your life?"

"That doesn't sound like her at all."

"That's exactly what she said when I was over last week. *Exactly*."

"She wanted me to join the leadership club. That's all."

"Oh yeah, that's all."

Eve pulled out her sketchbook and pencils. "Let me draw you."

Sara wrinkled her nose and stuck out her tongue.

"C'mon."

With a dramatic sigh, Sara lay back on the blanket and closed her eyes. "The life of a model."

"Sorry it's such hard work." She pulled her pencils out of the box and lined them up beside her on the blanket.

"You must be bored of my face by now."

"A little."

Sara plucked a pretzel off the blanket and chucked it at her head. She ducked it easily. Using the black pencil, she did a rough sketch of Sara's face and body, erasing and redrawing until she felt she had the proportions right.

Sara reached for a handful of sour gummy bears and popped them into her mouth one at a time. "Mom thinks I'm getting fat."

"It's a growth spurt. You always do that just before you grow another inch or two."

Sara tugged at her shirt, which clung to the area around her belly. "So I *am* getting fat?"

"Maybe you should stop eating so much candy?"

"Screw you." Sara stuffed a handful of the candy into her mouth. She chewed defiantly, cheeks puffed and lips glistening with sugar.

"Just trying to help. And now you look like an angry squirrel."

Sara sat up, blue eyes flashing. "Better than an anorexic poodle."

She didn't know what the word *anorexic* meant, but it clearly wasn't a compliment. She pushed a mass of curls away from her face. "Not cool. I can't help how I look."

"Exactly." Sara sounded like Donna in lawyer mode. She dropped the rest of the candy back in the bag and stared moodily at the pond below. Her eyes looked shiny. "Danielle and Margie can eat anything they want and still be skinny."

"But they're snots."

"Yeah. But they're *pretty* snots."

"They're giant stupid booger heads. You got the brains in the family."

Sara gave her a knowing look. "Leigh's okay."

"For a boy." She hoped Sara wouldn't notice the blush that heated her cheeks at the mention of his name. Time to change the subject. "I think there's room for a desk, if you want."

"What?"

"In my art studio." She loved how those words rolled off her tongue. "We can put a desk in there for you. You can have somewhere quiet to write."

The Adler home was many things, but quiet wasn't one of them.

Sara sniffed and wiped a sleeve across her eyes. "You'd do that?"

"We can get another key made at McGill's. I've got some money."

"I can pay for it. And we have some old furniture in the attic. I bet I can find something that would work." Sara turned to her, smile back in place. "Thanks."

"Just don't forget about me when you're rich and famous."

Sara giggled. "I never would. Doodlebug and Gumdrop forever."

She placed her hand over Eve's, their palms touching, and ran a gentle finger over Eve's wrist. It sent a shiver all the way up to her scalp.

"Our hearts are joined together," Sara said.

She completed the ritual, solemnly running her finger across Sara's wrist. "Always and forever."

Letting go, Sara said, "Maybe we can write something together? I'll write and you can do the drawings."

"Cool."

While they munched their way through their food, Sara outlined the story and Eve drew some sketches. As morning gave way to afternoon, heavy clouds rolled in and the river darkened to the colour of slate. The quicksilver plants rustled in warning and fat raindrops began to fall. A storm was coming in, and fast.

Eve tucked her sketchbook and pencils back into her bag. "This is going to get worse before it gets better. Maybe we should go search your attic."

Sara glanced up and nodded agreement.

Eve was zipping her backpack closed when Sara grabbed her arm. Surprised, she looked up and noticed how pale Sara had become. Her jaw worked in a funny, nervous kind of way.

"Are you okay?"

"I …" Sara stared at the forest on the north side of the Crook, and she automatically turned to look.

"No, don't!" Sara scooped an armful of picnic supplies and stuffed them into her bag. A plastic container upended, spilling a rainbow of candy onto the dirt. Her hands trembled. "Keep packing! Pretend everything's normal."

"What's going on?"

"Someone's watching us," Sara whispered out of the corner of her mouth.

"Where?"

"Don't look! Let's just get out of here."

"I bet it's Annabeth and her stupid girl gang. They have nothing better to do than follow us around and try to steal our stuff." Eve stood and scanned the treeline, blinking back raindrops.

Sara tugged at her sleeve. "Help me pack."

"They threw your scooter into the yard of Groaning House last week. Don't you want revenge?" Groaning House had been abandoned for as long as Eve could remember, and it was obviously haunted. Everyone knew it.

"But we got it back," Sara said.

"No. *I* got it back. I had to climb over the fence and dig through grass as high as my shoulders, while Snottsworth called you a scaredy-cat and kept hitting you in the arm. I want revenge, even if you don't."

There was a flicker of movement in the forest, as though someone had come close to the treeline before disappearing back into the shadows. Were they running? They probably were, the cowards.

Her heart kicked into high gear and she leaped forward, ready to give chase.

"Eve, no!" Sara grabbed her shoulder, pulling her back.

She was a half-foot shorter and twenty pounds lighter than Sara. Under normal circumstances she wouldn't have stood a chance. But conscious thought had slipped away, replaced by the primordial need of a hunter smelling blood.

"Don't be a chicken." She ripped free of Sara's grip and ran for the forest.

"What are you doing?" Sara called.

She was going to make them pay. That's what she was doing.

There was a flash of movement in the trees directly ahead.

"Hey!" Her voice didn't sound like her own. It was deep and commanding.

She thought she heard them giggle, and a white-hot rage swelled within her. She vowed that when she was through with them, they wouldn't find anything funny ever again.

"Hey, you glitter bitches! I'm coming for ya!"

"Eve!" Sara called from somewhere behind her. "Eve, *come back*!"

No way. The cesspool of anger and humiliation she kept stuffed deep inside had been unleashed. She was tired of feeling weak, of feeling like a stupid dreamer, of feeling as worthless as the crud on the bottom of someone's shoe. And since she couldn't attack the real source of her rage, the glitter gang would substitute just fine.

With a warrior-like whoop, she flew over rocks and tree roots without feeling the ground beneath her feet. She imagined them running ahead of her, now scared silent except for the panting of their breath. She bet they could feel her closing in.

She burst into a clearing and saw them directly ahead of her. "Gotcha!"

Except it wasn't them.

Her brain struggled to process this new reality, but her feet kept going.

It was a man. An actual *grown-up*. In the Crook, there was more chance of spotting a unicorn than a grown-up.

He ran with his jeans sagging around his hips. He tried to pull them up as he stumbled forward. He had black hair, which was dirty and tangled around his shoulders. His shirt clung to his back, wet from the rain. He gave a panicked look over his shoulder, and she saw that he had a hooked nose and a bushy black beard.

And then he tripped. Like a torpedo, he launched toward a stand of trees. When his head hit the broad trunk of a Douglas fir, it made a crunch so horrible she felt the reverberation in her bones. He hung in midair for several seconds, in defiance of the laws of gravity, and then fell in a crumpled heap. He rolled over with a winded moan and his gaze fixed on the sky above.

"Holy shit," someone said, and she looked up to see Sara's brother, Leigh, standing several feet away. The smoke from his joint fogged around him in a noxious cloud. He shook his head as though trying to clear it, and coughed out a cloud of smoke. Turning red eyes on her, he said, "Eve, what the hell?"

"He was," she paused for a gasping breath, "watching us. Me and Sara."

"Sara?" Leigh turned to look at the heap on the ground. The man continued to stare up at the sky, his eyes blank. Blood trickled from a cut on his forehead. His pants gaped open, revealing a tangle of black curls and a flesh-coloured tube that shrank back as she watched, like a snake retreating.

"Fuck," Leigh said.

"Is he dead?"

"I don't know." He flicked his joint away and it hissed out against the wet ground. Insanely, she had the urge to tell him that using drugs was bad, especially for an athlete.

S.M. FREEDMAN

Moving closer, Leigh jabbed a toe into the man's side. There was no response. He studied him for what felt like an eternity, his brow furrowed in thought.

"Eve!" Sara called from somewhere behind them, her voice warbling with fear. "Eve! Where are you?"

"Shit." Leigh pushed her toward the sound of Sara's voice. "Grab my sister before she sees this. Take her home."

"But …"

He pushed her again. "Just do it."

"But what if he's dead?"

"Don't worry." He ran a trembling hand through his hair, and she was struck by how much he looked like his sister. "I'll take care of it."

The sky ripped open in a blinding flash of lightning, and somewhere close by, Sara cried out. A moment later thunder rumbled. The rain came in a deafening torrent, and within seconds they were drenched.

Wiping rain out of her eyes, Eve took another look at the man on the ground. Did he blink? Turn his head a little? She wasn't sure, and for years after those questions haunted her.

"Go on." Leigh waved her away. Hunching against the rain, he lifted a thick tree branch from the ground near his feet.

"Leigh?"

He looked up at her, his hair dripping into his eyes. They were bloodshot, but dead sober. "Go now, Eve."

Without a word, she turned and ran back through the trees, calling for Sara.

NINE

EVE MOVED BACK AND FORTH between the silver and a confusing array of hospital rooms. Sometimes there was a sink to the left, sometimes to the right. Mirrors on the wall, or none. The hall door had a window, and then it didn't. There was a pink curtain, and then it was green, and then there was no curtain. Only the ceiling remained the same: white tile, fluorescent lighting.

She'd had seventeen surgeries. Or was it twenty-seven? She lived in a fog of procedures and therapies and medications. Only two words stuck in her mind: *decompressive craniectomy*. They'd sawed off a chunk of her skull to make space for her swelling brain, stuck it in a freezer, and then reinserted it like a piece from some horrific jigsaw puzzle. Beneath tight bandages, the area was bitingly numb, a constant reminder of what had been missing.

It was a detail she wished she could forget. Her other injuries were elusive, known not by their names but by their pain. Bones were broken, ribs were cracked — she had bruises, contusions, and internal bleeding. But the worst part was the cold. An arctic chill had frosted her skin and burrowed all the way to her marrow. No matter what she did, she couldn't get warm. It was another symptom of the brain injury, she thought they'd told her.

"Earth to Eve."

Blinking, she saw that a small table was set up in front of her. A deck of cards had been laid out in neat rows — hearts, diamonds, clubs, and spades.

"Umm, go fish?"

"Not quite," Leigh said. "I was teaching you how to play solitaire. Remember?"

She hadn't remembered that he was in the room, let alone anything to do with a card game.

"Did you lose time again?"

She hated the sympathy she heard in his voice. "I was never good at cards, anyway."

"I know."

"Could we do this another day?"

Without a word, he bent forward and scooped the cards into a pile. His hair was thinning at the top, showing some pink scalp underneath. She wondered if he knew.

"It's almost ten, anyway. Time for me to go home, and for you to get some rest."

She looked out the window. "It's that late? It's only just starting to get dark." Had she even eaten dinner?

"It's July."

"Oh. I'm getting worse, aren't I?"

"Not at all." He banged the cards into a neat stack and tucked them into their box.

"I've always known when you're lying."

He raised an eyebrow, but didn't look at her. "I doubt that."

This irked her because the truth was she didn't know anything anymore. So, she dug in even more, giving him a mulish look. "I always have."

"Then remind me not to teach you how to play poker."

"Would you just *look* at me?"

Sighing, he did. In the lamplight, his eyes looked almost black. She didn't like his beard, she decided. He probably thought it gave him the air of a serious doctor, but it hid too much of his face.

"What do you want me to say, Eve?"

"I want the truth."

He snorted as though understanding the lie.

It was her turn to look away. The parking lot below her window was nearly empty, pockmarked with circles of light cast by the lampposts. "You made it impossible for me ..." She trailed off, searching for the memory.

"To tell the truth?"

She knew without looking that his lips had pulled up in that angry half smile that made her anxious. She shook her head, grimacing at the numb feeling of the bandaged area rubbing the back of the chair.

"To *face* the truth." Yes. That felt right.

"About Sara?" How strange her name sounded on his lips, as though he hadn't said it in years. His chair squeaked as he shifted his weight. "Sara's been gone a long time."

Shock hit her like a flash flood. Sara was gone?

She looked down at her hands, noticed that someone had painted her nails a red so dark it was almost black.

The polish colour was called Very Berry Black Cherry. Yes, she remembered that. And with that, she remembered her friend. She'd had rounded cheeks and crooked teeth. Leigh's blue eyes. And a laugh like wind chimes in a storm.

She could feel the empty place in her heart where her friend had lived, and feel the loss burn her stomach like acid. But what had happened to her?

"I know how much you loved her." His voice was soft with something that sounded like forgiveness.

"Yes."

"It was nobody's fault." The words were sweetly said, but they festered like fallen fruit. "And it's been thirteen years."

"It's been *fourteen* years," she said, remembering if only for a moment. "I was only thirteen years old."

"So was she."

It sounded like an accusation, but of what? Her mind stuttered, trying to remember. Her gaze moved to the window, to the parking lot below. Time shifted and stretched.

"Eve?" Leigh sat in the chair closest to the door. In his eyes, she could see the flash of an ancient storm, buried deep within. What had they been discussing?

"What?"

"Remember what we used to say? 'Just you and me against the world.'" His voice was smooth and fragile, like the ice that covered the pond's murky waters in winter.

The pond. She remembered kneeling there in the moonlight, trying to see past the icy surface to what lay below, and listening to the rattle of winter brittle branches. She'd been terrified, but unable to look away. She'd needed to know, needed to see for herself.

She'd stayed until the frozen ground had turned her knees to stone, until the sting of the wind's icy breath had burned her wet cheeks into a fever. She'd been ill for weeks afterward, and her mother had been furious. That must have been before Donna decided it was safer not to care.

But what had she been looking for? That, she couldn't recall.

"What do you say? I think we could both use a fresh start."

"A fresh start," she said. "Why?"

"Because I've spent my whole life losing you, over and over again."

"Maybe I wasn't yours to lose."

The pain she saw in his eyes made her stomach churn with guilt. Why was she being so rude? He'd probably rearranged his whole life to be by her side, and this was how she repaid his kindness.

"I'm sorry," she said.

"My licence has been updated."

Her mind stuttered again, trying to cope with the abrupt change of topic. "What?"

"My medical licence. I've joined a private practice. Dr. Stephens wants to retire."

"I forgot about him. He's still alive?"

Dr. Stephens had seemed ancient when she was a child. She remembered how the ashen flaps of his face had tucked into themselves to form a neutral doctor's mask. But his clenched old-man fist had given him away, as had the *scritch-scritch-scritch* sound of him carving her referral into the notepad, as though seeking blood with the tip of the pen. She'd begged Donna to find her a female doctor after that, but Donna never had.

Now Leigh would take over Eve's old doctor's practice. She thought there was a joke in there somewhere and it was probably a bitter one, but she didn't have the energy to pursue it.

"So you're moving home," she said instead. "That's what you're telling me?"

"I thought you'd be happy?"

"I don't know what I am."

"Well." He dropped his gaze, momentarily at a loss. Then he blinked, and looked up at her with the old smile curving his lips. "We have lots of time for you to figure that out. I'm in no rush."

"All right."

"And you need to be more patient with yourself. Your memory will come back in time. The blank spots will fill in."

"Some things might be worth forgetting," she said, but the bite was gone from her words. Her eyes were gritty and dry, her eyelids heavy with the need for rest.

"Brain injuries take longer to heal than other injuries," he continued. "The brain is way more complex than a leg, for example."

"Yes." She suspected they'd had this conversation before. Many times, perhaps. "I feel like my mind's slipping on ice, trying to catch hold of something. But there's nothing to grab, so I just keep sliding around."

"I'm sure it's frustrating."

"Scary," she admitted. "What if I never get back to normal?"

"When were you ever normal?" He said it kindly, as though he appreciated that about her. "The trouble is, they just don't know. The neurologist and Dr. Jeffries —"

"Who?"

"Your psychiatrist."

"Oh, of course."

"They say this is normal after the kind of brain trauma you've endured. In most cases, it gets better. With time."

"Okay." She was starting to slur.

"You're tired." Leigh stood and tucked the deck of cards on the table beside a wilting bouquet of flowers. "Want some help getting into bed?"

"I'm fine."

He bent to kiss her cheek, and his beard felt prickly against her skin. She really didn't like it. It was too much like a mask.

"Get some rest. I'll see you tomorrow."

Once he was gone, she pushed herself out of the vinyl chair and shuffled to bed. She was still wondering whether to use the call button to request a pain pill when sleep overtook her.

TEN
Sara's Tenth Birthday

"RUN FASTER!"

The bag was heavy, and it sounded like it was full of glass bottles. It clanged painfully against her hip.

"I'm going as fast as I can. Stop pushing me!"

Sara didn't sound at all amused. Eve wasn't amused, either, but she laughed like an out-of-breath donkey. She'd really screwed up this time, and they were both going to pay for it.

She gave Sara another poke in the back. "They're catching up!"

Their breath puffed around their faces, adding to the fog that shrouded the low-lying ground along the river. They could barely see ten feet in front of themselves, though the way the path twisted, they wouldn't have been able to see much more than that, anyway.

The boys behind them shouted obscenities. They did, indeed, sound like they were closing in. This was no surprise, as they were several years older and fuelled by indignation.

"You said this was Annabeth's bag," Sara said.

"I thought it was."

They'd found the backpack leaning against a fence beside the skate park, and seized the opportunity. The previous week, Annabeth and her cronies had pulled a fire alarm during morning recess and told Mrs. Taylor that she and Sara were to blame.

Their parents had been called to the school, and their ardent denials hadn't done them a bit of good. Donna was still coming up with new and creative ways to punish her. Yesterday she'd spent forever digging clots of goop-covered hair out of the bathtub drain.

"Next time, could you be totally sure?" Sara huffed. "Because now we're going to die."

"Then there won't be a next time."

Clank-clank-clank went the bottles against her hip. They were going to leave a bruise.

Behind them on the left came the sound of someone crashing through the trees. It was a smart move, allowing whomever it was to approach them in a straight line. But the girls were fast approaching the railroad tracks, and beyond lay the dense greenery of the Crook. If they could make it there, she was pretty sure they could disappear along the hidden trails and mud-bogs.

"Come on, come on!"

"I don't want to die on my birthday," Sara said, but her nerves had taken hold and she giggled, too. "Why do I listen to you?"

"Because you're bored. Cross the tracks, we're almost there."

The boy smart enough to cut through the trees turned out to be Steve Ryder, a pockmarked pile of grease whom no one seemed to miss when he died of a drug overdose six years later, except maybe his parents. He crashed through blackberry bushes, seemingly unaware of the thorns that tore at his exposed skin, and sprinted the last few feet to the train tracks.

"I see you!" he bellowed, pointing an accusatory finger at them.

The girls squealed in response, sliding down the opposite hill toward safety. Three more steps and then they ran through the shadows of the Crook.

"Head for the pond!" Eve heaved the bag up to her chest and wrapped her arms around it, hoping to stifle the clanking. Cutting around her slower friend, she took the lead.

"We can foil them in the Foil!" Sara said, because some jokes never grew old. Eve rolled her eyes.

They slipped and slid down the path, wheezing and laughing. The closer they got to the river, the denser the fog became. The damp made her cough.

They passed through the clearing where, just over a year before, the man with the black beard had gone headfirst into a tree. She gave the incident no more than a fleeting thought.

"We're coming for you!" Steve Ryder hollered.

A deeper voice, probably Canton Forsythe's, added, "And we're going to *fuck you up*!"

He sounded berserk with rage, and she supposed that made sense. Canton was riding a winning streak in football and in life in general — and had a lot to lose if people found out he was drinking and doping with boneheads from the poor end of town.

She grabbed Sara's hand. "It's okay, Gumdrop. We're almost there."

"We're not going to make it," Sara said.

She was right. With an incoherent bellow, Steve Ryder flew out of the fog and slammed into Sara's back. Sara yelped in surprise and stumbled forward, knocking into Eve's shoulder as she fell. Eve spun around, just barely managing to stay on her feet.

Canton Forsythe slid into view, so angry his usually pretty head looked like a smoking tomato. Following behind him like the last two horsemen of the apocalypse were Kyle O'Neill and Jerry Moore.

Kyle was Annabeth's older brother, which explained the confusion over the bag. He must have stolen it from his sister, only to have Eve and Sara steal it from him. He stalked around behind Canton like a rooster on uppers.

Jerry was better known in the neighbourhood as "Slothboy." He bent over his belly and took deep gasping breaths, looking like he might puke on his shoes.

Sara lay in the mud near Eve's feet, having apparently decided that playing dead was her safest bet.

Sneering, Steve Ryder moved in on her. "Give us the bag."

"Up yours," she said in return, surprising herself as much as the others. Her heart gave a meaty *ka-thump* inside her chest and then thundered along at a maddening pace, as though eager to do its job while it still could.

"*What* did you say?" Steve's voice was dangerously soft.

Eve's was not. "Are you deaf as well as stupid? I said *up yours.*"

Sara groaned into a pile of wet leaves. Taking a few steps backward, Eve clutched the bag more tightly.

"That's not yours, bitch!" Kyle O'Neill jeered from behind Canton's back.

"Oh my *gawd*!" Eve pretended to grow faint from shock. "A rooster that talks? Someone get this bird his own show!"

Not waiting for their reactions, she turned and fled into the fog.

"Hey!" Steve shouted, and the chase resumed.

She spared a quick glance over her shoulder. She couldn't see anything but a rolling sheet of grey, but it sounded like all four horsemen were in pursuit. This was what she'd hoped for, as it would give Sara the chance to run to the baseball diamond where Leigh and his friends were practising. That meant Eve needed to evade capture for at least ten minutes.

She wished she hadn't swiped the bag in the first place.

Paradoxically, this thought made her even more determined to hold on to it. Stupidly stubborn, Donna called her, and she had to admit that on occasion her mother was right. But Sara would have been proud, because she was going to try to foil them in the Foil.

Eve launched headfirst into the tangle of quicksilver plants and then slowed her pace, moving silently. The silver leaves hung heavy and glistening like pearls. Branches loomed out of the fog to snag her clothing, soaking her in the process. In the eerie dripping mess, sounds were muffled and warped.

Pushing forward, she lost all sense of direction. Somewhere to her right the talking rooster shouted his frustration and, farther away, Canton called out orders for them to split up and search the area, his voice warbling in the thick air.

When she figured she was close to the middle of the quicksilver field, she eased down to a sitting position, crossed her legs, and gently laid the bag on her lap. The fog shrouded her, wetting her cheeks and hair with fine droplets. She slowed her breathing, trying to calm her racing mind and heart. The most important thing she'd learned from playing Seekers was that, to avoid capture, she needed to be calm. Over the years, she'd become really good at it, and she was rarely flushed out of hiding.

As she'd hoped, the boys proved inherently lazy. From what she could hear, they'd each chosen an easier job like searching the forest or the marsh grass along the river. Each of them was probably hoping someone else would take the Foil, as whoever did would come away with clothing that was soaked and tattered. She was learning that lesson first-hand, and was just hoping she could buy Sara enough time to return with Leigh. Maybe he'd bring some of his baseball buddies. Or his bat.

A giggle burbled up her throat, and she refocused on her breathing. In and out, in and out. As the minutes ticked by, she had more and more trouble staying calm. She was all too aware that this particular game of Seekers would have dire consequences if she lost. She did a few neck rolls to release some tension.

"Hey! Do you see that?" Steve Ryder said.

His voice was startlingly close, and she jumped. The bottles clanked, making her cringe. Had he spotted her?

Frantically, she scanned her surroundings. She couldn't see three feet beyond her nose, but that didn't mean they couldn't see her.

"Oh, shit!" came the reply, in a voice that was slow and slightly slurred. This must have been Slothboy. She'd never heard him speak before today.

"Dude, let's get out of here," Steve said. He sounded scared.

"We're not carrying anymore. Can't we just hang around and find out what they're doing? It looks like they're dragging the pond."

"Hell, no," Steve said. "Get within ten feet and they'll know you're baked."

"Shouldn't we at least warn the other guys?" Slothboy said.

"I'm not going to jail. They're on their own."

"Wait!" Slothboy said, but from the sound of it they were moving away.

Their departure did nothing to calm her nerves. In fact, it did quite the opposite. Were there really cops nearby? And if Slothboy was right, what were they looking for at the bottom of the pond? She could take a guess, and the idea sent her into a swooning panic.

She dumped the bag from her lap and crawled downhill, hoping she was heading in the right direction. She needed to take a closer look. If the police were really dragging the pond, she had to somehow find Leigh before he stumbled on to the scene. Not for a moment did it cross her mind that Sara would do anything other than run for her brother's help — or that Leigh would do anything other than pounce into immediate action when he heard she was in trouble. During the fleeting breaths of her childhood, some things were just a given.

Pausing to get her bearings, she heard the low rumble of machinery and some kind of flapping noise. She heard voices, too — *adult* voices. On hands and knees, she eased to the edge of the quicksilver and found a spot where she was well hidden but could see the pond below. The sun burned through the fog in patches now, and the pond sparkled blue and gold.

There were, indeed, police officers. Several wore diving gear. A tent had been set up near the pond's edge, and one corner had slipped from its peg to flap in the wind. The ground steamed, wisps rising toward the promise of blue sky above. Officers milled around with straight-backed authority.

She was too late to save Leigh. He rushed out of the fog and forest, baseball bat held aloft, and skidded to a cartoonlike stop. It would have been funny under other circumstances. Several officers sprang into action, reaching for their gun belts, but Leigh quickly dropped the bat and raised his hands in the air.

Moments later, Sara stumbled out of the forest behind him. She was red-faced and drenched in sweat, and now she was the one who looked like she was going to puke. One of the officers beckoned them forward. With reluctance, Leigh and Sara complied.

"Oh damn." Eve chewed on her fingers.

She couldn't hear the conversation that followed, but Sara did most of the talking. She seemed to recover her breath quickly, and waved her arms with animation while she spoke. Eve guessed she was giving a hastily modified version of their morning adventure, pegging them as the victims of four horrendous bullies. Sara pointed at Leigh, likely explaining how she'd sought her brother's help.

Not for the first time, she felt grateful for Sara's quick tongue and even quicker mind. The officer relaxed into attentiveness as Sara spoke, and she almost smiled at her friend's calm prowess. But one look at Leigh struck the smile from her face.

He stood beside his sister, looking stunned and pale. His gaze kept roving guiltily from the officer, to the divers in the pond, to a spot near where she was hidden. Backing up a bit, she wondered if Leigh had spotted her. But no, his gaze slipped blankly past her. As the conversation continued, he looked at the Foil with increasing frequency. Then he seemed to recognize what he was doing. He abruptly turned his back, facing the river instead. His shoulders pulled up to his ears.

His body language told her everything she'd never wanted to know. Her gorge rose with horror. She looked back the way she'd come, and then slammed her arm across her mouth and nose, gagging. She'd been too focused on finding a view of the pond to notice the scatter of clothing and bones she'd just crawled through.

As it turned out, it was Eve who puked that day.

ELEVEN

"WHAT HAPPENED TO YOUR BEARD?" she asked when Leigh squeezed through the door. He carried a takeout bag and wore a nervous grin. His cheeks looked raw and baby-fresh.

"You didn't like it." He placed the bag on the edge of the bed. "I brought Thai food."

"I didn't tell you I didn't like it!" She pressed the button to lift her bed into a seated position. "Did I?"

"You wish I hadn't shaved, then?"

"Well …"

Opening the bag, which smelled heavenly, he pulled out white Styrofoam containers.

"Coconut curry soup?" he said.

"That's my favourite."

"I also got lemongrass chicken, pad Thai, spring rolls, and mixed vegetables. Got to eat your greens. And if you're really good, I brought you something for dessert."

"Delicious. Thank you."

She took the bowl of soup and watched him make up a plate for each of them. "Have you been bringing me food a lot? It's not necessary."

"Your tongue would have died of boredom. I consider it my medical duty." He laid her plate on the swing-out table and placed a fork and napkin beside it.

"How long have I been here?"

"Too long," he said. "But you've had good news, I hear?"

"Oh?" She lost interest in her soup, which was creamy and had just the right amount of heat. It caused her upper lip and forehead to bead with sweat.

His forehead beaded with sweat, too, although he hadn't yet touched his soup. "You had a meeting this morning. With the doctors and your grandmother."

She continued to look at him, spoon held aloft.

"They think you're ready to go home. You'll have daily home care, of course."

"For real?"

"You've made amazing strides. You were as close to dead as anyone I've ever seen, and yet here you are."

"Here I am," she said, feeling the flames of anxiety lick at her skin. "Alive and ... well, not *well*, but ..." She paused. "I guess I'll take 'alive.'"

"Me, too. And you *are* well. You forget how much progress you've made."

"I forget a lot of things." She pushed at the soup with her spoon. Her appetite was waning.

"Eve, it's —"

"Normal. But I only remember you."

He paused with a forkful of broccoli halfway to his mouth. "What do you mean?"

"I only remember *you*. And Button, a little bit. But I don't remember any of the nurses, or other doctors, or that psychiatrist you've told me about —"

"Dr. Jeffries."

"Right, him —"

"Her."

"What?"

"Dr. Jeffries is a woman."

She flopped back against her pillow, food forgotten. "See? That's my point. How long have I been in this hospital?"

"You're not in the hospital." Leigh's voice was so quiet she could barely hear him.

"What?"

"You're in a rehab facility. And you've been here for six months."

"No." She looked toward the window, where she had watched the passing of the seasons. But it was no longer to her left. The sink had moved, too. It had been to the right of the door, and there had been an arrangement of flowers on the counter beside it. Now there was a mirrored closet and the door to what she guessed was the bathroom.

"Every day you have physical therapy with Gladys or James. Susan takes you sometimes, but you don't like her as much. You think she's bossy."

She shook her head, at a loss for words.

"And Dr. Jeffries works with you, too. Three times a week."

"Leigh …"

"I come to visit most evenings. And your grandmother is here every morning. She has breakfast with you. Do you remember that?"

She hadn't until he said it. But with the reminder, a few

memories surfaced: Button toddling forward with steps so quick she looked like she was riding a conveyor belt, or tsking at Eve's forgetfulness, or berating the nurses about a cut on Eve's leg that wasn't healing, or dunking her tea bag into a steaming mug while complaining that they only had Lipton's.

"Of course I remember."

She pulled the plate of food closer and took a bite of the chicken. Normal people ate dinner, and she was determined to be normal.

"Next week. You'll be home by the end of next week. With your grandma, and your art studio. Maybe you can start painting again?"

"Maybe."

"Have you been drawing? I brought you that sketchpad and some chalk —"

"Charcoal," she said, looking to where Leigh pointed. "No, I haven't been drawing."

Ignoring her, he flipped open the sketchpad. "This is different." His voice sounded thick in his throat.

"What is?"

He brought the sketchpad to her. "This isn't your usual style. Well, not like the stuff I've seen, anyway. I guess that's to be expected."

"Let me see." She reached for the sketchbook. Leigh pulled it into his chest, his brow creased with worry.

"What? Does it suck?" she tried to joke.

When he flipped the sketchpad open on his lap, she gasped. He was right. It was very different from her usual loose, colour-filled style. The drawing was done with thick, precise strokes, full of shadows. From the white page a man reached for her, pleaded with her, beckoned to her.

A memory arose from the swamp of her mind.

The storm had been raging. Rain sprayed from the tires of passing cars, pooled around leaf-clogged gutters, and pounded the canvas awning above her like a drumbeat calling her home.

"Take my hand, Eve."

Water dripped from the brim of his fedora and his eyes were the colour of fine amber, just like hers.

When he reached for her, she saw that his ring finger was missing from knuckle to tip. This had sparked a jolt of recognition that she hadn't, at the time, been able to process.

But now she could. It had to do with her favourite bedtime story. Night after night she'd said no to "Cinderella," no to "Goldilocks and the Three Bears," no to "Hansel and Gretel." She'd beg Button to tell her, once again, about the Polish printer and his hungry printing press. It was a true story, a family tale turned legend, and that made it all the more delicious.

As the story went, the printer had been in business a couple of years when he bought a new top-of-the-line printing press. All was well until the day he pinched his skin while closing the press. It wasn't a bad injury, and only one page was ruined by a smear of blood.

But that taste of the printer's flesh seemed to awaken a hunger in the new press. Accidents happened so frequently that the printer came home every day with new cuts and bruises. His wife begged him to sell the press. It was clearly bringing him bad luck, and someone in Rozopol had expressed an interest in buying it. He scoffed at his wife, told her he would not be swayed by superstition.

But he changed his mind the day the press ate his finger.

After the accident, he sold it to the printer in Rozopol, grateful that he'd lost a finger and not his life. Or so he thought until the infection set in.

His widow received the money from the sale the day after his funeral. Three weeks later, the Nazis froze all Jewish bank accounts, and that money was lost. Two weeks after that, the widow realized she was pregnant.

Their daughter was born inside the walls of the Warsaw Ghetto. The widow named the baby Batya, "daughter of God." Many years later, Batya would have a grand-daughter who couldn't pronounce her name properly, and instead would call her Button.

"Close the sketchbook," Eve said.

One eyebrow rose questioningly, but Leigh did as she asked. "It's really good."

"Please throw it out," she said through gritted teeth. "I don't want to see it."

"Are you sure?" He flipped through the sketchbook. "You've drawn him on every page. And you've really cap-tured something. Desperation. Or fear, maybe. Who is he?"

She opened her mouth to lie by telling him she didn't know, but instead said, "My great-grandfather."

"Really?" he mused, still staring at the drawing. "It's a shame to throw it out." One look at her face and he relented.

When he went to drop it in the bin in the corner of the room, she said, "No, please, not there!"

He sighed, but disappeared through the door.

By the time he returned, she'd regained much of her composure. And by the time he left, she'd forgotten about the sketchbook and the man in the fedora.

TWELVE

Eve's Fourteenth Birthday

THERE WAS A KNOCK on her bedroom door, and Eve told her grandmother to come in. She knew it was Button because Donna never bothered to knock.

Her grandmother wore her flowered bathrobe, the one that was threadbare at the elbows and smelled of cold cream. She moved into the bedroom, automatically tidying as she went. She picked up a pile of clothing from the floor and stuffed it into the laundry basket, closed the closet door, and smoothed the comforter over the foot of the bed before sitting down. Eve rolled onto her side and placed her head in her grandma's lap.

"One year," Button said, stroking the curls away from her temple.

That gentle acknowledgement gave her permission to let go, and she sobbed into the floral fabric of her grandmother's robe. Button stroked her hair, murmuring in Yiddish.

"Here," Button said, eventually, handing her a clot of tissues.

She mopped her face and blew her nose, which was painfully raw, and dropped the used tissues on the carpet.

"I'm going to work now," Donna said from the doorway. She wore a navy skirt and white silk blouse. Her high heels dangled from her hand. Her black hair hung glossy and perfectly straight to her chin, and her bangs were a severe wedge that ended just above her perfectly styled eyebrows.

"Okay." Rather than look her mother in the eye, she kept her gaze on Donna's feet. Pink nail polish showed through the tan fabric of her nylons.

"I'll pick up the cake on my way home."

"I don't want a cake."

"Then don't eat it," Donna said. "You're going to be late for school."

She looked up and accidentally met her mother's gaze. "No way. I'm not going."

How could Donna's eyes look like a younger version of Button's — or an older version of her own, for that matter — and yet be so chillingly different? Eve saw no warmth there, no caring, no kindness. Which was why she found it much easier to focus on Donna's feet.

"You're not going to mope around here all day," Donna said.

"Do you have any idea what school's like for me, now? I'm like a pariah. Do you know what kind of things the kids say to me?"

"Oh, I can imagine," Donna said.

"Whatever you can imagine, it's a billion times worse."

"You're a *Gold*, Eve. So, act like it."

"What does that mean?"

"It means stiffen your spine and keep going."

"Oh, yeah. Great. I'll just go ahead and do that." Donna padded away to the kitchen.

"Thanks for the pep talk, *Mom*!" Eve called out.

"Eve," Button said.

"Oh, you're welcome!" Donna called back.

They listened to the click of her high heels across the kitchen linoleum. The door creaked open and slammed closed, and a minute later they heard the rumble of Donna's car starting.

"I really don't want to go to school."

Button sighed and stroked the hair from her forehead. "I know."

"Do I have to?"

"It's not my place to go around your mother," Button said. "Just try to get through the day."

"I don't feel good," Eve said.

"I'd be surprised if you did."

"No, seriously. My stomach feels all wobbly."

"I'm sure you'll feel better once you've had some breakfast. You go on and get ready for school, and I'll make you some eggs. Okay?"

Her grandmother was almost at the door when she asked, "Do you think I'll forget her?"

Button turned. "Sara? I don't imagine you will."

"Right, but. Do you remember Grandpa Max? I mean, clearly?"

Button moved back into the room and sat back down on the foot of the bed. "Well, of course I do. He was my husband for almost thirty years."

"I'm sorry," she said, and the tears started again.

"What are you sorry for, *bubbalah*?" Button asked, stroking her back.

"I don't remember him."

"Oh," Button said, and Eve cried harder. "That's all right. You were very young when he died."

"I should remember him. It's awful that I can't."

"You don't remember anything at all?" Button asked.

"No. Well, I have one memory of him. We were at synagogue —"

"He used to take you to shul every Shabbos, so he could show you off to all his friends," Button said.

"Did he?" She sniffed. "I remember that I was wearing a frilly dress, and I felt very pretty in it because the skirt would go out like a bell when I twirled. But it was scratchy against my skin, and I felt all itchy. And Grandpa lifted me up in his arms, and he carried me up the stairs to kiss the Torah scrolls."

"Lovely," Button said, still stroking her back.

"And they were huge, and wrapped in beautiful fabric and silver casing. The lights above them were so bright I had to squint. And I could see our reflection in the silver, me with my hair all curled around my head and Grandpa Max wearing his big black hat."

She wiped her eyes and saw that her grandmother was smiling.

"He was a good man, my Max. A real *mensch*. And he loved you very much. Can you feel that?"

"Yes," she said. "I don't really remember him, but I still miss him."

"I miss him, too. And I haven't forgotten him, any more than you will forget Sara. But *di tseit brengt vunden un hailt vunden,* time brings wounds and heals them. It's natural to let her go a little."

Eve looked down at her lap. "Sometimes I can't remember her face clearly anymore. Or what her voice sounded like. And then there are other times when she's as clear to me as if she's right there beside me. But I'm worried. What if …"

Button sighed. "What if she keeps fading away?"

"Right."

"Hmm," Button said, looking sad and thoughtful at the same time. "You could paint a portrait of her? Do you think that would help?"

"Maybe."

"Or you could start a diary, write down things you remember about her. Or even write letters to her, telling her what you're doing or how you're feeling."

"That's a good idea," she said, even though she knew she'd never do it. She couldn't write with honesty because someone might read it.

Her grandmother smiled and patted her on the knee. "All right, then. I'll go make you some eggs."

Once Button had shut the door, she slipped her hands under her shirt and ran them across her breasts, which felt swollen and tender. She dug in her nails and twisted.

Not good enough.

She leaned over and tugged a small metal box out from between her mattress and box spring. She opened it and pulled out the razor nestled inside. She clamped it between her teeth and pulled up the sleeve of her pajama top. Her arm was covered with scabs in a cross-stitch pattern of grief and relief. She chose a clean spot and dug in with the tip of the razor, waiting for that pop of release. She watched in fascination as blood oozed from the wound. The surface pain was searing, but it soothed the deeper internal agony. She took a deep breath, pulled out the razor, and placed a tissue over the wound to stop the bleeding.

She could smell her breakfast cooking, so she hurried through her morning routine and made her way to the kitchen, tugging her sleeves down to cover her arms.

It was almost ten when she left the house, and though she had no intention of going to school, she still walked in that direction.

She paused at the entrance to the Crook, which sat green and silent in the fall chill. Labour Day had come and gone, taking the children with it. There was no one playing Seekers, or picking blackberries, or riding bikes along the Crook's paths and mud-bogs. There was just her, a walking wound in the shape of a girl.

She could picture her classmates sitting in neat rows with their heads bent over their desks, hear the catcalls and chatter of the lunchroom and the slap of new shoes on polished floors when the bell rang at the end of the day.

No one seemed to care about the gaping black hole that had opened up and swallowed her best friend. No one seemed to notice the absence of light. In kid-time, Sara's death was ancient history. So, they just kept laughing and chattering and flirting and bullying and learning, like everything was normal. Donna would say that life marched on, and she could either keep up with it or get trampled.

Well, she didn't feel much like marching.

She crossed the railroad tracks, smelling the ghost of sunbaked resin. Tendrils of fog snaked up the path from the river. She let them swallow her, feeling the damp weight fill her throat and lungs. It was just as foggy as the day she and Sara stole what they thought was Annabeth's bag, and the boys chased them into the Crook.

"We can foil them in the Foil."

Now she walked the path to the river like a tourist. Here was where the man hit his head against the tree. Here was where the boys caught up with her and Sara and demanded their bag of contraband. Here's where she escaped into the Foil.

Keeping to the path, she skirted along the edge of the quicksilver until she came to the high ground above the pond. This had been Sara's favourite spot, but after that day Eve insisted they find somewhere new.

She moved down to the edge of the river, where the prickling grass grew unabated. She could hear the water lapping against the shore, but she couldn't see it. Pulling off her backpack, she lay down. The grass punctured the fabric of her shirt and jeans, jabbing her like a million tiny needles. The fog rolled above and around her, kissing her with dampness.

"I wanted to tell you that I'm going to go to the police station this afternoon. To tell them what I saw."

"Oh, Sara, I'm sorry."

The only answer she received was the groaning of a tugboat somewhere on the river.

When she left the Crook, she turned in the direction of the Adlers' home.

It was probably a bad idea. She hadn't seen Mr. or Mrs. Adler in months. With each step she took, her anxiety grew. She made it as far as the sidewalk in front of their rambling green house, and froze there in indecision.

Both cars were in the driveway, and she could see the lights were on through the kitchen and living room windows. Despite the cloud of grief that seemed to permeate the air around the Adler home, she could still feel the warmth of the place. Filled to the brim with laughter and arguments and mess, it had always felt like a sanctuary from the cold quiet of her own home.

Would she still be welcome? And if not, could she bear the rejection?

She stepped back and was about to turn away when the front door opened. Mr. Adler stepped out onto the porch. He wore a tattered housecoat and slippers, and what was left of his hair puffed above his ears like cotton candy. Her first thought was that he'd shrunk. His chest caved inward as though half his internal organs had been removed.

"Eve." He lifted a hand in greeting. It wasn't exactly a welcome, but it was better than she'd hoped for.

Taking in a deep breath, she stepped onto the first paving stone, and the next, and the next, until she found herself at the bottom of the porch stairs. She'd bounded up and down them so many times over the years she'd ceased to notice them. There were six in total. The paint had worn away from the centre of each step, exposing the weather-beaten wood underneath. The porch listed like a ship in a storm, taking the stairs with it.

She couldn't seem to get her legs to work, so Mr. Adler climbed down to meet her instead.

She remembered when they'd redecorated Sara's room. The man who stood before her bore little resemblance to the man who'd cussed a blue streak doing battle against drooping wallpaper and a lack of right angles. His eyes were rimmed with purple, like he'd been punched in the nose. His cheeks were covered in grey stubble.

"Mr. Adler," she said. "I just wanted to …" She trailed off, not sure what she'd actually wanted to do. Apologize? Seek comfort? Go back in time?

"I wanted to see you." She couldn't meet his gaze.

He was silent for a moment, and then he said, "How's your grandmother?"

"She's okay. She sends her love."

"Tell her thank you."

Eve nodded miserably.

"Well," Mr. Adler said after another lengthy silence. "Thanks for stopping by." He turned and started back up the stairs.

"I'm sorry," she blurted.

He paused for a heartbeat, and then continued up the stairs.

As he reached the porch, the screen door banged open and Mrs. Adler stomped out, followed by their remaining children. She hadn't realized Leigh and Danielle were home from college.

"What do you want, Eve?" Mrs. Adler said.

"I just wanted to …"

"What?" Mrs. Adler said.

"Mom," Leigh said, placing a hand on her shoulder.

Danielle stepped forward, her pretty face twisted into an ugly snarl. "You have a lot of nerve, showing up here."

"I'm sorry," she said, backing away. "I'll just go."

"That's a good idea," Mrs. Adler said.

Eve turned and hustled down the path, feeling the burn of tears in her eyes.

She made it as far as her front yard before collapsing. She vomited half-digested eggs and toast, leaving a steaming pile of sick on the freshly cut lawn. Once there was nothing left inside her but burning shame, she curled into a ball and pressed her face against the wet grass, waiting for hell to open up and swallow her whole.

THIRTEEN

HER FINGERS TREMBLED on the paintbrush. It was from her favourite set, brought home from Paris. It was a high-quality mongoose brush, and only a few bristles had been lost in its decade of use. Since the accident, her memory had more holes than solid spaces. But as she thumbed at the layers of dry paint on the brush's shaft, it occurred to her that each fleck of colour told a piece of her story. And those memories, perhaps because they'd been preserved on canvas, were still accessible.

Here was the burnt sienna she'd used when Leigh brought a girl home from medical school to introduce to his parents. She'd barely left her studio all week, obsessively working on the stark landscapes of her Desert on Fire series.

Here was the cerulean blue she'd used the summer after Donna's death, when she'd created beach scenes of children splashing in ocean waves as puffy clouds rolled across perfect skies.

Her thumbnail scratched at the dark green she'd used to paint moss-covered trees — like the ones in the Crook, where secrets she could no longer recall were buried.

She frowned, trying to remember. It had something to do with Leigh. And Sara. Poor Sara, who hadn't lived long enough to have a first kiss. But what had happened to her? From the fog of her brain, all that emerged was the lonely sound of water lapping against the shore.

Shivering, she pulled the zipper of her sweater up to her throat. Perhaps in time she'd grow used to the way the cold gnawed at her bones and slowed the flow of her blood. She turned her focus to the canvas she'd set upon her easel. It had been primed with two layers of gesso, and sat ready for whatever story her brush wanted to tell.

Minutes ticked by, and the canvas remained untouched. Shaking her head in frustration, she set aside the brush and picked up the palette knife. She dipped it into the blobs of paint, mixing colours in search of inspiration.

Button had warned her to be patient with herself. So had Leigh, when he stopped by to check on her that morning. But she'd sensed the hope hidden behind their words, the desire to see some spark of the old Eve.

Closing her eyes, she willed her hand to steady. "You can do this."

The red light that filtered through her closed eyelids was soothing. She took several deep breaths, and without opening her eyes, continued to mix the paint until it felt right. Blindly, she reached for the brush. The soft squish under the bristles felt good, and her shoulders relaxed a little.

Perhaps it shouldn't matter what she painted today. It was bound to be terrible, so why not let go of her expectations? Why not focus on the feel of paint on the tip of her brush and the smooth promise of it gliding across the canvas?

"For today, that's good enough."

Not daring to open her eyes, she lost herself in the rhythmic sweep of brush on canvas, letting her mind drift into an artist's trance. Her eyes opened as the scene came to life before her: a pale summer sky, and below, the river was a grey snake with glistening green and blue scales. Along the trail edging the river, the brambles were plump with blackberries. Buckets in hand, children ran up and down, collecting fruit to be made into pies and jams. At dusk they'd haul their buckets home, arms scraped bloody and faces purple from blackberry juice.

"That's good."

The woman's voice came like the tinkle of wind chimes outside her studio, and it didn't startle her at all. It was nothing more than a conversation continued.

"It is, isn't it?" She dabbed her brush into the paint and then lifted it back to the canvas. "I always loved blackberry season. If you pick them at the right time they aren't even tart. Just sweet and juicy."

As she painted, the light in the studio grew dim. She'd have to turn on the lights soon.

"Do you think this boy should be holding a kite?"

"A yellow one."

The brush dipped. Humming, she continued to paint.

"More clouds in this corner?"

"Oh, yes."

Later, she asked, "Should I add some pink to the sky?"

"Silver."

"I don't like silver," she said, even as she grabbed the appropriate tubes and squeezed blobs onto her palette. She remembered when Hector brought the Escher collection into the gallery, how she'd obsessed over the reflective spheres.

She mixed ultramarine blue with cadmium yellow, and then added a drop of alizarin crimson. Once she was satisfied with the grey base, she began lightening with a bright white.

"What did Hector say about painting the colour silver?"

"That it should be painted like a reflection. I still don't like it." The brush touched canvas, adding delicate streaks of silver. She hated to admit it, but it was the right choice.

"Does it remind you of the Foil?"

"It makes me feel cold. Well, colder. But that's the head injury, they said."

"Who are they?"

She paused, brush held aloft. "It doesn't matter."

A bit of yellow ochre, a squeeze of black. She swirled the paint with her knife, watching the mossy green emerge. When she was satisfied, she dipped the brush and began to fill in the trees in the foreground.

"And who am I?"

She thought about it for a while, but felt her mind drifting. "Like Hector said, you're a reflection. I think this green is wrong. Maybe I should add more brown?"

"Lovely."

She was barely aware of the scraping sound as the studio door opened behind her.

"Eve," Button said, "it's pitch-dark in here." The overhead light flicked on, blinding her.

She dropped the brush and slapped her hands over her eyes. "Button, what are you doing?"

"I could ask the same. You've been in here for ten hours without so much as a pee break. Have you eaten today?"

"Umm."

"I'll take that as a no. Why are you painting in the dark?"

She tried to peek between her fingers, but the light stabbed her eyes. "I didn't realize it had gotten so dark." Now she could feel the aching stiffness in her legs and lower back.

"Oh, Eve." Button's shoes thumped across the floor as she moved farther into the room. Then she yelped like a cat whose tail has been stepped on. *Vey is mir!*

"What?"

"Your painting."

Dropping her hands, she squinted at the canvas. "Oh."

Gone were the children, the blackberry bushes, and the hazy summer sky. At the top corner, the river still lapped peacefully to the shore. But as it continued down to the centre of the canvas, it transformed into a thick, silver snake. It coiled over and around itself, scales shimmering with hints of green and blue. Red droplets of blood sprayed from fangs to flank. Instead of a tongue, a human arm unfurled from its mouth like a nightmare party whistle. The hand was delicate, the fingernails shiny with dark polish.

"It was called Very Berry Black Cherry."

"What was?" Button asked.

"Sara's nail polish." She turned away to retch.

* * *

"Well. It's really good," Leigh said. "I mean, disturbing. But really good."

"Should I clean it off?" she asked, going for the mineral spirits. "The paint is still wet enough … I think I can get most of it."

"Yes," Button said.

"No," Leigh said at the same time. "Why don't you see how you feel about it in the morning?"

"But the paint will dry."

"Worst-case scenario, you've wasted a canvas," Leigh said.

She studied the coiling silver snake. "It's really *awful*, isn't it?"

Standing behind her, neither Button nor Leigh answered.

"I mean, it's shockingly bad."

"No." Leigh placed his hands on her shoulders. The warmth of them was soothing, and she leaned into him without thought.

"It's actually … stunning. I mean, the technique is — I've never seen anything like it. But the subject matter is …"

"Awful." She wondered if Leigh grasped that it was his sister's hand dangling from the serpent's mouth.

"Yes," Button said.

She turned to look at her grandmother. In the natural lights of the studio, she looked pale. A shock of red highlighted each cheek, as though she were fevered.

"I'm sorry, Button." The painting felt like a betrayal.

Her grandmother opened and closed her mouth several times, and then said, "An artist shouldn't only paint pretty things."

"But I always have, right?"

"Well." Button gave a sad shrug. "Forgive me if I don't put this one up on the wall."

Tears sprang to Eve's eyes as she watched her grandmother leave.

"Of course," she said, but Button was already gone.

"Eve." Leigh turned her to him. "Are you all right?"

"I'm so cold."

Frowning, he pulled off his coat and wrapped her in its warmth.

"Come here."

He led her to the small sofa. They sat down, hip to hip, and stared at the painting. He wrapped a sturdy arm around her, and she eased into his heat.

"I wasn't lying when I said it's really good."

"But it's not what I painted."

"What do you mean?"

She hesitated, thinking of the blackberry bushes and the children with their buckets. It was a nostalgic scene, a summer day in the Crook. She'd tried to paint something safe and innocent, only to be reminded that she was neither.

"Nothing." She shook her head. "It just didn't turn out quite like I expected."

"Do they ever?" Leigh asked with a smile. "I remember your tantrums when you couldn't get a sketch the way you wanted it."

"I never," she said, but without much strength. She probably had.

"I used to enjoy watching you draw. You'd get so absorbed in what you were doing, the world around you didn't seem to exist. You had this passion, like your insides were on fire. I always loved that about you."

"And do you still?" she asked, surprising herself with the boldness of her question, with her bravery in asking it.

"I do," he said simply, one hand gliding over her curls and coming to rest on the sensitive spot above her collarbone. "It's always been you. You and me against the world, right?"

"Has it?"

"Maybe you don't remember," he said. "But yes. Always."

"I'm sorry," she said. "I remember some things. I mean, I obviously remember you. And that I had just the biggest crush on you when I was little." Saying that out loud should have embarrassed her, but it didn't.

"You did," he agreed with a smile.

"I remember that you seemed larger than life. You were Sara's perfect older brother. The star athlete, the popular kid."

"Well." He shrugged, gave her that smile that twisted her insides into a knot. "That might be true as well."

"But we were also close, right?"

"You spent so much time at our house, it was like I had a fourth annoying little sister. But we became friends, eventually."

"How?"

His smile disappeared, and he gave her an earnest blue-eyed look. "There was an accident. You don't remember?"

"An accident." She searched her memory and came up blank. "Did I get hurt?"

"No, not you. Somebody else did, though. And even

though you didn't mean to do it, it was kind of your fault. I covered for you so you wouldn't get in trouble."

"You did? That was nice of you. Thanks."

His hair hung into his eyes, and he brushed it to the side. The gesture was so familiar it caused her chest to tighten with something close to nostalgia.

"After that, we became friends. And then when Sara died …"

"How did she die, Leigh?"

"It was an accident," he said, and his voice grew husky. "A horrible, *horrible* accident. And none of us ever got over it."

His eyes had filled with tears, and her eyes started to burn as well. She didn't remember much, but she remembered her friend. *Our hearts are joined together, always and forever.*

"What happened to her?"

"I wasn't there," he said.

"Was I?"

"It wasn't your fault, Eve. People wanted to blame you, even my family …" He shrugged uncomfortably. "I guess when something so horrible happens, it makes it easier if there's someone else to blame. Someone who could be a target for all that anger."

"Yes," she said.

"But that was wrong. You weren't responsible. And I wish I'd been there to defend you."

"But you weren't," she said softly.

"I was in college. I came back once in a while, but no. I wasn't there. Not enough to make a difference. And I'm sorry about that; I really am."

She shrugged. "I don't really remember. And maybe that's for the best, huh?"

"Maybe it is. We've been through a lot together, Eve. We've *loved* each other through a lot."

She shifted on the couch, feeling uncomfortable.

"It's okay if you don't remember. But I did love you. And I think you loved me, too. We were really close, for a time. Because nobody else understood what we'd been through. So we … comforted each other. And loved each other, as best we could."

"How did it end?"

He shrugged, looking uncomfortable. "It was my fault. I wasn't ready to feel something so deep. I wanted to get away from my grief. Pretend that what happened to Sara hadn't happened. But every time I looked at you, I remembered. So it hurt, just being near you. And I didn't know how to make that hurt stop, except to walk away from you. So that's what I did."

There was a cold achiness inside her, like her body remembered the pain even if her damaged brain didn't. "I'm sorry, Leigh. I wish I could remember."

He laid a hand over hers, and she felt the warmth of him seeping into her bones and joints.

"But *I* do. I wasn't there for you when you needed me before. But I'm here now, and I'm not going anywhere. So, I'll be your memory. If you want me to."

Her eyes burned with tears again. "I do remember some things. I remember how you made me feel. You were the only one who could ever do it, Leigh."

"Do what?"

"Make a home inside my skin."

Rather than respond, he bent and touched his lips to hers.

FOURTEEN

Eve's Fifteenth Birthday

LEIGH DROPPED ONTO the blanket next to her. "I thought you'd be here."

She exhaled a thick stream of smoke. "I'm nothing if not predictable."

"On the contrary." He gave her that sideways smile that made her stomach do funny things.

She turned her gaze to the pond and the river beyond, tamping down the flutter of nerves. It wasn't hard to do; she'd had a lot of practice. Despite the day's unseasonable warmth, she zipped her sweatshirt up to her throat.

"The question is, what are *you* doing here, mister college man?"

"Pre-med now."

He took the joint from her fingers and brought it to his lips. "This shit kills your brain cells, you know."

"Too bad it doesn't kill your memories."

He took a deep drag and held the smoke in his lungs for several seconds, before releasing it in three short puffs. "I still keep trying."

"Yeah." She took the joint from him and filled her lungs with fire.

"I'm here for my parents. It's a hard day for them. For all of us."

Guilt prickled her skin. "How are they doing?"

"About how you'd expect."

Hooking his arms around his knees, he gazed at the pond. His limbs were long, but no longer lanky. Blond stubble dusted his face. His eyes were shiny with unshed tears.

"I don't know how you can stand to be here."

"I can still feel her here," she said. "Remember playing Seekers? How she'd always hide in the Foil?"

"I never played with you guys. I was too old and way too cool," he said with a small smile.

"You played with *me* plenty." She waited until he met her gaze, understood her meaning. In the pale light his eyes looked more grey than blue. In fact, they were the colour of the river the day it swept Sara away.

Rather than back down, as she'd expected, he held her gaze. "Ditto."

Uncomfortable, Eve tried to turn away, but he stopped her. Digging his fingers into her cheek, Leigh forced her gaze back to him.

"Stop ignoring me. We're all we've got now."

"Accomplices until the end," she said.

Rather than reply, he took the joint from her and sucked the last of it. Leaning in, he touched his lips to hers. The sensation was achingly familiar, a memory with teeth, and she opened to receive him. He blew the smoke into her mouth. Before she could think to stop him, his hands were on her shoulders, and then skimming down her arms.

"Leigh," she said, as close as she'd ever come to telling him no. The last of the smoke trickled from their mouths and dissipated, leaving no barrier between them.

He looked so much like Sara. It made her chest swell with aching grief.

Our hearts are joined together, always and forever.

He squeezed until her wrist bones ground together, making her eyes pop open.

"What's this?"

He shoved up her sleeve, exposing the line of healing scabs that laddered up her arm.

"What the hell, Eve?" His face was inches away, and his breath smelled like pot and grief. "Are you trying to kill yourself?"

She yanked her arm free. "I don't have to explain myself to you."

"Who else would understand?"

She pulled her sleeve down, staring sullenly at a passing tugboat on the river. It pulled a log boom, and the water spread in its wake in V-shaped ripples that lapped gently to shore. The boat's engine groaned as it passed, like metal scraping rock.

"Do you believe in hell?"

He considered. "Well, that depends. Are you asking about the hell we've created here on earth, or the one where the devil jabs you with his pitchfork for all eternity?"

"I'm serious, Leigh."

He shrugged. "I believe in things I can see. So, yes to the first one, and no to the second."

"Since I was six or seven," she told him, "I've had these recurring dreams where I'm sitting on this wooden bench, like a chairlift or something. There's a metal bar holding me in place. But instead of going up to the top of a mountain, it's going down into utter blackness. And I somehow know I'm riding into hell, and that the devil is waiting for me down there in his pit of fire, ready to eat my soul. And there's no escape, no matter what I do."

"Shit."

"When I die, where do you think I'll be going? We both know I don't deserve those pearly gates."

"Eve …"

"So to answer your question, no, I'm not trying to kill myself. I may have considered it once, but not now. I'm in no hurry to meet whatever's waiting for me on the other side."

They sat silently for several minutes. She stared at the river and Leigh hung his head toward his knees, appearing deep in thought.

"Well," he finally said, "I guess I'll see you there, then."

"Accomplices in eternity."

"At least we'll be together." His hand snaked toward her, palm up, and after a moment of hesitation she laid hers on top. His thumb traced the scar on her wrist, over and over, causing a strange tingling sensation to spread up her arm.

"Does Donna know you're cutting yourself?"

Eve gave a mirthless laugh. "The real question is, would she care?"

He sighed, stroked her arm some more.

"You have no idea —" She heard how her voice trembled, and resolutely pushed back the flood that threatened to drown her. "No idea what it's like around here now. The way people look at me."

"You haven't told anybody, right?"

"I'm not stupid."

"We'll make it through this," he said.

She searched his face, and saw that he really believed his words to be true. "But there's no *we*. You're not around anymore."

"It's temporary. I promised you that. I'm coming back once I've got my degree."

"So you've said."

"And *you* said you'd wait for me. Are you?"

She took a deep breath, feeling the trap he'd laid around her heart. "Of course I am."

"Good." He squeezed her hand, and then let it go to reach inside his coat. He handed her a small package wrapped in white tissue. "Happy birthday."

"What is it?"

"Open it."

Her hands trembled as she ripped the paper and lifted the lid of the jewellery box. Lying on a bed of white cotton was a dainty silver chain with a diamond-encrusted letter *S* that curled like a snake.

"Oh." Her eyes filled with tears, and the diamond fragments became a kaleidoscope of accusatory daggers. It was really just diamond dust; all she'd been able to afford.

"It was Sara's," he said.

"I know." Her hands shook too much to pick up the necklace. "I gave it to her."

"Here, let me help you."

He plucked it from the box and strung it around Eve's neck. The chain was short, made for a young girl. It cut into the base of her throat, strangling her with her own guilt. He fumbled with the tiny clasp, and when it closed he pressed his lips softly against the back of her neck.

He lingered there, breathing against her, letting her feel the press of his teeth and the damp of his tears. "Just you and me, right?"

"Right," she said, tears spilling hot down her cheeks.

Before returning home for cake and a *Golden Girls* marathon, she cleaned herself by the pond, shivering at the bite of icy water on raw flesh. Then she picked her way through the mud and marsh grass to the river. She stood on a log that was slippery and green with life, and watched the water lap at the rocks below. The wind picked up, stinging her cheeks and drying her eyes.

She reached for the silver charm digging into her throat, and yanked. The necklace sparkled in the dying light for just a moment before she let go. Rubbing at the welt on her throat, she watched it splash and disappear beneath the slate surface.

Feeling lighter, she turned for home.

FIFTEEN

BUTTON CLOSED THE LID of the toilet seat and sat down. Though it wasn't much past dinnertime, her hair was pinned up for bed, and she was wrapped in the flowered robe she'd had for as long as Eve could remember.

"I hope Hector is able to sell your paintings. Between the medical bills and all the hot water you've been using ..."

"It's the only time I feel warm." She slid deeper into the tub so soap bubbles popped against her chin. The heat tickled her skin into goose bumps, and, not for the first time, she felt grateful that Button had stopped Donna from modernizing the house. The claw-foot tub was a lifesaver.

"I know." Button gave her granddaughter a sad smile. "And I'm not *kvetching* —"

Eve laughed. "Oh, you're not?"

"Well, I shouldn't be. I'm so grateful to have you home, my Frida. Even if ..."

"Even if all you got back were broken pieces?" Under the water, she ran a hand over the ridges of scars that marked her belly and breasts.

Wiping at her eyes, Button forced a smile. "I'm afraid we're all nothing but broken pieces in the end."

"Wow, Grandma. Thanks for the pep talk."

Button's lips twitched. "The truth is rarely cheerful."

"That's why I don't like it."

Button sighed. "Then you won't like what I have to say."

"Is it about the art show? I know you don't like those new paintings."

"But I hope others do," Button said. "No, it's not about that. It's about Leigh."

"Then I don't think you'll like what I'm going to say, either."

"You've already said yes?"

She nodded, tears pricking her eyes. "Can't you be happy for me?"

"There's just something about that boy," Button said.

"What?"

"I'm not sure. But I don't think marrying him is a good idea."

"I *love* him."

"Perhaps you do," Button said. "But that's not enough."

"You've never liked him."

"Eve, I know what lies between you two —"

She sat up, causing water and soap bubbles to roll over the edge of the tub in a tidal wave. "No you don't."

Grabbing a towel, Button said her name in a warning tone.

"*Nobody* knows!"

"All right." Button's voice shook with the effort to remain calm. "You're right. I don't know everything, or maybe even almost anything. But I know enough to be concerned. To be concerned for *you*, my granddaughter."

Slightly mollified, she sank back into the warm water. "There's no need to be worried."

"I understand the temptation to be with him. He was Sara's brother. And *umglik bindt tsunoif* — misfortune binds together. But building a relationship on tragedy isn't healthy."

"No one else understands what I've been through." She ran her hands along her scars. "I don't mean just the accident, but before that, too. Yes, Sara … and other things. And maybe he doesn't understand everything either, but he comes the closest."

"When did it start?"

"When did *what* start?"

Button's face darkened with suspicion, and her voice shook with emotion. "Don't pretend you don't know what I'm talking about. *You and Leigh*."

"What kind of question is that?"

"Were you two …" It was the great unasked question and, as always, Button stopped before it was fully formed.

"I can't believe you'd ask me that. What do you take me for?"

"You've never dated anyone else, as far as I know."

"No."

"So how can you know he's the right one for you?"

"Because …" She paused, trying to think of how to explain it. "I'm like that egg that fell off the wall."

"Humpty Dumpty?"

"Right. And then Leigh came along, this boy I knew back when I was still whole. And he remembers what I've forgotten. And it turns out he's willing to help me glue the scattered bits of myself back together, and he loves me despite my missing pieces — despite being *half* the person I used to be. It's like some kind of miracle."

"It scares me," Button said.

"Why?"

"Because of all the things you've never told me. You have too many secrets."

"Yes." The word stuck in her throat.

"I've always been scared to know. Maybe that makes me a coward, but there it is. And now it's your secrets that scare me. All the things you no longer remember."

"Just because I'm injured —"

The veins in Button's forehead stood out as though ready to pop. "Your brain's a sieve, and things keep shaking through the holes and disappearing."

"It'll be okay, Button. I promise."

"What did you eat for breakfast this morning?"

Shaking her head, she said, "What does it matter?"

"It was less than an hour ago."

She sank back against the slick surface of the tub, trying to hide her surprise.

"You forgot it's morning, didn't you?"

"Of course not."

Button shifted forward, giving her THE LOOK. She was clearly just getting warmed up, and Eve had the sudden urge to duck her head under the water until she either passed out or her grandmother gave up.

"What was the last painting you worked on?"

"I —" She stopped, shook her head.

"Hector says it's like 'Modigliani meets the Grim Reaper'?"

"I don't remember it."

"I didn't think so." Button looked at her with a mixture of grief and appraisal. "I think he might be dangerous."

"Leigh?" She gave her grandmother an incredulous look. "He's a *doctor*."

"*A dokter un a kvores-man zeinen shutfim.*" Doctors and grave diggers go together.

"For goodness' sake. Doctor's *swear an oath* to do no harm."

"There were rumours when you were kids, things people whispered out of the corners of their mouths."

"What kind of things?"

Her grandmother's cheeks flushed with either embarrassment or anger. "Parents were cautioned to keep their young daughters away from him."

"That's ridiculous. He was the football star *and* he was on the honour roll *and* he was gorgeous. *Everyone* loved him, and yes, a lot of younger girls had crushes on him. He was probably the most popular boy in the whole school."

"You spent a lot of time around him because of your friendship with Sara. You always denied that anything ever happened —"

"And that's the truth."

"As far as you can remember now." Button shook her head. "And when that horrible tragedy happened with his sister, I have to admit I wondered ..."

"Now that's ridiculous. Truly."

"Is it?"

"There's no way Leigh would have ever hurt Sara. *No way.*" Eve shook her head, trying to push the memories back into the cave in which they belonged. But it was too late, and a few of them slipped through.

Sara's tears fell on her upturned face, landed on her cheeks and lips, salt mixing with salt.

"What is it?" Button asked.

She began to shake — suddenly she was achingly, bitingly cold. She imagined her skin turning to frost, and her bones into hollow husks buried deep within glacial ice.

Button reached over and touched her forehead. "Are you all right? You feel so cold."

"I'm sorry I hurt you. I never wanted you to get hurt."

"He's not the danger."

"What?"

"It's *me.*"

"Oh, Eve, that's not true." With a dismissive wave of the hand, her grandmother stood to leave.

Determined not to let Button escape as she always did, Eve rose from the tub. She stood there, dripping, scarred, and naked. She hid nothing, willing her grandmother to finally see the beast inside the woman.

"It's me, Button. It's always been *me.*"

For one moment, she saw understanding in her grandmother's eyes. Then Button turned away, fumbled for the bathroom door, and was gone.

She sank back into the tub, shaking so violently her teeth rattled. She was so cold. When had the bath water turned to ice? She dug a toe into the plug's metal ring and pulled it. The water gurgled as the tub drained.

When it was empty, she replaced the plug and turned on the hot water full blast. Heat caressed her frigid body like a kiss in the moonlight. Relaxing, she hummed as the tub filled. She let the memory of Sara and that day at the river sink back beneath the surface of her mind. Best not to remember.

When Button brought her a steaming mug of tea, she sat up and smiled at her in thanks. Button nodded stiffly in return, and left the bathroom.

With a frown, she eased back into the tub and wondered what she'd done wrong.

After her talk with Button, there was no ceremony or fanfare. There were no flowers or bridesmaids or table linens to worry about. There was just a quick trip to the courthouse followed by takeout sushi for two, which they ate picnic-style on a towel spread over the hotel room's bed. Leigh wanted to buy a cake, but she vetoed that idea in favour of chocolate-dipped strawberries and champagne — things that didn't remind her of her birthday, didn't remind her of death.

"It's been a good day," she said dreamily, curled like a shrimp under the electric blanket they'd brought from home.

His fingers twined with hers and squeezed. "One of the best."

"I'm glad for the privacy tonight. You swear you don't mind moving into Button's home?"

"It's your home, too," he said. "And the doctors felt it would create less confusion for you."

"Did they?"

"Do you remember getting lost walking home from the library?"

"Yeah," she said, although she didn't.

"The police had to bring you home. You didn't recognize a couple new buildings on Yew Street, so you didn't know which way to turn. But you don't have that problem at home. Am I right? You've never forgotten where you are?"

"I don't think so," she said. "But it's familiar. It's where I grew up, and the only place I've ever lived. Well, except those couple months in Paris." And her two "vacations" at Riverbend Psychiatric Hospital. But he didn't know about those.

"Exactly. And nothing's changed in your house since we were kids."

"Button's allergic to renovations," she said, and he chuckled.

"So, no, I don't mind. I want to do whatever's best for you."

"Okay."

For a time they dozed under the comfort of electric heat. Then he asked, "What's it like? This forgetting?"

"Hmm …?" She pulled back from the brink of sleep. "Oh. It's weird, I guess."

"Describe it for me."

"Well," she said, snuggling deeper into the blankets, seeking the warmth of his body. "There's two parts to it. The first is my memories from before the accident. That's like one of those disc things theatres used to use to play movies. What are those called?"

"Film reels?"

"Right. It's like the film is damaged, so when it feeds through the machine it flickers back and forth between perfectly preserved parts of the movie and chunks that are black or too blurry to see properly."

"And the second part?"

"The second is the way life is for me since the accident. And that's more like …" She paused, debating how to describe it. "Like living behind giant red curtains."

"What?"

"Remember when I was eight, I played one of the orphans in a community theatre production of *Annie*?"

"Vaguely."

"I'd have to find my starting position onstage in the pitch-dark, and wait there until the curtains came up and the stage lights came on, and they were so bright I could barely see for a while. We'd do the scene, I'd say my two lines, and then the lights would go out and the curtains would drop. And then I would be —"

"Back in the dark."

"Yes."

"Okay. So, now you have moments that are like being onstage with the lights off?"

She sighed. "No. I guess that's where the similarity ends. When I was onstage I couldn't see, but I was breathing and thinking about my lines and filled with nervous energy. It was like taking a pause, waiting for something to begin. This is different. I'm either not aware of myself, or …"

"Or what?"

Or I'm in the silver. She shrugged. "Or I guess I just don't exist."

"Shit, Eve," he said. "That's terrifying."

"Yes." She rolled over to face him. In the dim light, he looked like he'd been chiselled from shadows. She reached over and touched his cheek, reassuring herself that he was real. His skin was warm under her fingers, rough with the first hint of stubble. "Except I keep coming back, don't I? And I guess if I don't, I won't know the difference."

"But *I* will," he said, and she caught his tear with her finger. "I don't want to lose you."

"You mean you don't want to lose the last few scraps of me."

"Yes." His voice warbled over the word. More firmly, he said, "And those scraps are enough for me. I promise."

She pressed her lips to his and tasted strawberries.

Some time later, she said, "It's been a good day."

His fingers twined with hers and squeezed. "One of the best."

"I hope I'll remember it."

He sighed in answer, squeezing her fingers more tightly.

Through a gap in the curtains, she watched the sun rise on her first day as Eve Adler. She felt scrubbed clean, ready to begin again. Curled against her back, Leigh's breath dampened the curls at the base of her neck.

For a moment, she was almost warm.

SIXTEEN

Eve's Eighteenth Birthday

"I SAID I DON'T WANT CAKE."

"It's a bran muffin, dear."

The nurse's voice was dry, almost bored, as though nothing could surprise her anymore. And probably nothing did. Certainly not the poor excuse for humanity she'd become. And in this place, her "break with reality" probably seemed quietly mundane.

"I don't want a muffin, either."

"No one does," the nurse said. "But this ain't the Ritz. Take your meds and I'll be on my way."

She picked a green pill out of the paper cup and placed it on the table, then swallowed the rest.

The nurse nodded at the pill on the table. "That one, too."

"I don't know what it is, so I'm not taking it."

"It's for anxiety."

"I don't have anxiety."

"Take that up with Dr. Jeffries. I can't leave until you take it."

The nurse hovered over her until she swallowed the pill and opened her mouth for inspection.

"Good girl." The nurse patted her on the shoulder, like she was a pet.

"It tastes like cat vomit."

"How do you know what cat vomit tastes like?" the nurse asked, but she moved away before Eve could answer.

The pill had some kind of truth serum in it. She'd been too hard to break, and this was their new way of tricking her into admitting the things she'd done. But this wasn't her first rodeo. With her tongue, she nudged the pill from where she'd stashed it, in a soft flap of gum left over from the removal of a wisdom tooth. When no one was looking, she plucked it from her mouth and stuffed it into the muffin.

"Gotta eat, sweetie pie," a nurse in pink scrubs chirped as she passed. She was maybe five years older than Eve, tops, and that was way too young to be dishing out condescension.

A wave of resentment crested within her, but she couldn't sustain the emotion. Instead, she picked some raisins off the top of the muffin and chewed them unenthusiastically. They tasted like chemicals. But then again, everything tasted like chemicals. And while it cut through the lingering taste of coconut cake, it wasn't much of an improvement.

Dumping the rest of her breakfast in a bin by the cafeteria door, she shuffled back to her room. She kept her gaze firmly on her slippers, avoiding eye contact with the other denizens of the psych ward. Most were harmless: loons and addicts and depressives, but some were worth avoiding.

The woman next door, for example, who thought Eve was the reincarnation of the husband she'd supposedly killed. Then there was the hag who spoke only in Bible verses, called her "sister," and obsessed over saving her soul. Eve had tried to explain that it was a pointless venture, but to no avail.

Shutting the door behind her, she crawled into the narrow bed. Her "sister" had left her another note. She read it quickly, then balled it up and tossed it aside. The meds were starting to kick in. Her face felt numb and her muscles buzzed and jumped, as though plagued by random jolts of electricity. She closed her eyes, trying to ignore the sour taste on her tongue, and sank into a fitful sleep.

"Your grandmother is here."

"Huh?" Eve unstuck her face from the damp pillow. Her eyes were so puffy she could barely see. Had she been crying again?

"Visiting hours."

A nurse stood in the doorway, her arms folded under her breasts. Her head was framed by the fluorescent lighting in the hallway, so her face was in shadow.

She felt slow and stupid. Or perhaps she was drowning. "What?"

"Your grandmother. In the lounge."

"Oh." She sat up. The bed pitched beneath her and her eyeballs rolled back into her head.

"I'll let her know you're on your way," the nurse said. "Better clean yourself up first."

Cold water did little to help, and she shuffled down the hall with her slippers flapping, her robe gaping open, and her hair in a damp pile on top of her head. Her mind felt reasonably clear, but her eyeballs kept drifting and rolling, causing her to stumble. She must have absorbed some of whatever was in the new pill. It sure was messing with her.

"Hello, my Frida," Button said as she approached, wincing at her appearance.

Eve must have looked terrible. Though she cared, she lacked the energy to do anything about it.

"Hi, Button."

Button was, as always, impeccably dressed. But her eyes were puffy and red, her skin mottled, and her nose raw.

"Happy birthday, my dear girl."

She leaned into her grandmother's embrace, and wished she could burrow there forever. She pulled away while she still had the strength, and motioned Button to a chair.

They sat across the table from each other, awkwardly formal. To her right, the window dripped with condensation. It was fogged, and she used her sleeve to clear it, peering at the grounds below. There was nothing to see but concrete and puddles. Her eyes rolled upward and she saw the ceiling.

"How are you?" Eve asked.

Button made small talk for a while. She'd joined a book club, she was attending synagogue on Saturdays, the apple tree in the side yard had unexpectedly died and she'd had to hire a service to come cut it down.

"They tore down the Adlers' old house," Button said, slipping it in as casually as she could.

Mr. and Mrs. Adler had sold their home the previous winter and moved back east to be near their remaining children.

"Now they're building one of those three-storey monstrosities."

"That's good," Eve said.

"Good?" Button tsked. "I suppose they call it progress, don't they? Everything has to be new, and as big as possible. And no need for a yard, but they need twelve bathrooms. Who, I ask you, needs that many toilets?"

"It's a lot to clean," Eve said.

"Exactly." Button shifted in her seat, as though getting down to business. "How are you?"

Eve shrugged. "Apparently this ain't the Ritz."

"I hear you're not eating. Or participating in the group sessions."

"I go to them. I just don't have much to say."

"Eve, how are you going to get better if you don't try?"

Her gaze rolled down to the table. She ran a finger over the graffiti etched into its surface. To most people the etchings would seem like nonsense, but she understood them. They were messages from whatever waited for her in the underworld.

"The harp polisher leaves Bible verses on my pillow. Yesterday it was: 'If your hand causes you to stumble, cut it off.'"

Her gaze rolled upward, and she saw Button grab the collar of her sweater and bunch it tight against her throat.

"What's happening to your eyes?"

"Another one said: 'Better to enter life maimed than enter hell with two hands.'"

"Should I call a nurse over?"

"I kind of like that one —"

"Eve, you're worrying me."

"But not as much as Sodom and Gomorrah. That's juicy."

"Your eyes," Button said.

"It's the meds. Take it up with Dr. Pill Pusher."

"Dr. Jeffries? I'm sure he knows what he's doing."

"She."

"What?"

"You're sure *she* knows what she's doing."

"Oh …" Button said, momentarily flustered.

Eve's gaze roamed to the side. Rain splatted against the window. "Do you know what meds they're giving me? Do they go over that stuff with you?"

"No. Legally, you're an adult —"

"And *legally* I signed myself up for this adventure. But we both know that's bullshit. Oh, stop it." She slapped her hands over her eyes, but it did no good. She could feel her eyeballs moving against her palms. "You practically hog-tied me to get me to agree. Maybe you thought you were protecting me, but it makes me look like I'm hiding something."

"Eve —"

"Is that detective still harassing you?"

"Don't worry about that."

"How many times has he been by?"

"Just a few. It's fine."

She pressed harder against her eyelids. "Stop answering the door. He has no right to keep after you like that."

Button was silent for a moment. "But we have nothing to hide."

"He's digging. He doesn't have anything on me, or he'd be showing up with a search warrant. Don't let him upset you like this."

"I've dealt with much worse than that."

She let her hands drop to the table. Her gaze rolled downward, and she saw how jagged her fingernails had become, and how her hands trembled. "I guess you have."

Button sighed. "Oh, Eve. How did we get to this point? Donna's gone, you're in this horrible place, and everything is *fercockt*."

"I'm sorry," she whispered.

"Maybe I've lived too long." Button's voice clogged with emotion.

She managed to look up. "Please don't say that. You're all I have left in this world."

Tears and mascara ran a jagged course along her grandmother's wrinkled cheeks, exposing the fault lines in her foundation. How much more could Button take before she broke into a million pieces?

"And *you're* all I have, my Frida. So, you have no choice but to get better."

"All right. I'll try."

The tears dried as quickly as they'd come. Her grandmother gave her a look like flint against steel. "You're going to participate in group therapy. And start eating."

"Yeah. Okay."

"And let Dr. Jeffries help you."

"But she doesn't want to help me. She's trying to give me the rope to hang myself with."

"That's simply not true."

Eve's eyes rolled upward, and she forced them back down. "'For you have turned justice into poison, and the fruit of righteousness into wormwood.' That one resonates, doesn't it?"

"What?"

"That was the note on my pillow this morning. I've turned *justice* into *poison*. That's no coincidence, is it?"

"What are you saying?" Button said. "I don't understand."

"And this new pill. The little green one."

"I don't —"

"Don't you *dare* try to tell me you don't know about this pill."

Shaking her head, Button balled the collar of her sweater tighter against her throat. "Please, dear. You're not well."

Those words were the match to Eve's fuel. Jumping up, she shouted, "What's in that pill, Button? Tell me what's in that pill!"

"You're scaring me. Please …"

The orderlies descended, pulling her away from the table.

"Tell me the truth! I want to know the truth!"

They dragged her from the room. The last she saw of her grandmother, Button was huddled in her chair like a dog waiting to be kicked.

They carried her past her room. She screamed and bellowed, her eyes rolling like marbles. As they passed schizos and weirdos and mopers and dopers, they all gawked at her like *she* was the crazy one.

Through a set of double doors, down another long hall, and into the Quiet Room. They lifted her onto the bed and one nurse straddled her while the others strapped her down. A needle pricked her arm, and her blood rolled through her veins like lava.

"Not so mundane now, am I?" Her voice warbled and slowed, like a record player with dying batteries.

The room narrowed to a pinprick, and she was gone.

SEVENTEEN

"YOU'RE TWO YEARS LATE for your party, my darling."

Hector's voice dragged her from the fog of quicksilver and into the high-gloss atrium of his art gallery. It was an assault on her senses, with needles of light stabbing her eyes and the crowd's chatter like daggers in her eardrums. But she could smell the citrus and lavender of Hector's aftershave, as familiar as her own home. A warm arm wrapped around her shoulders and held her steady.

"But you know what they say, better late than never. Oh, you'll have to forgive me; it seems all I'm capable of tonight are clichés."

She looked up and saw the sheen in his eyes. His hair was slicked back, his skin impeccably smooth, his eyes like fine chocolate. "And here's another one. You really dodged a bullet there, my darling."

Her body was like a broken vase put back together with glue and steel rods. "I didn't dodge anything."

The words tore at her throat, as though she hadn't spoken in a long time. She coughed and tasted bile. A low-level tingle of nausea travelled from her stomach to her chest and up into her throat, where it sat like a lump, threatening to cause trouble at any moment. The white marble staircase at the far end of the gallery throbbed in time with her heartbeat, as though beckoning her to escape before it was too late.

Hector turned to watch the crowd, a look of satisfaction on his face. The turnout was good. His arm tightened around her shoulders, and she knew he was deciding upon the right moment to step out of the shadows.

"Are you ready to fly, my nightingale?"

"I can barely walk," she said.

"No need." Before she could protest, he dragged her forward. The crowd shifted and sighed around her. Their faces were moon masks of bloody lips and wolfish teeth. Frightened, Eve stepped back, dodged out of Hector's grasp, and lost her balance. She would have fallen, if not for Leigh grabbing her by the elbow.

"Hang tight, Mrs. Adler. You've worked too hard to turn chicken now."

Like warm clay, his body molded against hers and held all her fractured pieces together.

"Oh my God. Do you see?"

"See what?"

His hand pushed firmly against the small of her back, steering her forward. She saw the back of Hector's perfectly coiffed head bobbing through the crowd several feet ahead of them.

"Why are they all so pale?"

"Oh, Eve," he said. "Not tonight, okay?"

"But —"

He steered her into a cloud of perfume surrounding the women Hector called "shelfers." Plastic-skinned and bedecked in jewels, they were the trophies high-end lawyers, politicians, and local celebrities mounted on their shelves. They perched precariously on their stilettos like skeletons in Chanel, and were the true bread and butter of the art world. She understood her job, so she plastered on a smile.

"Darling!"

Like a pet, Eve was passed from one bony embrace to the next. No heat to be found, only cold hearts and cold hands and cold smiles. She greeted them politely, kissed powdered cheeks.

Leigh's hand remained warm against her back, a guide through the onslaught. She was at a noticeable disadvantage in her flat shoes, speaking pleasantries into one set of expensive cleavage after another.

She leaned forward, overwhelmed by the sudden desire to motorboat an enormous set of breasts on display in front of her. She giggled madly at the thought, and Leigh yanked her away, finding some free space beside the bar. A line had formed, but those people were more interested in alcohol than in an artist who was coming unhinged.

He bent over her. "You've got to get it together."

She hiccupped into his face, and his lips twitched with momentary humour.

"For heaven's sake. You just laughed at that woman's boob job."

"Guess the gallery's lost a benefactor." She giggled, tears squeezing from her eyes and rolling down her cheeks, likely taking her mascara with them.

"What's so funny?" Leigh sounded frustrated. Rummaging in his pocket, he came up with a crumpled tissue and handed it to her.

"Nothing. Nothing's funny." It was the truth. She wasn't really laughing; she was screaming upside down. "Did I paint something?"

But he wasn't listening. "There's Hector."

Once again, Leigh's hand pressed the small of her back. "Come on, it looks like he's ready to open the doors."

Hector stood by a red ribbon strung across a set of closed doors. He smiled with ease, laughing and nodding at those who crowded around him, but his gaze was also scanning the room. Searching for her, Eve supposed.

"Is it like theatre? Do I say 'break a leg'?" Leigh asked.

"I'd rather not break anything tonight."

His hand slipped lower and squeezed. "Good luck, then."

As they moved toward Hector, the nausea churned inside her. She wondered what they would do if she vomited on her shoes. This thought loosed another brief fit of giggles.

"Ready, my darling?" Hector asked, looking relieved to see her. He extended a hand, and she clutched it like a life preserver.

"Let's roll," she said. "The suspense is killing me."

Patting her hand, he turned to the crowd. Hector was made for moments like this, where he could show off his wit in a charmingly self-deprecating way. It drew people to him, no matter their wealth or culture.

She tuned him out, fixating on the scissors he held in his hand. She didn't like scissors, she realized. They were vicious tools meant for cutting, severing, and untethering. And these ones were silver, a bad omen. Her smile grew stiff and forced.

Hector was doing a good job of wooing the crowd. Holding up the scissors, he paused dramatically, letting the applause and laughter build.

"What did he say?" she said to Leigh, feeling panicked.

Leigh's attention was on Hector's show. "What?"

"*What's* the exhibit called?" But she didn't need his answer. There was a banner above the door. It hung twelve feet across, was boldly lettered, and was impossible to miss. And yet she *had* missed it, until this moment.

The Resurrection of Sin.

"What happened to *The Other Side*?"

That got Leigh's attention. Turning to look down at her, he shook his head sadly. "Oh, Eve."

"What? Leigh ... *what*?" She reached for him, frantic, and found his hands. They were so warm, and she was so cold she felt she could disappear.

"Ready?" Hector whispered out of the corner of his mouth.

"Absolutely," Leigh said with a bright smile, and then turned back to her. "*The Other Side* closed two years ago. While you were still in the hospital."

Hector raised the scissors to the ribbon.

"Oh, of course." Tears of confusion burned her eyes. "So, what show is this? What have I painted?"

But her voice got lost in a cacophony of applause.

The ribbon was cut. Hector smiled, but his eyelid

twitched. He was nervous. Did he not believe in her show? Or was it because she'd become so unpredictable?

"Ta-da," Hector said, and the doors to the exhibit opened. The crowd surged around them as though they were rocks in a stream.

"Want to come see?" Leigh asked.

"It's a powerful show," Hector said, giving her hand a reassuring squeeze. "Come on, darling. They'll want to pester you with questions, get their money's worth."

"I don't —"

"Here we go," Hector said with false cheeriness as they guided her through the doorway. It was the same tone a nurse used when wheeling a patient to the shock-treatment room; she'd heard it plenty, and her gorge rose in response.

They led her to the opening wall of the exhibit. The painting was massive, eight feet across by ten feet high, and for a moment she was stunned silent by the logistics required to paint such a large canvas, especially in her small studio. But the painting itself …

It was titled *Persephone, the Pale Queen*. An army of thick black feathers funnelled up to the top of the canvas, a cocoon from which a woman emerged, naked and bathed in moonlight. She reached heavenward, grasping with dirt-smeared hands at a tattered silver rope. But her gaze was turned to look below her, tears spilling down a vulpine face covered in purple bruises, her hair a cloud of blood-dipped curls. Her breasts were plump globes, engorged and blue-veined, nipples dripping blood rather than milk. The blood ran in rivulets over an abdomen swollen with pregnancy, and fat red drops fell from the black dagger of her pubis.

"Holy shit," she said.

"Isn't she magnificent?" Hector said.

"She's *me*!"

Hector's voice rose, speaking to the crowd that gathered around them. "Isn't the desperation in her expression haunting? As the story goes, Persephone was forced into marriage by the god of the underworld, Hades, when she was no more than fourteen. Notice how the interplay of light and shadow highlights the juxtaposition between hope and despair?"

"Remarkable," someone said, and others murmured agreement.

Hector took a step closer to the painting, clasping his hands behind his back and smiling beatifically. "Remarkable, yes. Persephone fought to regain her life among the living, but because she'd eaten some pomegranate seeds in the underworld, she couldn't be completely freed. So she lived partly in the land of the living, and partly in the land of the dead."

"Tell me," a woman said, nudging closer to Eve. Her face was powdered to a paper finish, her eyes shiny blue marbles. "Was your accident the inspiration for this painting?"

Eve shook her head and tried to step away, but the crowd surrounded her from all sides.

"Oh, look, it's already sold!" Hector said, clapping his hands. Others joined in as a slender woman in a tight suit stepped forward. As she placed a red sticker on the plaque beside the painting, the applause grew.

"Wonderful!" Hector said. "Shall we move on?"

"I think I'm going to be sick." Eve's stomach heaved as though proving the sincerity of her words.

Hector didn't hear her. He was bouncing, waving his arms to draw the crowd forward. He always said the first sale was the hardest, but if it happened early one could expect a deluge.

"This way." Leigh pulled her along.

People turned, smiled, and pushed closer to her. They took up all the air in the room, and she couldn't breathe.

Everywhere she turned, she saw her own naked body. Her breasts were caked with blood, her midsection rounded with pregnancy, her eyes wide with terror and desperation. She'd never felt so humiliated, so exposed — so nauseated.

In one painting, a metallic serpent coiled around her torso. The tip of the snake's tail disappeared into the black curls between her legs. Vicious fangs pierced the flesh near her nipple.

Around a corner, she saw another behemoth of a painting. In this one, the right side of her face was grotesquely purple and misshapen, as though someone had taken a shovel — or a thick tree branch — to her head. Her mouth was open in a silent scream, her teeth black with blood. The serpent had her pinned to the wood-planked seat of a chariot, its silver body coiled around her waist and neck.

It looks like a chariot, but it's actually a chairlift. And we know where it's going, don't we? Down and down and down.

Deep within her abdomen, she felt a sharp stab of pain. The nausea crested, causing her to retch.

Leigh grabbed her arm. "Are you okay?"

"I'm going to be sick."

"She needs air!" Leigh shoved toward the emergency exit. Slowly, ever so slowly, the crowd parted before them.

He pushed and pleaded, dragging her in his wake. She shut her eyes, focusing all her energy on not vomiting.

An alarm sounded. Cool air hit her face. He closed the door behind them with just moments to spare. Everything came out of her with such force it knocked her to her knees.

"Lord have mercy." He laughed nervously and skittered out of her way.

"I'm sorry," she whimpered. "Oh, damn, I've ruined my dress."

Rather than move away from her and the puddle of vomit, he lowered himself to the concrete. Leaning against the emergency exit door, he watched her with weary eyes.

"What the hell, Eve. This was supposed to be a big night for us."

"I'm sorry," she said again.

"I'm making an appointment with Dr. Jeffries."

"Please don't. I hate her."

"But this, whatever this is, is beyond my scope."

"I promise I'll do better. Please, just give me another chance."

He shook his head. "You need medical help. A full workup."

"Not her. I need a different kind of doctor."

"What? Why?"

Without warning, she spewed vomit on Leigh's new shoes. He yelped and tried to get away from the onslaught, but to no avail.

Once finished, she said, "Because I think I'm pregnant. Again."

EIGHTEEN

Sara's Fourteenth Birthday

"I SAID I'M TAKING YOU," Donna told her.

"I promised I'd go. You don't need to police me."

"Apparently I *do*." Donna's mouth was turned down in a surly grimace, as though she'd been sucking on lemons.

"Fine. But why does it have to be *today*?"

"I've already rearranged my schedule to take the day off work. I told my secretary I was planning a special mother-daughter day." The irony twisted Donna's mouth even more.

"And Button? Do we tell her?"

Donna shook her head. "It would kill her."

"I know," Eve said softly.

"She thinks I'm taking you to get your ears pierced — which I will. After."

"All right." Her stomach rumbled a threat.

"Can you eat some toast?"

"Yes," she said, although she wasn't sure.

"Then make yourself some. I'm going to take a shower."
She paused at the kitchen doorway and turned to look at
her daughter. "Your grandmother will be back from her
walk soon."

"I'll act like nothing's wrong."

Donna tipped her head to the side, considering. Her
pillow had teased the hair above her right ear into something resembling a bird's nest, and this visible imper-
fection eased the tension around Eve's heart just a little.

"You probably don't need to. She'd expect you to be
sad on Sara's birthday." Donna studied her for so long
she felt her cheeks prickle with heat. "And so would I."

"What does that mean?"

Donna was a master at firing the last shot, and she
was already gone.

Eve rolled the tin of maple syrup back and forth in
her hands, examining the snow and maple trees on the
label. She'd been working on a couple of winter scenes,
and was satisfied with how she'd done the bare branches
and dead sky, but painting snow made for a particular
challenge.

Water rumbled through the pipes as Donna turned
on the shower and, a few minutes later, the front door
opened and slammed closed. Button entered the kitchen
with a hopeful smile on her face. It didn't quite reach
her eyes.

"Good morning, my Frida." She bent to kiss Eve on
the top of the head, and placed a gentle hand on either
side of her face. Whatever Button saw in her expression,
it extinguished her attempt at a smile.

Stroking Eve's curls, she asked, "Are you okay?"

Her grandmother's sympathy brought immediate tears to her eyes. "No."

"Me, neither."

A little later, Donna entered the kitchen and found them curled around each other. "Time to get dressed."

Donna wore crisp black slacks and a charcoal silk blouse. It was the same outfit she'd worn to Sara's funeral.

"Eve," Donna said, when Eve didn't move fast enough for her liking.

"All right." She pulled reluctantly away from her grandmother and wiped her damp cheeks.

"Fifteen minutes," Donna said as she left the kitchen.

There was a piece of lint near the ankle of Donna's perfectly pressed pant leg, and Eve found her eyes returning to it again and again. It seemed the safest place to look, as it lowered the risk of accidentally meeting her mother's muddy gaze.

The compassion she saw in the nurse's face was somehow even worse. She saw no judgment there, and it made her want to press against the nurse's ample chest and weep. It made her want to unburden the giant load of secrets she kept stuffed around her heart. But if she did, how many lives would come crumbling down?

"So, are there any questions?" the nurse asked, looking from her to Donna and back again.

Donna's legs were crossed, and the top one kept bopping up and down like someone was hitting that reflex spot near her knee with an invisible hammer. "I think you've explained it very clearly. Thank you."

The nurse moved a bit closer to her. "How about you, Eve? Do you understand what will happen during the procedure?"

Eve kept her gaze down. "I think so."

"Are you comfortable with the risks? As I said, they are low, but it's important to know what potential complications might arise."

She tried to nod, but her head wouldn't move.

"Eve," Donna said.

"Yes, I understand."

"If you're uncertain in any way, we have counsellors you can speak to about your options."

"That won't be necessary," Donna said.

"Eve?" the nurse asked.

"It's okay."

The nurse considered for a moment, and Eve got the impression she was debating whether to push more on the counselling.

Perhaps Donna thought the same. In her courtroom voice, she said, "How much longer will this take? We've already been here for an hour."

The nurse spoke to Eve, rather than Donna. "We'll start with a blood draw and ultrasound, and then you'll speak to a counsellor. While this is going on, your mom will fill out some paperwork."

"She doesn't need to speak to a counsellor. The decision has already been made."

"The counsellor helps your daughter through the emotional aspects of the procedure, Mrs. Gold —"

"Ms.," Donna said.

"My apologies."

"So, how much longer?"

"The actual procedure takes about fifteen minutes, but there will be recovery time after. And of course there are things to do before the procedure. All in all you should expect to be here for about five hours."

"Another five hours? Are you serious?"

The nurse's mouth tightened. "Perhaps four at this point."

Donna checked her watch. "We have an appointment across town at three."

"I really don't care about getting my ears pierced today."

"It's not that." Donna waved a hand in exasperation. "Can we get moving?"

"Certainly." There were cracks forming in the nurse's professional mask. "Come with me, Eve, and we'll get you all set up."

Donna stood and tucked her purse under her arm, preparing to follow them.

"Please wait here, Ms. Gold. Sabrina will bring you the paperwork."

Without waiting for a response, the nurse opened the door and ushered Eve from the room. She closed the door behind them, perhaps a little too firmly.

"Do you have cramps?" Donna asked, steering around the back end of a delivery truck that had parked with its nose across the sidewalk.

"I'm okay." She stared resolutely out the window. The day was bleak, rain falling in fat drops. Seemed about right.

"Did they try to talk you out of having the procedure?"

"They offered me a discount if I referred a friend."

"That's not funny," Donna said.

"You're right. I don't have friends."

Silence descended, save the *swish-swish* of the windshield wipers. They headed east into farmland and forest, an area she'd never seen before, but she couldn't be bothered to ask where they were going. She watched the passing landscape, hands gently pressing her aching abdomen.

"I don't suppose you're willing to tell me the name of the boy, now?"

She remained silent.

Donna's lipstick had rubbed off except for a rim of dark red around the edge. "I didn't think so."

At a stoplight, her mother turned to look at her. Under her eyes was a dusting of black mascara. "You may not understand this now, but I did this to give you the opportunities I never had."

"What opportunities?"

The light turned green, and Donna turned back to the road.

Eve lost herself in dozing misery, face turned to the window. She awoke some unknown time later as Donna pulled into the circular driveway of a three-storey brick building.

"Where are we?"

There was a placard above the door that read Riverbend Psychiatric Hospital.

"Mom?" Panic hit her like a freight train. "What are we doing here?"

Donna turned off the engine and grasped the steering wheel. She gripped until her knuckles were white. "I'm afraid we won't be getting your ears pierced today."

"What's going on? Why are we here?"

The large double doors opened, and two burly men wearing scrubs exited the building and climbed down the steps.

"I think you need a break. And some help, because frankly I don't know what to do with you."

"You're leaving me here? Are you crazy?"

"It's only temporary," Donna said. "They can help you here. They can figure out …"

"Figure out *what*?"

"What's wrong." Donna's eyes filled with tears, and the sight of them was terrifying. Had she ever seen Donna cry before? "Because there's something really *wrong* with you, Eve."

"I promise I'll be good. Better than good! Just please don't make me go in there."

"Let's just talk to them."

The orderlies, or whoever they were, had reached the car. One of them opened Eve's door, and she kicked at him.

"Eve, don't!" Donna said.

He reached in and unbuckled her seat belt. His pores were huge and dripping sweat.

"Get away from me! What are you doing?"

"Don't fight him," Donna said. "You just promised you'd be good."

The orderly hauled her out of the car and wrapped her in some kind of full-body hold that locked her arms across her abdomen.

"Hey, don't touch me! Mom, please!"

Donna didn't move. She stared out the windshield, gripping the steering wheel with such force the veins in her arms popped. Tears streamed down her cheeks.

The other orderly closed in, and they moved her toward the stairs.

"Mom! *Mom*!"

Finally, *finally*, Donna exited the car.

Her chest lightened with hope. They were going to have a meeting, Donna had said. So she would have a chance to convince her mom, and whomever else they'd be meeting with, to let her go home.

Donna strode stiffly to the trunk of the car, popped it open, and pulled out a small suitcase. Without looking at her daughter, she carefully placed the suitcase on the bottom stair, turned, and walked back to the car.

"Mom?"

"This is for your own good, Eve." Donna climbed behind the wheel and closed the door. The engine roared to life.

"Where are you going?"

The car rolled forward, tires spraying water, and angled down the circular drive to the street.

"Mommy!"

The car reached the edge of the driveway and the brake lights flared. It turned right and disappeared from view.

NINETEEN

ICY FINGERS SLID into her vagina. They pushed against her cervix, seeking the warm nest of her womb. If they found it, she was certain the amniotic fluid would freeze solid, the unborn skin would crystallize, and the tiny heart would be stilled.

"Noooooo."

"*Eve,*" the woman's voice beckoned. "*Eve, come here!*"

She opened her eyes. Her hands gripped the cold metal of an enormous garden gate. It rose skyward in a complex weave of cherubs and skulls, snakes and eagles. She gripped a handle shaped like a scythe.

Behind her lay the unending field of quicksilver plants. Twice her height, their branches tangled together in an impenetrable phalanx, covered in leaves that looked like a million pieces of tinfoil. The icy wind stirred them awake to rattle and hiss.

It was *so cold*. And yet she stood naked in snow that was ankle-deep. Her skin was marble, her belly rounded over the small life that burrowed inside. Her son. She could feel his heartbeat, steady and warm within her freezing body. This time, she vowed she would protect that little life.

She tried to push and then pull the gate open, but it wouldn't budge. When she tried to let go, she realized her hands were fused to the metal like a tongue to a pole in winter. The wind was an icicle between her legs, stabbing at the warmth of her womb.

"Please don't hurt the baby."

"There is no baby."

Her abdomen cramped, a breathless pain. She bent forward, trying to curl around the warmth in her centre. But her hands were still locked on the gate, so all she could do was writhe in breathless agony.

"Eve ..." The voice came from everywhere: from the wind, from the rolling fog, from the snow beneath her feet — and from somewhere inside her broken brain.

Or perhaps it came from whatever was behind her in the quicksilver. There was a dark splotch out there, like blight on a piece of fruit. It moved like smoke in the corner of her eye — forming, dissipating, and reforming so quickly she never caught more than a glimpse, but she knew it was moving closer.

"Please stay away!"

"Why do you demand so little of yourself? How long can you pretend?"

"Mom?"

The black splotch shifted and reformed. She tried to pull away, certain that if she saw the face behind the voice, her mind would shatter.

Tears crystallized on her eyeballs, froze on her cheeks. "No! Stay back!"

"This is your chance." The dark shape solidified into something more or less human. It had arms and legs, and a strangely misshapen head. *"Look at your reflection. Remember. See the truth behind your lies."*

"No!"

"And atone for what you've done."

"Leigh! Help me!"

At the sound of her voice, the darkness cracked open like an eggshell, revealing fissures of blinding white light.

"You can't run forever."

"Leigh!" she screamed again and again.

The shell shattered, revealing yellow morning light. She burrowed into the fur of her husband's armpit, too relieved even to weep.

"Stop that!" He wiggled away from her. "It tickles!"

"Sorry." She burrowed closer, sniffing at the musk of his skin. He felt so warm, so *real*. "I had another bad dream."

"Can't you think of better ways to wake me? You could at least try doing that lower down."

His hand roamed over her curves, warming her chilled skin. Rolling her onto her side, he pressed against her back.

"Don't. I'm as big as a house." She was slow and pendulous and aching in every reknitted bone.

"Maybe." He cupped a firm hand around the globe of her belly. In response, the baby stirred to life, kicking against the walls of her abdomen. "But you're *my* house."

"I have to pee."

"What else is new?"

"But Leigh ..." she said.

"Don't worry, this will only take a minute." His breath was hot against her ear.

"You say that like it's a good thing."

He laughed against the back of her neck, dampening her curls.

It was Sunday, and Leigh didn't have to work. He brought her breakfast in bed, waking her from a fitful slumber.

"Rise and shine, mama." He stroked the hair off her forehead. "Hey, look at that, you've got more greys this morning."

"What?" She pushed herself up with some effort. Leigh propped a couple of pillows behind her back and reorganized the comforter to cover her pale legs.

"Many women get grey hairs during pregnancy," he said. "It makes you look distinguished."

"Hmph. Hey, I don't need the tray. Look!" She placed the bowl of oatmeal on top of her belly and grinned at him as it balanced there. "Ta-da!" Just as she said it, there was a definitive thump from within and the bowl toppled.

Leigh caught it just before it hit the blanket. "Don't think he liked that."

"You little gremlin," she told her belly. "You're already trying to make a mess."

Leigh set the bowl on the night table. "Let me feel."

She obliged, sinking back on the bed and closing her eyes as his hands probed her belly.

"I think he's turned."

She opened her eyes to see him smiling at her.

"I can't feel his head. It must be deep in your pelvis —"

"No wonder that's hurting so much."

"But I'm pretty sure this, right here, is his backside, and up here is a knee and a foot."

As he felt the firm lines of his son buried beneath the taut flesh of her belly, his gaze grew far-off and dreamy. He looked just as she imagined he'd have looked all those years ago, if given the chance. It made her chest ache with a strange mixture of grief and gratitude.

"I don't think it will be much longer," she said.

"Just four more days until your C-Section."

"Right." She shook her head as she remembered. The doctors thought a natural labour was too risky, with her broken pelvis. "I just meant I think he's ready to come out."

He lowered the nightgown over the swelling of her belly, helped her into a more upright position, and handed her the bowl of oatmeal.

"This is our last Sunday." He wriggled his eyebrows and lowered his voice ominously, making her smile. "How would you like to spend it?"

"Sleeping."

"I can get behind that. But let's go for a walk this afternoon. It looks like it's going to be a sunny day."

Leigh was an avid runner. She couldn't understand the passion he felt for something that seemed pointless and painful to her. A slow lumber down the street was about all she'd be able to manage, but it seemed like a good idea. She nodded her agreement.

Sitting on the edge of the bed, he asked, "What was your dream about?"

"What dream?"

"You said you had a bad dream. And you cried out. You don't remember?"

She shook her head. "What was I saying?"

"Something about the baby."

The skin on the back of her neck prickled.

"Vivid dreams are common during pregnancy," he said. "It's the hormones."

"I know. I've always dreamed vividly at certain times of the month."

Scooping oatmeal into his mouth, he looked pointedly at her bowl. Obligingly, Eve lifted a big spoonful to her mouth.

"I think I'll catch the ten o'clock NFL game. You can call me if you need anything."

She spat her oatmeal back into the bowl, making him jump. The taste was thick and bitter on her tongue.

"Is there maple syrup in this?"

"We're out of brown sugar."

Memories oozed to the surface like blood from a wound.

"You have the worst mother in the world."

There was nothing to evacuate from her stomach, but she heaved and heaved, anyway, and the baby kicked furiously in response.

"Little do you know how much I've protected you."

"Why did you *do* that?" she asked.

A bland expression on his face, he handed her a glass of water to rinse her mouth. His hair was damp from the shower, and he pushed it out of his eyes. "Do you want something else instead?"

"No. Just get it out of here."

142

After he took the bowl away, she eased under the blankets and closed her eyes. With trembling hands, she stroked her belly beneath the cotton nightgown.

"See the truth behind your lies."

Her stomach felt cold, like a water balloon pulled from the fridge on the hottest August days of her childhood. The baby pushed against her hand, reassuringly strong.

"I won't lose you again," she said, and felt a sharp jab in return, as though he was telling her that all would be well.

TWENTY

Sara's Fourteenth Birthday

"HELLO, EVE," the doctor said crisply, moving around the desk and dropping a folder on the glossy surface in front of her.

She propped a pair of rimless glasses onto the bridge of her nose and opened the folder. Studying the page, her mouth moved as though in silent conversation. Whatever it was about, she seemed to come to an agreement with herself.

She gave an emphatic nod, and then peered at Eve over the top of her glasses. Above the rim her eyes were like arctic ice; below they swam distortedly behind the thick lenses. Her hair was pale, slicked back into a tight ponytail, her face full of sharp angles. Her eyebrows were drawn with severe strokes, high-arched as though she were eternally surprised, and there was an incongruous smattering of girlish freckles across her nose and cheeks.

"I'm Dr. Jeffries," she said. "I head the juvenile wing here at Riverbend."

Eve's gaze dropped to her lap rather than face the intensity of the doctor's eyes. There was a lengthy silence that she was probably supposed to fill. She bit her lip and waited.

Eventually, Dr. Jeffries asked, "Why don't we talk about why you're here?"

"My mom thinks there's something wrong with me."

"And what do you think?"

"It's better when I don't."

"When you don't what?"

"Think."

The sound of a pen scratching across paper, reminding her of Dr. Stephens writing the referral for her procedure. *Scratch-scratch-scratch.*

"Tell me more about that," the doctor said.

Eve shrugged and looked out the window. The wind had picked up, and dark clouds rolled angrily across the sky. The earth below them was lost in a haze of hard rain. Her abdomen cramped in the same rolling, angry kind of way. The pad between her legs needed changing.

Dr. Jeffries began talking about Riverbend and its facilities, and describing the intake procedure for a new patient.

Barely listening, she pictured Donna driving home through the sudden deluge. Imagined her leaning forward, frowning, unable to see through the windshield. Perhaps she'd meet another car around a sharp curve. Its headlights would blind her. She'd overcorrect and end up nose-down in one of the deep ditches they'd passed on the way here. The car would slowly fill with water while Donna screamed and cried and banged on the windows, to no avail.

"Is something funny?" Dr. Jeffries asked.

"What?" She turned away from the window.

"You laughed."

"No, there's nothing funny."

"And yet you're smiling. Fill me in?"

"You wouldn't get it."

"Try me," Dr. Jeffries invited.

She turned back to the window instead. Listened to the scratch of pen on paper.

"You seem angry. Are you mad at your mother for leaving you here?"

Instead of answering, Eve nodded at the diplomas on the wall behind the doctor's head and asked, "How many years of school does it take to become a psychiatrist?"

"Well." Dr. Jeffries leaned back in her chair. "A bachelor's degree takes four years, usually. And then medical school, residency —"

"So, a lot. And a lot of money, too."

"Yes."

"If I were you, I'd ask for a refund."

"Why is that?"

"Any dumbass could figure out I'm mad at my mom. Wouldn't you be?"

She expected anger. Instead, Dr. Jeffries leaned forward, propped her elbows on her desk, and gave her a direct look. "Under the circumstances, I'd be furious."

"Circumstances?"

"I'm not going to pretend I understand what you've been through this past year, or how you're feeling. But I *am* here to help you sort through it."

"So, write the prescription and be done with it."

"Pardon?"

"Isn't that what psychiatrists do? Give people drugs that make them act normal?"

"Sometimes medication is needed. Or other forms of therapy. But the first step is to figure out the root of the problem."

Root of the problem. For some reason, that made her think of the flowers in the Adlers' backyard, the ones that looked like daisies.

"We're here to help you sort all that out," Dr. Jeffries said.

"Maybe some people aren't worth helping."

"Pardon?"

Making a decision, Eve asked, "Do you believe that some people are born evil?"

The doctor pursed her lips, giving it some thought. "I believe that we all have a mixture of good and bad within us, and that what happens to us throughout our lives makes us choose one direction or the other."

"You've never had a patient who turned out to be a monster? Beyond your help?"

"No," the doctor said firmly.

"Hmm." She turned back to the window, swallowing back something that felt like disappointment. The rain was closing in. It pounded on the concrete outside the window, darkening the day into an early dusk.

"Let me be clear," Dr. Jeffries said. "I've treated people who have done vile things, things you'd say were evil or against our moral code. But that doesn't mean they're evil people. Just damaged."

"Damaged."

"Or ill. But in my experience, almost all damage can be repaired, and illness can be managed. With honesty and hard work from the patient, and the correct medical and psychiatric treatment."

Eve slumped in her chair.

"We're here to help you through this. You're an intelligent young lady and a talented artist. You have a lot going for you and a lot of years ahead of you."

"That file." She nodded at the open folder on the desk. "It's all stuff my mom told you?"

"And medical records. But yes, your mother has provided us with a lot of information. Does that bother you?"

"She's never had one nice thing to say about me. So, yeah."

"That must be very frustrating."

"Mustn't it."

"Do you feel misunderstood by your mother?"

"That's one way to put it."

"How would *you* put it?" Dr. Jeffries asked.

Eve snorted. "Nope. I'm not falling into this trap."

"You think I'm laying a trap for you?"

"I tell you all about my awful relationship with my mom, I confess all the shitty things I've done or ever thought of doing. Then you write it all up in a fancy report for her, so she has the evidence she needs to lock me up for good." Eve shook her head emphatically. "No freaking way."

"Why do you think she'd want you locked up for good?"

She looked pointedly around the room. "Gee. I don't know."

"Eve, I hear you. Since you're a minor, I can't promise you complete confidentiality. I'm obligated by law to keep your mother informed about our sessions. But I understand how difficult that makes it for you to confide in me, so my policy is to protect your confidentiality, as long as there's no risk of harm to you or anyone else."

"And what if that harm has already happened?"

Dr. Jeffries shifted forward in her seat. "Are you talking about your friend Sara?"

"I'm not going to talk about that," Eve said, and then in the next breath she asked, "Are the police reports in that file, too?"

"Not the interviews. But there is a letter from Detective Baird, written at your mom's request, I believe."

"Of course there is."

"It sounds like the detective was rough on you." Dr. Jeffries shook her head. "Four hours of interrogation."

"Is that the time for you to beat?"

"I'm not a police officer. I'm a psychiatrist. I'm not trying to trip you up or get you to confess to some kind of crime. I'm trying to build a rapport with you, so that I can figure out how to help you."

"What if I did confess to a crime, like everyone wants me to? What would you do then?"

"What kind of crime would you be confessing to?" Dr. Jeffries asked, her face setting into a carefully neutral mask. Yet there was a flash of hunger in the doctor's eyes that made Eve pull back from the edge of truth.

"Murder."

Dr. Jeffries blinked, took a deep breath, and leaned forward. "Whose murder?"

She let her legs fall open, exposing the sopping stain on the crotch of her pants.

"You're bleeding."

"I guess my mom didn't mention the 'little procedure' she forced me into, just before she dumped me here."

Dr. Jeffries's mouth opened and closed several times, then she shook her head. "I'm sorry, Eve. I had no idea."

She stood and moved toward the hall. "Let me call Dr. Murphy — I think you need some medical attention. That's a lot of blood."

"I would have called him Gabriel," she said, but the doctor had already left the room.

TWENTY-ONE

"IT'S A CAUL."

Leigh's voice pulled her from the silver. She lay on her back, and a pale pink sheet rose up from her chest toward a ceiling of white tiles and fluorescent lighting. The lower half of her body was missing.

There was a squawking noise coming from the corner of the room, beeping sounds, and the raised voices of several people talking all at once.

"Leigh?"

"I'm right here." He leaned over her, wearing green scrubs. The colour made him look ill. "Do you understand what I said? The baby was born with a caul."

"What's that?" He'd missed a spot under his chin when he was shaving. Her gaze fixated on the surviving sprout of hair.

"It's a sac around his face and body. They're working to remove it right now."

"The baby," she said. "He's here? I want to see him." She tried to push herself upright.

"Whoa," someone on other side of the sheet said, her voice rising with panic. "Hang on, Mrs. Adler."

"Stay still, Eve. You're not stitched up yet," Leigh said.

"Is he okay?"

"He's fine," a woman said, moving into her line of view. She wore a medical mask over her mouth and nose. Above it her eyes were the pale colour of moonlight on a lake, her brows high-arched, her grey hair pulled tightly back into a scrub cap.

"We've cut holes in the caul so he can breathe, but removing it is a delicate procedure. It's wrapped around his ears, and then attached at different points along his body. We need to go slowly so we don't tear his skin."

"Tear his skin!"

"Mrs. Adler." A man wearing scrubs and a mask peered around the sheet. "Your legs are moving. Can you feel it when I do this?"

"What? No."

"What about this?"

"No!"

"She just kicked me," someone said. His head disappeared, and from the other side of the sheet he ordered an increase in the medication going into her epidural.

"Can I see my son?"

The woman with the pale eyes said, "You can see him as soon as we have him cleaned up. It's a full caul, of uncertain origin —"

"What does that mean?"

"It means it's not amniotic in nature. Not to worry, once we remove it your son will be just fine."

"A cocoon caul," Leigh said, his voice awed. "I've never seen that before."

"Me, neither," she said. "It's a bit of a shock, isn't it?"

"Yeah," Leigh said.

"A cocoon caul?" A memory rose to the surface. Donna had once said that Eve was born wrapped in a dark caul. "I was born like that, too. Please let me see him."

"I'm not sure." The doctor's eyes widened and she turned to Leigh for guidance.

"You said he's fine. So, why can't I see him?"

"It's just a bit shocking," Leigh said, and the doctor nodded in agreement.

"Why?"

"The caul covers his whole body. And it's not transparent, so …" He shrugged.

"What colour is it?" she asked, and then terror struck. "It's not silver, is it?"

"Oh, no," the woman said. "It's dark. Alarming to look at, but not completely uncommon."

"I need to see."

The woman looked at Leigh, who shrugged in defeat. She disappeared and returned a minute later with a squirming black sac.

A sewer-like smell hit Eve's nose, and she gagged. "Oh my God, what *is* that?"

"That's your son."

"She just kicked me again."

"Mrs. Adler, you need to stay still," the man said from the other side of the sheet.

The thing in the black sac undulated, like an alien creature pushing out of a cancerous growth.

She closed her eyes and turned her head. "Get it away from me."

"Eve," Leigh said. "It's okay."

He kept talking, issuing reassurances, but in the darkness of her mind she quickly lost track of his voice. She heard a rustle and hiss, like quicksilver leaves coming alive in a storm, and somewhere beyond she heard the tinkle of laughter.

"Breastfeeding is the natural way to feed your child! How else can he get the proper nutrition he needs to grow big and strong?"

Eve opened her eyes and saw a laundry basket sitting on the table in front of her. "Button, please —"

"I saw this documentary about all the horrible chemicals they put in that stuff. Haven't you heard of Monsanto? You want to feed my great-grandson poison?" Button was in such a snit she was literally spitting her tea.

"That's not true." Eve struggled for calm. "And I'm not saying I'm going to use it, but I wanted to have some just in case."

"In case of what?"

"In case he's hungry, and I'm not making enough milk. In case I lose time again, or wander off, and you or Leigh need to feed him!"

Button's mouth drew down in displeasure. "There's no need to yell. You'll wake the baby."

Squelching the urge to point out who had started the argument, she said instead, "Maybe just once you could say something that doesn't make me feel like I'm doing a shitty job as a mom, okay? It reminds me of Donna."

Button recoiled as though she'd been slapped, and that was the final straw.

The tears spilled from Eve's eyes and became icy rivers on her cheeks. She swiped angrily at them. "Damn it! I'm such a mess!"

"It's the hormones." Button handed her a tissue and watched her with less sympathy than Eve might have hoped for. "Mop yourself up. There's no need to be carrying on like that."

Button grabbed a toppling pile of burp cloths and began to refold them, stacking them neatly on the table in front of her.

"Thanks," she said in a tone that was less than grateful. She didn't have the energy to do anything more than sit and stare blankly at the laundry basket.

Button folded a swaddling blanket into a neat little square. "Either join me for a cup of tea, or go lie down."

She stumbled to her bedroom, but her head had barely settled into the groove of her pillow when she heard the first wavering cry from her son's room.

"Damn it." She wasn't sure she was even capable of getting up. Maybe if she waited a minute, he'd quiet down and go back to sleep.

The squawking grew louder. On the dresser, next to a crystal vase full of wilting roses, the lights on the baby monitor flashed in sync with the baby's cries. She moaned and rolled over, the first step in a process that she hoped would ease her upright.

Through the monitor, she heard the squeak of her son's bedroom door, followed by Button's soft coo. Eve relaxed back into the pillows and closed her eyes.

"Hello, Gabriel," Button said in the high-pitched voice she reserved for babies and puppies. "Did you have a good *shluf*?" There was a rustling noise as Button lifted him out of the bassinet, followed by the grunting squawk of a baby searching for sustenance.

"Hang tight while we get this diaper changed," Button said. "And then we'll bring you to your mama, okay?" The squawking became a full-blown cry, and Button cooed and hushed and murmured reassurances.

"There now," Button said as the baby quieted. She pictured her grandmother lifting the swaddled bundle and tucking it expertly against her warmth as she carried him from the room.

Blearily, she pulled herself into a semi-seated position against the pillows. She was just pulling her nursing bra aside when Button slipped into the room.

"Here we are," Button said to the bundle in her arms. "Here's Mama."

She was surprised at the weighty warmth of him. He immediately started to root for her nipple, grunting like a truffle pig, and she shifted forward to help him.

Button reached over and made the necessary adjustments. "Bring the baby to you, not the other way around. Remember?"

"Right."

"It'll come naturally soon enough."

"Ouch," she said as the baby latched on.

Button stuck a finger into his mouth and broke the seal, much to the baby's obvious distress. "Like this. He needs to open his mouth wider. If it hurts like that, he's not taking enough of the breast into his mouth."

With Button's help the baby latched on more comfortably.

Eve settled back against the pillows. "Thank you."

"I'm glad I'm of some use," Button said, stroking the fuzz on the baby's head.

"I don't know what I'd do without you," she said with complete honesty.

Button flushed with pleasure, but waved off the compliment. "You'd manage."

"Or I'd forget he was here and go out, or leave him on the change table while I went to make tea, or something."

"You're too hard on yourself."

"I can't even remember what he looks like unless I'm looking right at him."

"Oh, Eve."

She looked down at her nursing son. "I forgot he has dark hair, and that there's a bald patch at the back where it's rubbed off. And what about his eyes? Are they like ours, or blue like Leigh's?"

"He has your eyes, sweetheart," Button said softly. "Having a newborn is a challenge for anyone. And the doctors warned us that the hormonal changes and lack of sleep could make the symptoms of your head injury more acute. But it's only temporary. Babies grow. Before you know it he'll be sleeping through the night, and it will all be easier."

"What if I lose time or forget about him, and he gets hurt?"

"Leigh and I are here to help."

"What if it's never safe for me to be alone with him?"

Button shook her head, sighing. "You worry too much. One day at a time, okay?"

She swallowed back a wellspring of tears and nodded.

"I think he's ready for the other side." Button helped her get the baby nursing properly on the other breast, and then turned to leave. "I'll come back in a few minutes."

"Please stay."

Button shook her head. "You need to start trusting yourself more. You may have problems with your memory, but there's nothing broken about your mothering instincts."

Button left before Eve could argue.

The baby's mouth grew slack and he released his hold. She lifted him to her shoulder and rubbed his back until he gave a juicy burp. "That's better, huh?"

She laid him against her legs and they looked at each other with curiosity. He did indeed have her eyes, amber in colour and with a pronounced downturn at the outer edges. She wondered if he'd end up with her dark curls, too, or whether he'd be fair-haired like Leigh.

She stroked a finger up over the snub of his nose, along the red skin at his eyebrow, down the soft roundness of his cheek, and into the damp fold between his chin and neck. He squeaked and wiggled madly, making her smile.

"Does that tickle? Sorry."

His gaze locked on hers, full of innocence and trust — clearly he was unaware of the mess he'd chosen for his mother.

A while later, Button took him away, dimming the lights as she left.

Eve pulled the covers up to her chin, trying to get warm, and let her mind drift into the fuzzy place between sleep and waking. She heard Leigh come home, heard the brief and stilted conversation between him and Button, and then the sound of a football game playing on the television in the living room. She drifted deeper into the blackness of her mind, following the voice that called to her from beyond the quicksilver.

Eventually, the smell of Button's chicken cacciatore motivated her to get moving.

"Bad dream?" Leigh asked when she stumbled into the dining room. "I thought I heard you call out."

"The usual," she said.

"What's the usual?" Button moved to get up.

Eve stopped her with a wave of the hand, grabbed a plate off the sideboard, and ladled food onto it.

"The accident," Leigh said, and she didn't correct him. He sorted through a stack of papers on the table beside him. He placed bills and other important mail into a small pile, while old grocery lists and coupon mailers went into a recycling bin by his feet. He paused once in a while to take a forkful of food.

Plate in hand, she paused to look down at the sweet bundle in the bassinet. He was wrapped in a fuzzy green blanket, his eyes closed and mouth slack with sleep. His hair was a fringe of dark fuzz. She wondered what colour his eyes were.

Leigh held up a scrap of paper. "You writing poetry now?"

"Of course not."

"It's your handwriting," he said.

"Let's see it." Button took it from him and slid her reading glasses onto the bridge of her nose. Her fork dropped with a clatter.

"Are you okay?" Leigh asked.

Without a word Button stood up and carried her nearly full plate of food back into the kitchen, leaving the scrap of paper on the table.

"What —" Leigh said, but his words were cut off by a loud crash from the kitchen.

"Zol es brennen!"

Eve dropped her plate on the table and ran for the kitchen, Leigh not far behind.

"Button! Are you okay?"

"Just clumsy."

The plate had smashed at her feet, splattering chicken, pasta, and tomato sauce across the linoleum floor. She reached for the roll of paper towel and bent forward.

"I'll clean it up." Leigh grabbed the roll from her hands.

"What's wrong, Grandma?"

Without looking in her direction, Button said, "I'm feeling a bit *fertummelt.* I think I'll go lie down."

"Do you need help?"

Button pulled away from her touch. "I'm fine. You see to the baby."

She followed Button back into the dining room, where Gabriel mewled in his bassinet. He'd kicked free of his blanket. She lifted him into her arms and followed her grandmother down the hall toward her bedroom. When Button closed the door firmly behind her, Eve turned and carried Gabriel back to the kitchen.

"What was that about, do you think?" Leigh asked.

"I don't know." She bit her bottom lip. "Do you think she's maybe losing it a little?"

"That grandma of yours is as sharp as a tack."

"Sharper than me, right?"

He gave her a sideways grin. "I know when to keep my mouth shut."

"Would you go talk to her?"

"Should I burst into her bedroom with my medical bag? She'll *love* that."

"I just want to make sure she's okay. What if she's having a stroke or something?"

"She's not."

"How do you know?"

"All right," he said with a sigh. He put the broken shards of Button's plate in the garbage and dropped the dirty paper towels on top. "But have my medical bag ready. I'll need it when she bites my head off."

She plucked the scrap of paper from the table and tucked it in her pocket before carrying Gabriel, who kicked and bellowed complaints, into the bedroom she now shared with Leigh. Rocking the baby back and forth, she pulled the paper out of her pocket and sat down on the bed. There were four lines of poetry, written in her distinctly elegant script.

> *Bloodroot is red*
> *Sara turned blue*
> *The roses aren't real*
> *And neither are you*

Gabriel shrieked and went stiff in her arms. She rocked him faster.

There'd been a vase of roses on the dresser, right next to the baby monitor. She was sure of it. But now there was nothing else on the glossy wood surface except her hairbrush, a bottle of nail polish, a tube of nipple cream, and a package of baby wipes.

When Leigh entered the room, his head still in its rightful place on top of his neck, she asked, "Is she okay?"

"She's fine. Nothing to worry about."

"Good."

"Is he hungry?" Leigh asked.

"What? Oh, yeah, maybe that's the problem." She pulled her shirt open and settled back against the pillows. Gabriel latched onto her nipple with ferocious hunger. "Ouch."

Leigh lifted the baby off her breast and resettled him in a more comfortable position. "Like this."

"How come everyone's better at this than me?"

"You'll get the hang of it soon enough."

"Maybe. Hey, did you throw out those flowers? They were barely wilted."

"What flowers?" Leigh asked, pulling off his shirt as he moved to the closet.

"The ones on the dresser."

He looked puzzled, then shrugged. "I don't remember them. Maybe Button threw them out."

"But …"

"But what?" His pants dropped to his ankles, and he kicked them into the corner of the room.

"Never mind."

He climbed under the blankets and laid his hand gently against the curve of Gabriel's fuzzy head. "Is seven-thirty too early for bed?"

"Not anymore, it's not."

"That's good, because I'm exhausted." He was snoring a minute later.

TWENTY-TWO

Eve's Sixteenth Birthday

"WHAT'S THAT SMELL?"

Leigh pushed through the kitchen door as though it was still something he did every day, causing Eve to jump and drop the spatula she'd been holding.

His hair was cut short, with stiff spikes gelled up at the front. He wore track pants and a tank top, which showed off a *V* of golden chest hair. Most dismaying was the baby caterpillar crawling across his upper lip.

"Who do you think you are, Tom Selleck?" She bent to pick up the spatula and dump it in the sink.

He stroked his moustache self-consciously, then leaned against the door. Wrinkling his nose, he said, "Seriously, what are you making?"

"It's supposed to be linguini. But I think it's going to end up being garbage."

"Oh. It smells good."

Wiping sweat off her face with a dishcloth, she said, "I can always tell when you're lying."

He grinned. "Fine, it smells like farts."

"When did you get in?" She moved to him without thought, but stopped while there was still several feet between them.

"Late last night," he said. "Mom picked me up."

"You didn't call." Eve winced at the plaintive tone in her voice. Clearing her throat, she added, "I didn't think you were coming this year."

"Neither did I until I got on the plane."

"How long are you staying?"

"I'm leaving tomorrow morning. I have a paper due on Friday, so I need to get back."

"Short trip," she said, trying to hide the mixture of relief and disappointment in her voice.

"Are you coming to the celebration my parents are having this evening?"

"No."

As though she hadn't spoken, he said, "They're releasing balloons from the pier at dusk. It seems kind of stupid to me, but I'm not going to tell them that. We all have to do whatever we can to get through the day."

"I can't go," she said through numb lips.

"Do you know what people think, when you're not there?"

"I don't care what people think."

"Do you care what they say?" he asked.

"Just what *do* they say?"

He gave her a pointed look, as though she should know perfectly well what people were saying. She did know, and it didn't help that they were right.

Motioning to the sink where Donna's good stockpot sat smoldering, he said, "That doesn't look good."

She was grateful for the change of subject. "I didn't put enough water in with the noodles. I think the pot is ruined. Donna is going to be pissed."

"What else is new. Is she home?" The question was asked far too casually.

She debated not answering, but only for a moment. "She and Button are out getting the cake. I said I'd make dinner."

"How long do you think they'll be gone?" She knew the look in his eyes very well.

"I need to start dinner from scratch."

"This is salvageable. Do you have more noodles?"

"No."

He pulled the lid off the pot of sauce that sat bubbling on the stovetop and then quickly dropped it back in place, recoiling from the pungent steam that fogged up around his face.

"What the hell *is* that?"

She put her hands on her hips. "Clam sauce."

"I stand corrected. It's not salvageable." He turned off the burner.

"Why not?"

"Did you clean and sort the clams first?"

"Of course I did."

"It smells like at least one of them has gone bad. And your sauce is gritty."

"Gritty? What would make it gritty?" She moved over to the stove and lifted the lid. She had to admit that the smell was atrocious.

"I'm guessing it's the sand."

"Shit." She put the lid back on the pot. "Now what am I going to do?"

He pulled out his phone and scrolled through the contact list. "You're going to order a pizza because you shouldn't be cooking dinner on your birthday. Besides, Button won't eat shellfish; I don't know what you were thinking. Don't worry, I'm paying," he said when she opened her mouth to protest. "Happy birthday."

"I don't want your money."

"You can pay me back, then."

"Donna won't let me have a job, remember? No job, no cellphone, and no freedom."

"You'll think of some other way. You always do."

"And what does that make me?"

Instead of answering, he put the phone to his ear. As he placed the order, she took stock of him, noting how tall he was, how broad his shoulders had become, and how big the hand was that wrapped around her wrist like a shackle. She wondered what he would do if she ever said no, then she reminded herself why she couldn't.

He stuffed the phone into his back pocket, smiling down at her. "Forty-five minutes to an hour, they said. Plenty of time for me to give you your present."

"Leigh." It was a weak protest.

"Come on." He pulled her to the bedroom.

"I'm doubling my course load to graduate a year early," she told him afterward. "Donna said she'll pay two years of college tuition if I do, and Button promised to send me to an artists' retreat in Paris next summer."

"That's great," he said sleepily. "I always said you were smarter than you gave yourself credit for."

This rankled for some reason, and she shrugged away from him. He didn't seem to notice.

"Well, I'll miss you next year," he said.

"Why? Where am I going?"

"Whichever school you choose, they'll be lucky to have you." He yawned widely. "Oh man, I don't think I've ever been so tired."

"But ..." She shifted to look at him. His eyes were closed, lashes a dark fan against his cheeks. His breathing deepened as though he was falling asleep.

"Leigh?"

"Hmm?"

"I thought ... I mean ..." she trailed off, unable to find the words. The silence stretched, and, eventually, she managed to ask the question. "Aren't you moving back here this summer? Once you graduate?"

His eyes opened, and he looked at her blearily.

"Wasn't that the plan?" she prodded. "You'd move back, and I'd go to Emily Carr, and we'd both be living here?"

"My plan is medical school."

"I know, but ..."

"Damn! I better get going," he said, looking at his watch. He rolled away from her and sat up. "I told Mom I was going for a run. She'll be wondering why I'm not back yet. And *your* mom could be home any time."

"You were going to apply to medical schools around here."

He found his shirt and pulled it over his head.

"Leigh?"

"Is that really what you want? I'm never sure with you."

"Don't throw this back on me. That was the plan." She felt like a broken record. "*Your* plan."

"Right," he said. "I know it was."

"So where are you applying?" she asked.

"Five different schools," he said. "On the east coast. I think I have a shot at getting into at least one of them. My grades are excellent, and I scored well on my MCATs."

"But why not here?"

"Those are better schools."

"But what about me?" She hated the hurt that infused her words, hated the sting of tears she felt in her eyes — hated him most of all. After all these years, after all of his demands and promises, after all the secrets she'd kept and lies she'd told ...

"I'm doing this for us. How can you doubt that? I *promise* we'll be together."

"You *promised* you'd come back after you graduated."

"Please don't," he said. "Not today, of all days."

"Then when? I never see you!" When he didn't respond, she asked, "Is there someone else?"

"You know, I came here today because I needed comfort. I needed to be with someone who understands everything that happened to me, someone who knew Sara — and someone who knew me *before* she died."

"Someone?"

"You! Of course I mean you. What was it that you said last year? Accomplices until the end, remember?"

"Which one of us is dying, Leigh?"

He flushed, but looked her square in the eye. "Enough people have died already, don't you think?"

"What's that supposed to mean?"

"It means I'll keep my mouth shut if you do. Now I really have to go." Leigh stood, pulling up and zipping his pants. "Can we talk about this later?"

"When?"

"Soon. We'll figure it out."

It felt like a dismissal. Pulling her shirt over her head, she followed him from the room. He'd entered through the kitchen, like a friend. But he was leaving through the front door, like a stranger — and she realized that this might be the last time she ever saw him.

He turned from the front porch to look at her. Moths danced in the light above his head. His eyes were full of tears. "Eve."

Her stomach clenched with anticipation. Maybe he'd changed his mind, decided he really couldn't live without her any longer.

Instead, he pulled money out of his pocket and held it out to her. "For the pizza."

She stared at him, mouth dropping open.

"Go on, take it."

She could barely see him through the blur of tears. "Two years ago," she told him. "I killed our baby."

Before he could react, she closed the door in his face.

TWENTY-THREE

EVE STOOD IN the kitchen when the fog lifted, her hand on the cozy that covered Button's prized teapot. It warmed her palm, highlighting the chill in the rest of her body.

"Say Nana," Button said.

Her grandmother sat on the bench by the kitchen table, and a baby waved his arms at her from a high chair. Button dropped a few Cheerios onto the tray, which was already smeared with banana and cheese. The baby wore a plastic bib with a giant cartoon tractor on the front. His hair was a sprout of dark curls, his round cheeks shiny with food.

"Say Na-na." Button said it more slowly, moving her mouth in an exaggerated way.

"Nnnnna!" He chortled and waved chubby fists. A chunk of banana flew from his hand and hit Button's cheek.

"Na-na," Button said, wiping her cheek with a dishcloth.

The baby clasped his hands together. His face turned red with mounting pressure, and he let out a high-pitched squeal that reminded her of a kettle on the boil.

She saw that his eyes were the colour of amber just like hers, and with that everything clicked into place. The world around her made sense again, and she awoke to her place within it.

She had taken a break from her studio to grab a snack. She was preparing for her third art show. The baby was her son. His name was Gabriel.

Button dropped more Cheerios on the tray. "You've almost got it. Say Nana."

"Nnnna!"

"What a good boy! You bring me such *naches*." She handed over more Cheerios. He grabbed a fistful from the tray and stuffed them into his mouth.

"No fair," Eve said. Her throat felt dry and painful. She poured tea into her favourite cup and took a sip. The warmth was soothing. "*Mama* should be his first word. Payback for the cracked nipples and drooping belly."

She took a candy bar from the cabinet, tore open the wrapper, and dunked a square of chocolate into her tea.

"Maybe you should quit eating so much junk food, if you're worried about your weight."

"Chocolate is the only thing keeping me sane," she said around a gooey bite.

Button rolled her eyes and turned back to the mess in the high chair. "As for the cracked nipples, you're doing that to yourself. He's past a year. There's no need to breastfeed anymore."

"He likes it."

"Of course he likes it. But he doesn't need it. You're spoiling him."

"You can't spoil a baby, right, Gabe?" She moved over to the high chair, found a clean spot, and planted a kiss. His head smelled like banana and lavender shampoo.

He gave her a sticky smile before stuffing another fistful of food into his mouth.

"And if you *can* spoil a baby, you're doing a fantastic job at it."

"I'm his great-grandma."

"Gurg!" Gabriel dropped Cheerios out of his mouth and pumped a fist in the air in apparent agreement, making both women laugh.

"Rock on!" Eve pumped her fist in the air, and he squealed his delight. "Are you okay to put him down for his nap? I've got to get back to the studio."

"What are you working on?"

Button asked it casually enough, but she remembered how much her new style of painting disturbed her grandmother. She didn't come into the studio anymore, nor did she want any of Eve's new pieces to cross the threshold of their house. This was fine with Eve. She didn't like her new paintings, either, even if they made her a lot of money.

Since *The Resurrection of Sin* art show at Hector's gallery, everyone seemed to want an Eve Gold painting. There were four downtown galleries currently selling her artwork, and she'd been approached by six more. She'd also recently finished a commission with the Aquilini family for a series of portraits. And for those who couldn't afford an original, she'd signed a generous contract with Hector to reproduce several of her paintings as giclées.

S.M. FREEDMAN

She could barely keep up with the demand, and her fatigue and stress intensified the symptoms of her head injury. She frequently lost time, was easily confused, or found herself drifting in and out of silver dreams with no real understanding of who she was or what she was doing.

The worst of it came when she'd left Gabriel in a baby swing at the park and wandered away. Someone had called CPS and remained with Gabriel until they arrived. Eve was missing for hours, and her disappearance ended up on the evening news. Search dogs found her the next morning in the Crook. She was near the field of quicksilver, unconscious and bleeding from a gash on the head.

The upshot of the whole miserable experience was that she now had a social worker dropping in at unexpected times, and she was forbidden to be alone with her son. Her guilt only served to increase her stress, which worsened her other symptoms. Sometimes Eve felt like she was drowning.

"Eve?" Button said.

"Sorry, what?"

"I asked what you're working on." Button was wetting a cloth at the sink and didn't turn to look at her granddaughter. But Eve knew her mouth was turned down at the edges, the way it often was these days.

"Oh. I'm playing with painting in negatives. Here, let me."

She took the cloth and wiped Gabriel's face. He opened his mouth and sprayed her with soggy bits of Cheerios.

"That's disgusting, dude," she told him, wiping her arm. Gabriel seemed to think it was very funny.

"What's painting in negatives?" Button asked.

"Hector suggested it, and I thought I'd give it a try. I start by colour-washing a blank canvas. And then instead of painting the actual object, like a tree or whatever, I'm painting around it to define its edges."

"Well, that sounds interesting. So, you're painting trees instead of people?"

"Kind of. Hector asked me the other day why I thought my work since the accident was so different. I mean, is it because of the head injury?"

Button shrugged. "I'd imagine so."

"It got me thinking, though. Before the accident, I painted whatever caught my eye and captured my imagination. I was trying to harness the beauty of nature, or of some everyday object, or a person. It was like taking something external and putting my own spin on it."

"And now?" Button asked.

She sighed. "And now it's like my eyes have turned inward. I'm painting what I see inside myself, what I fear, what I don't understand."

Button looked at her sadly. "What do you fear?"

"I don't know," she said, although she knew exactly what she feared. It waited for her in the fog and quicksilver.

Button tilted her head to the side, examining her granddaughter shrewdly. "Do you want to know what I think?"

"I'm not sure."

"I think whatever it is you're afraid of, you're trying so hard to run away from it that it comes out in your paintings and in your dreams. It's like your own personal devil keeps rising to the surface."

"My own personal devil," she said.

"Yes. And the only way to chase away the devil is to face him head-on."

"How do you do that?"

Button studied her as though debating whether to push forward or retreat. Gabriel decided for her, shouting "Uppa!" He reached for Button, waving his arms.

"Are you sure it's all right?"

"Of course." Button's smile almost reached her eyes. "Come on, Gabe. Let's go play for a bit, and then we'll have a nice *shluf*." She lifted the squirming boy out of his high chair and carried him toward the living room. "Grab your sweater if you're heading back to the studio. You look cold."

She *was* cold, but that was nothing new. She lived with permafrost biting the marrow of her bones.

She stood in the kitchen, eavesdropping as she drank the rest of her tea. Gabriel was playing with his new favourite toy, a set of plastic giraffes that made different noises when hit against something solid. One made a whooping sound and another sounded like a spring being loaded. Gabriel favoured the one that sounded like a whoopee cushion. He banged it repeatedly against the floor and giggled each time it made a farting noise.

"You're such a boy," she whispered, and heard Button say the same thing in the living room.

A smile curled her lips. She drained her tea and headed for the studio, leaving her mug in the sink.

"She's getting worse," Button said.

Eve paused in the hallway outside the kitchen door, listening.

"It's the lack of sleep. The stress," Leigh said quietly in return. There was a clanking sound of the kettle being placed on the stovetop, and then the click and whoosh of the gas fire being lit.

"Don't tell me that," Button said. "That's *bubba maisa* and you know it!"

"Language." Leigh sounded amused.

"She's getting worse," Button said again, stubbornly.

"Maybe. But I don't think we should sound the alarm yet."

"She barely remembers to feed her child or change his diaper. Not because she doesn't care, but because she *forgets* he *exists*."

"Now, that's not true," Leigh said, and Eve realized how much he sounded like her; in denial, they called it.

"What happened at the park, then? I'm telling you, she does things like this every day. If I weren't here —"

"And we're so grateful you *are* here," Leigh said.

She imagined her grandmother making that sweeping arm gesture she used when something wasn't worth acknowledging. "I'm not looking for a pat on the head. She spends hours in her studio —"

"Her paintings are in demand."

"She won't eat or even come out for a breath of fresh air if I don't force her to do it. And Lord knows I hate going anywhere near her studio. I can't even look at what she's painting."

"I think they're pretty good," Leigh said. "Maybe a tad—"

"They're the devil's work."

"Since when do you believe in that?"

"Since I saw my granddaughter *die* and come back a different person!"

Her grandmother's words were like a gut-punch. Eve slapped her hands over her face so hard her eyes watered from the sting. Behind her closed eyelids, she saw a man wearing a fedora.

"Take my hand, Eve."

At the touch of his fingers, the top of her skull had popped open. The inside of her head became a wind tunnel spiralling toward a blinding, horrifying white light.

"She's running from something." Button's voice was so soft she could barely hear her. She wished she couldn't. "And whatever it is, I think it's catching up to her."

"What do you think she's running from?" Leigh asked.

She whipped to the opening, toward light that screamed — and somewhere beyond, she'd felt certain she would find her reckoning.

"From the abyss," she whispered into her hands.

"I don't know," Button said with a sigh. "And she's not saying."

"Look, this is what happens with head injuries. There's no straight path to recovery. The brain is a complex organism —"

"You've explained all this before. Last time you used the circuit-board analogy."

"Well, it's true," Leigh said.

She pictured him shrugging in that one-shouldered way that was either endearing or annoying, depending on the circumstances. The fridge door opened, and she heard the clank of bottles hitting each other — Leigh grabbing a beer. There was a pop as he twisted off the cap.

"I'm telling you," Button's voice lowered in a way Eve knew all too well. It was her "Button knows best" voice, and to ignore it was to set off fireworks. "This isn't happening because of her head injury. There's something going on at a deeper level, with her *neshama*."

Leigh choked, then hacked and spluttered, clearing liquid from his lungs. "What? You think there's something wrong with her *soul*?"

"Don't act like it's a ridiculous concept. You grew up with a mezuzah on every door of your house. Even if your family never kept Shabbos, or only attended shul on the High Holy Days —"

"Eve was raised the same way."

"Yes, she was. Donna put no stock in religion. But my grandfather was a great rabbi, and I was learning at his knee before I could talk. Eve grew from those roots of belief."

"All right, I hear you."

"What do *you* believe in?" Button asked.

Eve lifted her head, curious what his answer would be. Above her was the painting she'd done of the café on the Rue Saint-Honoré.

"I'm a man of science," he said.

"*Vos iz der chil'lek?* The one doesn't counteract the other."

"I suppose that's true."

"When that Lexus hit her, how long was she dead?" Button asked.

"The estimate was about ten minutes."

Ten minutes.

"And what do you think happened to her during that time?"

"She's never said."

She was dead for ten minutes.

"I keep wondering," Button said. "Where she was, what she saw."

Eve put her fingers in her mouth and bit down.

"Probably nothing. I think you're letting your imagination get the best of you," Leigh said.

"I watch her in her studio sometimes."

"Yeah?"

"She doesn't know I'm there, of course. But when the baby is sleeping, sometimes I sneak out back to watch her. She talks, you know."

"Lots of people talk to themselves," he said.

"It's not like that. She talks to the corner of her studio where that old desk and chair sit. The one where your sister used to do her writing."

"Oh."

"A few times this summer, when the windows were open, I heard her, too," Button said.

"What was she saying?"

"She wasn't speaking in English."

"What?" Leigh said. "She doesn't know any other languages."

"No, she doesn't. And it doesn't sound familiar. It's guttural like German, but with soft uplifts like French or Italian."

"Shit."

"What are you doing?" Button asked.

"Calling a colleague at the hospital. She needs to be evaluated. I wish you'd told me this sooner."

"That's why I didn't."

"Why?"

"Because I knew you'd want to have her tested. Maybe committed to Riverbend."

"Damn straight," Leigh said.

"And I don't think she can survive being there again."

Eve dropped her head back to the wall, biting her bottom lip.

There was a weighty pause, and then Leigh said, "What do you mean, *again*?"

"Just please put down the phone. There's more." Button cleared her throat, and then continued resolutely. "I heard another woman speaking, too."

"She must have had the radio on," Leigh said.

"No."

"Or maybe —"

"No," Button said again.

"I just don't buy it," Leigh said.

"I *heard* her."

"Have you asked her about it?"

"Would *you* want to ask her that kind of question?"

"Yes." Leigh's voice shook. "You bet I would ask her."

She didn't realize she was moving until it was too late to stop. She stepped into the yellow light of the kitchen, walking with the stiffness of a marble statue come to life.

"Go ahead," she said through numb lips. "Ask me anything you want. But I have a question for you, too."

Leigh swallowed hard. He stared at her, eyes wide and blue like the river in summer. "I think we should get you to the hospital," he said instead. "Have them do an MRI, a psych evaluation —"

"Why didn't you tell me?"

"Tell you what?" Button asked.

"That I died during the accident. That I was dead for *ten minutes*."

"The paramedics revived and stabilized you before they took you to the hospital," Leigh said. It wasn't really an answer.

"You should have told me."

Button wrapped her warm hands around Eve's. "When Donna died, I would have followed her to the grave if not for you. When I think how close I came to losing you, too …" She shook her head. "But *Baruch Hashem*, you came back."

TWENTY-FOUR

Sara's Seventeenth Birthday

"BUTTON?"

Eve knocked on the door to her grandmother's bedroom. "Grandma? Are you ready to go?" She paused, listening, but heard nothing. "Button?" She knocked again. "The limo is here. It's time to go."

"In a minute," Button said faintly from the other side of the door. Her voice sounded clogged and wobbly.

"Are you okay?" She winced at the stupidity of the question.

"Just … just a minute, dear."

"I'll wait outside, then. Okay?"

"Yes, fine," Button said.

There was a knock on the front door as she was slipping her feet into a pair of Donna's heels. Her feet were half a size larger than Donna's had been, and the shoes pinched her toes excruciatingly. She relished the discomfort. It felt like penance.

"Just a moment!"

She tottered down the hallway and opened the door, expecting the impatient limo driver. Instead, Leigh stood solemnly on the porch. He wore a charcoal suit with a dark blue tie. Since the last time she'd seen him, on her sixteenth birthday, he'd let his hair grow out and had shaved off that awful moustache. She hadn't expected ever to see him again after that day — the day she had closed the door on him, both physically and emotionally.

The memory of their last meeting was there in his eyes; she could see it adding to the weight of all they carried between them. She wondered how much more it would take to break him, the way she had broken. She wondered if he was breakable.

"I'm sorry about your mom."

She stared at him, at a loss for words.

He shifted from foot to foot, not meeting her eyes. "And I'm sorry about the last time …"

She continued to watch him, letting the silence stretch and enjoying his discomfort.

"What about all the other times?"

He met her gaze, looking perplexed.

"Do you feel bad about all the other times, too?"

He opened his mouth to respond, but didn't get the chance.

"Hello, Leigh," Button said stiffly, coming up behind her. She wore a large brimmed black hat, angled down over one eye, and an oversized pair of dark sunglasses. She looked like an old-time movie star playing the part of a grieving mother. In comparison Eve felt sloppy, a skinny kid adrift in her mother's curve-hugging dress.

"Thank you for stopping by, but we must be going." Button nodded at the limo idling in the driveway.

Leigh stepped back and the heels of his shoes tipped over the edge of the first stair. Grabbing hold of the railing, he nodded at Button. "I'm very sorry for your loss, Mrs. Gold."

"Thank you." Button's lips pursed as though she'd tasted something sour. She pushed past Eve, gave Leigh a wide berth, and stumped down the stairs in her sensible black shoes.

"Come along, Eve."

She didn't follow right away. "Are you coming to the funeral?"

"I'm helping my parents pack stuff into storage. They're listing the house."

"They're moving?"

He nodded. "We're doing a remembrance thing for Sara later, but I was planning to come to the funeral first." He frowned, watching Button make her way across the lawn. "Just say the word and I'll stay away."

Ashamed of her weakness, she said, "You should come. If you want."

"All right."

For different reasons than her grandmother, she gave him a wide berth as she moved past him down the stairs, tottering only a little in Donna's high heels.

He touched a fingertip to the back of her hand, opening the conduit between them. "Can we talk? I mean, not now. But later today, or tomorrow?"

Stiffening her shoulders to hide the wobble going on a little lower down, she remembered what he'd said to her the last time they'd been together, and repeated the lie back to him. "Soon. We'll figure it out."

"Eve …"

She crossed the lawn with mincing steps to keep her heels from sinking into the soft grass, and climbed into the dark interior of the limo.

"What's he doing here?" Button asked once she'd closed the door.

"I don't know."

"I never did trust that boy. It was a terrible tragedy, what happened to his sister. But there's something not quite right about him. He's like, *az me lozt a chazzer aruf afn bank, vil er afn tish*, the pig you give a chair to, and next he wants a table."

She barely listened. From behind the safety of the tint-ed glass, she drank him in like a recovering addict looking at her fix. He stood on the stairs, watching the limo pull away. His mouth was turned down, his shoulders slumped, his hands stuffed into the pockets of his suit pants. For the first time since Donna's death, she felt tears burn her eyes.

"Eve," Button said.

She turned around, giving Button a guilty look.

Button pulled down her sunglasses and examined her over the top of them. She wasn't certain what her grandmother saw, but whatever it was made Button's eyes tighten to slits.

"What?"

"*Der ponem zogt ois dem sod*, your face tells your secrets."

She shook her head, giving her grandmother a confused look. All the while, she tried desperately to stuff her emo-tions back into the box where she normally kept them.

"Please tell me there's nothing going on between the two of you."

"Of course not."

Button raised an eyebrow, and she squirmed.

"Nothing?"

"Nothing. I swear."

"Well that's good. Because if there *was* …" Button trailed off and turned to look out the window at the grey landscape. They spent the rest of the ride to the cemetery in silence.

"What can we do for you, Detective Baird?" Button's voice echoed, extra loud, from the front door.

Eve froze with the top half of her body stuck inside the fridge, where she'd been rearranging platters to make room for one more — she'd never realized how many versions of tuna and noodles there were — and closed her eyes in silent appeal.

Pleasantries had never been the detective's strong suit. Sure enough, he got straight to the point. "I'd like to speak to your granddaughter."

Detective Baird's voice was unforgettable. It rumbled deep in his throat, reminding her of the way the old bloodhound next door, Oliver, had yowled when he smelled prey. A train had run over the dog when she was eleven — no such luck when it came to Detective Baird.

"What for?" Button said.

"Is she home?"

"This isn't a good time. We've just returned from my daughter's funeral. Perhaps —"

"That's why I'm here."

Eve's head snapped up so quickly she banged it on the fridge light. Wincing, she backed out and let the door swing closed on the untidy stack of tinfoil-wrapped platters. She looked around the kitchen, frantic, caught between the instinct to run and the understanding that there really wasn't anywhere for her to go.

"Well," Button said in a high-pitched voice, and Eve could picture her clutching the collar of her bathrobe, pulling it tight against her throat. "I'm sure you can understand this is hardly the right time —"

"I can come back with a search warrant, if you'd prefer."

The inside of her head felt like it was swelling, a balloon full of ringing panic. Her vision went fuzzy and her legs threatened to give way. She might have given up right then, if not for the quiet knock behind her.

She whirled to see Leigh peering at her through the small window at the top of the kitchen door. He was soaked, hair plastered to his forehead and dripping into his eyes.

"Eve?" His voice was muffled through the door. "Can we talk?"

She pounced on her chance, grabbing the tin of maple syrup off the table and flying across the kitchen. She opened the door onto a gust of wet wind and thrust the tin at him. "Take this!"

"What?"

"Take it!" She shoved it into his chest, hard enough to make him wince.

Leigh grabbed it before it could fall. "What's going on?"

"Please! If you *ever* loved me even a little bit, you won't ask any questions."

He looked down with incredulity at the tin of syrup in his hand.

"Throw it in the river or something," she said, and then issued a short, bitter laugh at the irony.

He shook his head, trying to hand it back to her. "I don't know what you've got yourself into, but I don't want any part —"

"Listen to me, you steaming pile of chicken shit. Detective Baird is at the front door. Remember him?"

His eyes widened.

"Do this for me, or I'll tell him everything. And I do mean *everything*."

His mouth dropped open. "Eve!"

She was as surprised as he was by her threat, but desperate times and all that. "I've been protecting you for a long time."

"Ms. Gold?" Detective Baird said. "I'd like a few minutes."

The sound of heavy footsteps in the hall stopped Leigh from saying anything more. Stuffing the syrup into the inside pocket of his coat, he faded into the wet night.

"Going somewhere?" Detective Baird said behind her.

Shutting the door, Eve turned to face him. "Where would I go?"

The detective had put on weight around the middle. His moustache was bushier, too, but his eyes were just the same. They were the kind of eyes that saw everything.

She went through a quick internal debate, wondering how best to portray herself to the detective. He wouldn't buy frail and broken-hearted; maybe numb denial would

189

work better. Or she could just be herself. This idea held a certain inelegant appeal.

She lit the burner under the kettle, even though it was still warm from recent use. She had no desire to drink another cup, but it gave her something to do besides look at Detective Baird.

"What can I do for you? I'm sure my grandmother explained that this isn't the best time."

"It's never a good time, Ms. Gold."

"Please, call me Eve."

"Sorry." He sounded anything but. "I guess that reminds you of your mother?"

She was determined not to take the bait. "Would you like some tea?"

"What I'd like, for once, is the truth."

She was glad her back was turned. Pulling the tea box out of the cupboard, she said, "'Everything we hear is an opinion, not a fact.' That's Marcus Aurelius."

"I'm not much for philosophy," the detective said. "But here's a quote I can get behind. It's by William Lloyd Garrison. 'I will be as harsh as truth, as uncompromising as justice … I will not retreat a single inch.'"

"That sounds like a threat."

"Only if you've done something wrong."

Eve turned and leaned back against the counter, giving him a tight smile.

He returned it, his eyes like those of a hawk hungry for whatever lay beneath her skin. "If you come clean now, you'll be charged as a juvenile."

She forced a laugh. "Charged with what?"

"You think what happened to Sara is funny?"

Like the scream of a ghost on the river, the kettle began to whistle. It was bad timing, and the hairs on the back of her neck prickled to life. "Far from it."

She poured steaming water into the teapot, gave the tea a quick stir, and put on the lid to let it steep. "What I find funny is that you think I had something to do with it."

"And what I *don't* find funny is the number of people around you who have come to an unfortunate end."

"I'm not sure who else you're talking about, but I'd guess it was bad luck."

"Hmm."

He was getting under her skin, like he always did. "What's that supposed to mean?"

"As far as I can tell, the only bad luck these folks had was in knowing you."

She felt suddenly exhausted, and slumped against the counter as though someone had dropped a weight on her shoulders. "Are we just about done? I'd like to take a bath and then sleep for about three days."

"Trust me, *Ms. Gold*, you'll know when I'm done."

"You still think I did something to Sara?" Eve said, shaking her head.

"I think I haven't heard the whole story."

"And who else?"

Detective Baird pulled a photo out of his pocket and held it out. The man had bushy black hair and a bladelike face. "Ever see this guy?"

"No. Who is he?"

"Thomas Mahoney. A vagrant who went missing eight years ago."

She looked at him incredulously. "When I was nine."

"He liked little girls."

"What does that have to do with me?"

"Nothing, necessarily. But his remains were found a football field away from where we're standing right now. In a place called the Crook, where I'm told all the local kids used to play. Including you. There were several complaints about him hanging around the area, watching the neighbourhood girls. So, I'm thinking, maybe you ran across him at some point?"

"No."

"Are you sure? Here, take another look." He held out the photo.

She didn't even glance at it. "You think a nine-year-old is capable of hurting a full-grown man? What have you been smoking?"

"Maybe not most nine-year-olds."

"I think that's enough, detective." Button stood in the kitchen doorway, her arms crossed over her chest. She pointed her bony chin in the direction of the door. "Time for you to leave."

He ignored her, watching Eve carefully. "I've been a police officer for forty years, and if there's one thing I can spot, it's a sociopath."

"I didn't know the police academy handed out psychology degrees," she said.

He stepped closer, trying to use his height and girth to intimidate her. She would have stepped back if she hadn't already been propped against the kitchen counter.

"I've put a rush on your mother's toxicology reports."

"Good."

"Not the best mom, was she?" he asked softly. "I'm betting what she did to you when you were fourteen is just the tip of the iceberg."

She shook her head. "I don't know what you're —"

"They found bloody spittle around her mouth. Hyperaemia was observed on her stomach lining. Do you know what that is?"

"Should I?"

"It's usually caused by an irritant poison."

"Poison!" Button said from the kitchen doorway.

"He's just trying to scare us. Don't fall for it."

"They're testing for *everything*. Garden poisons, barbiturates, cleaning solvents, cosmetics, kitchen cleaners, mushrooms. You name it, they're testing for it."

"*Es vert mir finster in di oygn.*" Button slid sideways, and Eve grabbed her before she fell. She led her grandmother to the kitchen table, eased her onto the bench.

"She buried her only daughter today. Where's your compassion?"

"If you poisoned her, we'll find out."

"Thanks for the warning, but I'm not worried." Stroking her grandmother's cloud of curls, Eve said, "Let me get you some tea. And maybe an oatmeal cookie?"

"I wouldn't eat anything your granddaughter offered, if I were you," Baird said.

Button closed her eyes and sobbed.

"Please leave. Can't you see what you're doing to her?" Eve said.

Detective Baird watched Button dispassionately for a moment, and then shrugged. "I'll see you soon."

She listened to his heavy footfalls as he crossed the dining room and living room, followed by the opening squeak and hollow slam of the front door. The front porch shook as he descended the stairs. A moment later there came the rumble of a car engine, and the sound of tires slicing through puddles.

"Are you okay?" she asked her grandmother. "Should I call the doctor?"

"Eve." Button opened her eyes.

"Yes? What do you need?"

With a hand that shook badly, Button reached across the table and touched the ring of rust where the tin of maple syrup had sat for as long as she could remember. Running a gentle finger over it like she was touching a baby's cheek, she looked up at her granddaughter with eyes that were watery and wild with fear.

Her heart hammered in her throat. "What is it, Grandma?"

But all Button said was, "I think I'll take my tea in the bedroom."

TWENTY-FIVE

"WHEN CAN I GO HOME?"

"We're not sure yet." Leigh still wore his scrubs, and there was a stain on the shirt that looked suspiciously like blood. Her gaze was drawn to it again and again, perhaps so she wouldn't have to see how her husband looked off to the corner, or above the bed, or down at his fingers … or anywhere else to avoid looking at her.

"Is it hard for you?" she asked.

"What?"

"Having a psycho for a wife."

"Eve —"

"Do you tell anyone, the other doctors and nurses you work with, that your wife is locked up in Riverbend?"

Leigh opened his mouth, and then perhaps thought better of whatever he was about to say. He shook his head, and his gaze travelled up to her face for just a moment. "Dr. Jeffries will be here soon to discuss your results, and a plan of action."

"She's a bitch."

"Eve," Leigh said. "I get that you're scared. But we're all trying to do our best here."

"Screw that. Your best is locking me up like some kind of criminal."

He scrubbed a hand across his face, so hard she heard the rasp of his stubble against the palm of his hand. "You know what's bothering me? You've been here for five days —"

"I have?"

"And you haven't asked about Gabriel. Not once."

"Oh."

"Did you forget about him?" he asked, and she could hear the fear in his voice.

"Of course not. What kind of an awful person would forget about their child?" Even to her own ears, her protest was too strident.

"Not awful. Just in need of help."

"I don't —" But she was cut off as the door to her room opened.

"Mrs. Adler." Dr. Jeffries strode purposefully into the room. "Dr. Adler." She extended a hand to Leigh, who stood to shake it.

Dr. Jeffries looked exactly as she had the last time Eve saw her, right down to the pale slick of hair, the ice-coloured eyes that swam behind thick lenses, and the incongruously girlish freckles dusting her nose and cheeks.

"I have the results of the MRI and the neuroplasticity workup. Comparing the results to those done six months after your accident, we can see some interesting anomalies."

She took the only seat in the room and crossed her legs. She wore tweed pants and brown shoes with pointed toes. Flopping the thick chart open on her lap, she said, "The good news is, there's significant improvement in areas of the brain that weren't directly impacted in the accident. But I found this part curious."

She turned the folder so Leigh could see. "Take a look at the hypothalamus."

Leigh frowned. "Huh."

"Eve, did you have trouble getting pregnant?"

"Not at all."

"Any difficulty breastfeeding?"

"No."

"We had to supplement with formula," Leigh said. "Because her milk production was poor."

"Right."

"Do you sleep well at night?" Dr. Jeffries asked.

"Most of the time."

"She rarely sleeps," Leigh said at the same time.

The doctor looked from one of them to the other, but neither elaborated.

"Do you often feel too warm? Or too cold?"

"Cold," Leigh said.

"I can never get warm."

"And when did that begin?"

"Um." She paused, thinking. "It's been a long time. I rarely think about it anymore."

"It's been getting worse lately," Leigh said. "She's been wearing sweaters while the rest of us are sweating in T-shirts."

"I'm not surprised, considering what I see here." The doctor nodded at the chart in her lap. "Your hypothalamus function has deteriorated significantly since the last time we ran these tests. It's responsible for many functions, including helping to control the pituitary gland. This can affect everything from sleep patterns to reproductive issues to the body's ability to regulate temperature. Your blood tests show that you've become hyperthyroid, and your estrogen level is higher than we would like. But medication can bring both these issues under control."

"Well. That's good."

"Yes," the doctor said. "That's all very good news. However, there are other issues of concern. Your husband believes there's been a decline in your cognition since the birth of your son."

"If he says so."

"You don't agree?"

She shrugged, glancing at Leigh for guidance. The bloodstain on the front of his scrubs, which she remembered as being about the size of a nickel, had grown to several inches in diameter.

"Eve?" Dr. Jeffries said.

"Sorry. What?" She turned back to the doctor, who watched her with a mixture of interest and concern.

"Your husband tells us that you're having increasing moments of forgetfulness, and you're also experiencing some aural hallucinations." Dr. Jeffries leaned forward, giving her an earnest look. "This is not uncommon after a significant head injury. It's also fairly common for this to start happening years after the initial injury. However, this level of psychosis —"

"Psychosis."

The doctor held up her hand, smiling. "It's a term that's bandied about very liberally in popular culture, with negative connotations, but in medical terms all it means is a break from reality."

198

"A break from reality. Uh-huh."

"This woman who visits you while you're painting —"

"I don't want to talk about her."

"I'm afraid we must. If we're to get to the bottom of this problem, we'll need to have some open and honest communication."

"Not about her."

"Hmm," the doctor said. "Are you afraid of her?"

"Of course I am."

"Is she telling you to do things you don't want to do?"

"Like what?"

"Like hurt yourself? Or hurt others?"

She shook her head. "No. Nothing like *that*."

"Then what?" Leigh asked, reaching out to stroke her hair. "What is she saying?"

"I don't remember." She was on the verge of tears, her body quaking with pent-up tension.

The doctor leaned back in her chair, watching her.

"What?"

"Well, how can we know if it's safe for you to be around your child, or your grandmother and husband, if we don't know what she's telling you to do?"

"You're saying I'm not leaving here."

"I'm saying it's hard to treat something when we don't know exactly what it is. However, I suspect that the presence of this woman is a symptom of your poorly functioning hypothalamus. And that's good news."

"How?"

"Because with the right treatment, we should be able to eliminate this symptom and many others."

Eve grew suspicious. "And how do we do that?"

"Science is a marvellous thing." For the first time since entering the room, the doctor's smile seemed genuine. "By isolating the areas in your brain that have been damaged, we can go in and fix them."

"You're going to shock me again."

"Again?" Leigh asked.

She turned to him and froze. The stain on his shirt had grown to the size of a dinner plate. It was perfectly round, bright red, and glistening wet.

"Oh my God, Leigh. You're bleeding."

He looked down. "Where?"

"Your chest."

He pulled the shirt away from his chest, craning his neck to examine it, and then looked at her with raised eyebrows. The doctor gave her the same look. They couldn't see the blood.

"Never mind. Just a trick of the light, I guess." It was thick and gelatinous, oozing down the front of his shirt and glopping onto his pants.

Leigh turned to the doctor. "Do you really think an ECT is the best way to go?"

"I understand the concern," Dr. Jeffries said. "But much of the stigma still associated with this kind of treatment stems from a time when it was used in high doses, without any specific targeting, and without general anaesthetic. It's a completely different procedure now."

"I've heard *that* before."

Dr. Jeffries went on as though Eve hadn't spoken. "I'm talking about targeting a precise location in the brain with electrical current, which triggers a brief seizure. There is minimal risk, and potentially a lot to gain."

Drips of blood hit the linoleum floor by Leigh's feet —
plop-plop-plop — and oozed toward Dr. Jeffries's pointed
shoes.

"How quickly do you usually see results?" Leigh asked.

"It's cumulative," the doctor said. "Sometimes we see
results almost immediately, but usually things really begin
to improve after the third or fourth procedure. Every time
the brain has a seizure it releases hormones, and this is
where the work really happens."

"No fucking way," Eve tried to say, but her voice didn't
make it past her throat.

"Quite frankly, this is the only possible solution I see,"
Dr. Jeffries said to Leigh. "If the results are good, I expect
Eve will be able to go home to you and your son."

"And if not?" Leigh asked.

Dr. Jeffries shrugged. "I'll give you two some time to
talk. Dr. Adler, if you'd like to arrange a meeting, I'm
happy to go over the procedure in detail with you."

"Thank you for your time, Dr. Jeffries." Leigh stepped
forward to shake her hand and his shoes made a squelching sound.

"Of course." When the doctor departed, she left a trail
of bloody shoeprints in her wake.

"Well," Leigh said.

Eve raised a hand to stop him from getting any closer.
"Get out."

"I understand if you're scared. But we really need to
talk about this."

Holding grimly to the last of her self-control, she said,
"I need some time alone. Okay?"

"We need to talk about this."

"Tomorrow."

"Well." Leigh looked at his watch. "If I leave now I'll be home in time to tuck Gabriel into bed."

"Yes. Do that."

He leaned over to kiss her, and a clot of blood splatted onto the blanket. Eve pulled back, her gorge rising. With a sigh, he moved away.

"Eve," he said at the door. "We'll get through this together, like we always do. Just you and me, right?"

Plop.

She bit down on her tongue, unsure if she was going to scream or vomit.

The door clicked closed behind him. She managed to hold on until his footsteps had faded down the hall, then she gave in to her horror. Retching, she kicked the soiled blanket off the end of the bed.

She grabbed the pillow and rammed it against her face, blocking her view of the room. But as clearly as if her eyes were still open, she could see Leigh's footprints smearing gelatinous clots of blood.

The flowers looked like daisies, but they had blood at their roots.

She screamed into the pillow until she wore herself out. Eventually, she slept. Her dreams were full of silver things soon forgotten, and she awoke to the sun shining through the blinds and birds chirping outside the window.

Wrapping her wool sweater around her shoulders, she climbed out of bed and stumbled groggily to the bathroom to relieve herself. Her head felt stuffed and thick, her eyes bleary from tears and sleep.

The sound of her urine hitting the water reminded her of the previous day's blood. Stretching out one pale foot, she pushed the bathroom door open. From what she could see, the floor was clean.

"Motherfucker."

She wiped, flushed, washed her hands and face with water as warm as she could get from the tap, and then brushed her teeth. Feeling slightly more human, she moved back into the bedroom. She examined the floor carefully, even getting down on all fours to look beneath the chair Dr. Jeffries had been sitting in. There was nothing but faded linoleum.

Relieved, she sat back on her haunches, a smile spreading across her lips. And then she saw it: a small smear on the metal leg of the chair, dark red like old ketchup.

TWENTY-SIX

Sara's Eighth Birthday

"CAREFUL, YOU CAN'T pull them out like that. Here." Sara broke the flower off at the stem and slipped it into Eve's hair. "They look like daisies, but they're not."

"What are they?"

"Bloodroot flowers. They don't normally grow around here."

"How do you know that?" The flowers were pretty. They had yellow at the centre and delicate white petals.

"Duh. It's called a library."

"Oh. Yeah." She tucked a flower behind Sara's ear. "Donna always says you're too smart for your own good."

"How can you be too smart for anything?" Sara asked.

"I don't know. She's always saying things that don't make sense."

They sat with their backs pressed against the fence in the Adlers' yard, sipping glasses of iced tea and pretending to do their homework. Their books were spread around them in a fan, but spelling lists and times tables were far from their minds.

The day was unusually warm, and it made both girls feel lazy and slow. Indian summer, her mom had called it. She didn't know what Indians had to do with the weather, but the air was hot and sweet, a reminder of the long sticky days of freedom just past.

On the other side of the yard, Margie and Danielle lay sunning themselves on towels. Though there was a two-year age difference between them, most people couldn't tell them apart. They were everything Sara was not: skinny, bitchy, and stupid.

Today they wore matching red bikinis, and their bony bodies were greasy with suntan oil. They each had one ear plugged into Danielle's iPod, and their heads bopped side to side with the music.

In the driveway, Leigh bounced a basketball and threw it with such perfect precision it barely ever touched the metal ring on its way through the hoop. Eve didn't think she could get the ball through the hoop even once, but sports weren't really her thing.

If Sara hadn't been sitting next to her, she would have pulled out her sketchbook and done a couple hasty drawings of him. She already had a stack of them tucked between her mattress and box spring, to look at on nights she couldn't sleep.

"Want to know why they're called bloodroot?"

"What?"

"Stop staring at my brother like that. It creeps me out."

"I wasn't staring."

"Sure."

"Why are they called bloodroot?"

"Because their roots are as red as your face is right now."

Eve stuck out her tongue.

"Look." Sara dug in with a stick and flipped up a clump of dirt and roots. Red goop oozed out.

"Eew."

"It looks like blood, right? But thicker."

"You're going to get it on your pants."

Sara scooted over. "You don't want to drink it."

"Why would I even *think* of doing that?"

"Seriously. This sap is really poisonous."

"Oh, yeah?" Eve eyed the goop with interest.

"Yeah. You shouldn't touch it, either. It'll burn your skin."

"Shouldn't you tell your mom about it?"

"No way," Sara said. "She'd rip them out."

"Well, yeah, that's the point."

Sara gave her a devilish smile. "But what if I need to poison someone?"

"Ha-ha."

"Seriously. I read all about it. Because it doesn't normally grow here, no one would even guess where the poison came from."

"Sara, that's creepy."

"Don't you ever think about things like that?" Sara asked.

"No."

"Not even when Canton Forsythe pulled down your pants in the gym?"

"Maybe you should write a story about it instead?"

"That would be like a confession. I'd totally get caught."

"You're not, like, serious? Right, Sara?" She was starting to feel distinctly uncomfortable.

Sara narrowed her eyes and gave her a villainous look, and then she giggled. "Gotcha!"

"Jerk."

"But it really is poisonous, so be careful," Sara said.

"I wonder what it tastes like."

"Gawd, Leee-*eigh*!" Sara turned his name into four syllables of sisterly condemnation. "Don't sneak up on us like that!"

He stood above them, dripping sweat, with the basketball tucked under one arm. From her vantage point he was about a million miles high, and she had to crane her neck to see him. The sun was behind him, creating a golden glow around his head.

"Hey, Doodlebug."

"And *don't* call her that," Sara said.

"Whatever you say, Gumdrop."

Sara's face turned red. "Those names are *secret*."

"Wanna see a trick?" he asked Eve.

"Sure."

"No," Sara said at the same time, but Leigh ignored his youngest sister. He threw the ball up into the air and caught it on his index finger, setting it to spin.

"Cool," she said, trying to act like she wasn't that impressed.

He threw the ball so it sailed high up into the air, and then caught it with the index finger of his other hand and set it spinning.

"Wow!"

He tucked the ball back under his arm and gave her that slanted smile that always made her stomach flip over. "Thanks. I've been practising that trick for months. Why don't you ever come watch me play?"

Eve shrugged, grinning up at him.

Sara rolled her eyes. "Uh, because your games are at night? She has a *bedtime*, dummy."

"No, I don't. I can come sometime."

Leigh pushed golden hair out of his eyes. "Rad."

"What are you *talking* about? You mom would kill you," Sara said.

"Donna doesn't have to know."

Leigh gave her an approving nod. "I always knew you were cool."

The heat started in her chest and rose up into her cheeks. "Yeah."

"Oh my God, would you guys just *stop it*?"

"Next game is on Friday. Maybe I'll see you there?"

She burned like one of those firecrackers that fizzed along the ground, spitting and spinning sparks of colour and heat. "Cool."

Leigh turned and strutted off to the house, basketball tucked into the crook of his arm.

Sara made a gagging noise. "I'm going to use that bloodroot on myself."

"Hey, Sara!" he called from the porch. "Catch!"

The ball flew so quickly Sara barely had time to lift her hands before it hit her face. Danielle and Margie laughed.

"Leee-*eigh*!" Sara bellowed, jumping up to chase him.

"Happy birthday, doofus!" Leigh turned and waggled his backside, then slipped into the house.

TWENTY-SEVEN

IN SPITE OF EVE'S PROTESTS, the first ECT was scheduled for Monday morning.

"You'll be groggy and possibly confused from the anaesthetic," Leigh said as they waited for the nurse to return to wheel her wherever they were going to do the procedure. He shifted nervously in his chair, his hand sweaty against hers. "And it may impair your memory. But just remember, that part's temporary —"

Although terror churned her insides into a stew, she laughed.

"What?"

"How am I supposed to remember that it's temporary, if my memory is impaired?"

The side of his mouth curled up in a half smile. "I guess I'll remind you again in the recovery room."

"You'll stay with me the whole time?"

"Dr. Jeffries is letting me observe the procedure, and I'll come with you to recovery. I promise I won't leave your side today."

"You love me, don't you?"

"I love your boobs," he said.

She smacked him in the arm, and he laughed.

"That's what you get for asking such a ridiculous question."

"I'm just scared. You really think I'll be okay?"

"I know it."

"I guess I can't get any more messed up than I already am."

He squeezed her hand, but didn't bother to respond. They stayed that way until the nurse came back with her IV.

"We're starting the drip now. Just lay back and relax."

She shook all over, like a puppy at the veterinarian.

"Leigh ..." Her words sounded slow and sluggish in her ears, like a record winding down.

"Right here," he said, and then she was gone.

Quicksilver rattled and hissed around her, dripping with fog. Eve moved downhill toward the river. Branches snagged and tore at her clothing, and iridescent leaves left icy slug-trails on her cheeks and arms. Somewhere below was a pile of clothing and bones.

The woman moved beside her, a dark shadow barely seen through the branches.

"You were never a good listener."

"That's true," Eve said.

"When will you end this charade?"

"This is no charade. It's my life, and I want it back."

"You think that's possible?"

"If I can get rid of you, then maybe."

"Don't you get it? I'm the only thing that's real." She probably wanted to say more, but she didn't get the chance.

The field of quicksilver exploded with excruciating blue shock-light. Eve both heard and felt a sizzling snap, and then she smelled her own flesh burning.

For just a moment she remembered everything. She remembered the accident, and shaking loose from the centre of her brain to whip around her skull like a pea lost in a tornado. She remembered every other moment of her life; all the bad things she'd done and the people she'd hurt.

She screamed into the light. She screamed and screamed and screamed — until the darkness smothered her in welcome annihilation. Seconds or eons later, she began once again to rebuild.

"I'm warm."

Leigh smiled at her. "That's wonderful."

"It *is* wonderful. Like being in a bath without getting wet."

"How are you feeling, otherwise?"

"Hmm? Oh, okay I guess. What happened?"

"You had the ECT, remember?" he said.

"Oh."

"It went well. No repercussions from the general anaesthetic, which can be a concern. But you handled it like a champ."

"Well, that's good," she said dreamily. "Hand me a bucket. I'm going to throw up."

Cleaning her up after, he said, "That's a common reaction to the anaesthetic. Nothing to worry about."

"Not worried." She closed her eyes. "Leigh?"

"Yes?"

"I think she's gone."

TWENTY-EIGHT

Sara's Ninth Birthday

LEIGH YANKED OPEN the door to her art studio, making Eve shriek and drop her paintbrush. It hit the floor in a splat of bright yellow.

"There you are. I've been looking *everywhere* for you!"

She placed a hand against her chest. Her heart thundered beneath her ribcage like it was trying to escape. "You scared the crap out of me!"

"Shh!" He eased through the door and closed it behind him, looking around with interest. "So, this is the famous art studio. Sara's so jealous she's turned green."

"Why is she green?"

"Green with envy." When she continued to look at him in confusion, he waved it off. "Never mind."

Bending to pick up her paintbrush, she tried to ignore the eruption of nervous heat that started in her belly and climbed all the way up to her scalp. He must have been there to talk about the maybe-dead man in the forest — a conversation she'd been awaiting this past week with no great enthusiasm.

But she also felt nervous that he was seeing her studio, as though each painting would expose to him a little piece of her soul. She pressed into the corner near Sara's desk to give him room.

He moved through the studio with interest, his lanky body seeming to take up more space than it should. "I can see where you got the name Doodlebug. What's this one? It looks like my back fence."

"Sara says those flowers are called bloodroot." She thought about telling him the sap was poisonous, but didn't.

"Is that me?"

"Yeah," she said casually, but her flush deepened. With sudden panic, she realized how many of her other paintings he was in, like her own personal *Where's Waldo?* What if he noticed? He'd think she was a total creep!

Faced with this mortifying possibility, she decided to dive face-first into the only thing that might distract him.

"Was he dead?"

The back of Leigh's neck was covered in a soft fuzz of hair, golden-white in the natural light. "Yeah, he's dead."

"Oh. Um, I'm sorry you had to …"

He turned to face her, watched her squirm. She felt like she'd missed something, but she couldn't think what it might be.

"Thank you?" She was unsure about the etiquette in these sorts of situations.

"Do you want to know where …?" he asked.

"The pond?" she said, and then shook her head emphatically. "I'm sorry. Maybe I don't want to know."

"But you know what he was doing there, right? Why he was watching you?"

"Sure."

He looked her up and down, as though judging whether or not he should believe her. "Well, anyway. I wanted to make sure that we're cool."

"Oh. Yeah." She nodded, although she felt more lost by the moment.

"Because I don't want us to get in trouble."

Her stomach wobbled like a ship in a storm. "Trouble?"

"With the cops. I mean, they might think that we, you know, *murdered* him or something. Because of what he was doing."

"But we didn't!"

"Look, it's okay. If you tell me you didn't do anything wrong, I'll believe you."

She let go of a breath she didn't know she'd been holding. "I didn't. I swear. I — I thought he was Annabeth and the glitter gang. That's why I chased him. And then he tripped."

He considered, and then nodded. "I figured it was something like that. But the cops might not understand."

"You don't think? Maybe if we tell them together —"

"Sure, if we'd gone to them right away," he said, his brow furrowed in thought. "But a week later?"

"I guess that doesn't look too good."

"No one knows we saw him. And no one will ever find his … him. I promise."

"But he must have a family, or someone looking for him?"

Leigh shook his head. "A man like that? I doubt it."

"That's kind of sad," she said, and he gave her a strange look.

Her head was starting to hurt. She rubbed her temples, thinking it through. "So, maybe we shouldn't do anything?"

He looked thoughtful, and then nodded agreement. "You might be right. I don't want either of us to go to jail. But it means you can't tell anyone."

"For sure."

"Because if someone finds out, we'll be in big trouble. And I'm older than you, so I might end up in jail for a long time. If you told someone —"

"I would never." She shook her head emphatically.

"Not even Sara."

"Right. Not even Sara."

He moved closer, and she automatically took a step back. "So I can trust you."

"You can. I swear."

Leigh stopped a couple feet away from her, so she had to decide whether to stare at his chest or crane her neck to look up at his face. She chose his chest. It seemed safer.

"One thing I'm wondering about," he said.

"What?"

"Why am I in so many of your paintings?"

She felt tears of humiliation sting her eyes. "I'm sorry," she said, not even sure why she was apologizing.

"Do you have a crush on me?"

Eve stared miserably at her feet.

"I can't trust you if you're not honest with me. Okay?"

"Okay."

"So no secrets?"

She nodded.

"I promise I won't tell anyone that you like me. You know why?"

"Why?"

"Because you and I are the same. I don't think anybody really understands you. For sure not your mom. Maybe not even your grandma, or Sara. You feel pretty alone, don't you?"

"Sometimes."

"I feel that way, too."

"You?" she asked, finally looking up into his face. "But you're so popular, and you're good at sports, and ..."

"But no one really gets me."

She was stunned. The idea that Leigh Adler — *the* Leigh Adler — might feel just as lost as she did? It didn't seem possible.

"I think you're really different." He said it like a compliment.

Her cheeks warmed yet again — this time with pleasure. "Thanks."

After a moment of silence, he asked, "So, are we cool?"

"Yeah."

He gave her arm a quick squeeze. His hand was so big it wrapped all the way around her biceps with room to spare. After he let go, the skin he'd touched crawled with heat for a long time, like she'd been branded.

Moving to the door, he told her, "I've got to get to football practice. Are you going to come watch me play sometime?"

"Yeah, okay. Sure."

"Are you coming to dinner tonight? Mom is making Sara a chocolate cake."

"Yeah, I'll be there."

"Cool." He ducked out the door.

For long minutes after he left, she picked at the drying paint on her fingertips, her stomach rolling with unease. The whole conversation had been unsettling. She felt like she'd missed something important, but whatever it was remained elusive.

Without cleaning her brushes, she left the studio and went to her bedroom to lie down.

TWENTY-NINE

BEFORE SHE STARTED to slip, they had several good years. They were peacefully forgettable, filled with the monotony of easy days. The electric blankets went into storage. Leigh grew his medical practice, Button grew obsessed with making jams and preserves, and Gabriel grew from baby to toddler to preschooler.

"*D-O-G* spells dog," Gabriel said, his chubby fingers tapping the tablet screen until he received a chime of success.

"Well done, sweetie." Eve stroked burnt umber onto the canvas.

"*C-A-T* spells cat." There was another ding.

"You're going to be reading before kindergarten at this rate," she said.

"I read already. How you spell snake?"

She called out the letters and the tablet chimed.

"Good job, Mommy."

"Thanks," she said with a laugh.

"Mommy?"

"Mm-hm?"

"Button said you was sick when I was a baby. She said you was in the hospital."

"Did she, now?" She turned to look at her son and noticed how the sun cut through the blinds at just the right angle to turn his dark curls into a golden halo.

"Hang on. Don't move." She grabbed her phone and snapped a picture. Showing him, she said, "See? You look like an angel."

"*Mommy*, angels aren't real."

"Then how am I looking at one right now?" Turning to clean her paintbrush, she asked as casually as she could, "So, what did Button tell you?"

"She told me you was sick. Are you sick now, Mommy?"

"No, sweetheart, I'm all better."

"So, you're not going to die?"

"Gabriel!" She turned back to her son. "How do you even know that word?"

Gabriel pointed in the direction of the house next door. "Missy's cat died and she put it in a hole in the backyard."

"Oh." She laid the paintbrush aside. "I'm sorry to hear that. I know she loved her cat very much."

"She told me that people die, too."

"Well, yes. But only when they're very old, like Missy's cat."

"Is Button very old?" His amber-coloured eyes were wide with worry.

"She's older, yes. But she's still very healthy and active. I hope she'll live a long, long time."

"Me, too." Gabriel gave an emphatic nod, his curls flopping across his forehead. He needed a haircut.

"When are *you* going to die, Mommy?"

"Not for a long time," she told him firmly.

"But what if you get sick again?"

"I wasn't sick in my body, sweetheart. Something went wrong in my brain. Remember I told you that my head got hurt really badly, once?"

He nodded uncertainly.

"Well, it made me think funny things for awhile. That's why I was in the hospital, so they could fix it."

"Like Bob the Builder fixes things?"

"That's right."

"Did they use a skew diver?"

"Something like that."

Gabriel kicked his legs, banging the sofa beneath him. *Thump-thump-thump*. "What happens when you die?"

Her stomach twisted with nerves. "I don't know."

"Button says good people go to heaven. But I don't know what that is."

"I guess it's a nice place."

"What about mean people? Do they go to a mean place?"

She patted his shoulder. "Let's go grab some lunch, Gabe."

"Mommy." He squirmed away from her. "Your hand is so cold!"

She stuffed her hands into her armpits, trying to calm the immediate swell of panic. Because he was right, her hands felt like blocks of ice.

"Maybe you *are* sick? 'Member when I had that fu and you put lots of blankies on me?"

"Flu," she said.

"I'll make you soup." Gabriel's chest inflated with pride. "Button showed me how. Come on!" He tugged at her shirt.

"Don't forget your stuff," she said.

Gabriel picked up the tablet, which had a neon yellow cover, and then tried to scoop up his pile of Hot Wheels cars.

"Why don't I take your tablet?"

"Thanks, Mommy."

They moved slowly across the backyard to the kitchen door. Through the window she saw her grandmother ferociously scrubbing the kitchen counter, a silk scarf tied around her head to protect her curls.

Jars of spiced apples sat on the windowsill, cooling after their hot-water bath. The smell of sweet cinnamon tickled her nose, and her chest tightened with something that felt an awful lot like grief.

For the first time in forever, she felt *so cold*. The ice seeped, quickly and inexorably, into the marrow of her bones. What was next? Would she start losing track of time again? Would she hear the silver tinkle of laughter? She could feel the confusion closing in on her like a fog.

Gabriel pushed through the kitchen door and dumped his cars on the table, where they clattered and rolled. "Mommy has the fu!"

"What?" Button asked, dropping the cloth and moving toward her granddaughter.

"Don't get too close. I might be contagious."

Button's face pinched with worry. "Maybe you should go lie down?"

Eve tried to give her grandmother a reassuring smile, but her face moved with the stiffness of a mask.

"Come on." Gabriel dragged her to the bedroom. "I'll tuck you in and get Doc McStuffins. She'll give you a checkup."

She crawled stiffly under the covers, while her son disappeared and returned moments later with a pile of blankets from his bedroom. He laid them on top of her, one at a time, and propped his Doc McStuffins doll on the pillow beside her.

"You rest now," he said in a stage whisper, and then tiptoed away.

She burrowed beneath the weight of the blankets, tears leaking from her eyes and pooling in the cups of her ears.

"Gabe said you're sick." Leigh leaned across the bed to feel her forehead. "You feel cold."

She gave him a plastic smile. "I'm nice and toasty."

"Sore throat? Headache? Anything like that?" She heard the hope in his voice.

"Yes," she lied.

"You're rundown," he said. "You've been working too hard."

Her fourth art show, *Lost Homeland*, was launching at Hector's art gallery the following week, and she was nervous. It was a series of abstract portraits exploring the fear and hope of refugees who had fled war-torn countries.

A Syrian Boy was her favourite of the twenty-painting series. The boy was the same age as her son, but lacking the chubby good health of Gabriel's privilege. He'd lost an eye during a sniper strike, and the eyelid was a twist covering the sunken well of his eye socket. In contrast, the remaining eye stared with a haunting clarity that told his story more deeply than words.

She'd also painted *Waiting*, a portrait of the boy's mother and older sister. She'd captured them from behind, standing side by side at the window of a dingy Downtown Eastside motel room. Beyond the window was an endless grey winter rain. The mother clutched the back of her daughter's dress with fierce, muscled strength.

The husband had sold everything they owned to pay the cost of his family's escape, promising he'd find a way to join them as soon as he could. Every day, the mother explained, she stood watch at the window. Every night she dreamed that he'd died.

"Have you had any hallucinations?"

"No," Eve told Leigh truthfully. "I'm just rundown, like you said."

"You need to take better care of yourself." He stroked the hair off her forehead, and they both pretended not to feel the difference in their temperatures.

"I just need a couple more hours to finish the last painting."

"Not tonight, okay?"

"I'm not leaving this bed tonight. Promise."

"Gabe and I will bring you your dinner. He's making you a card, too. Act surprised when you see it."

They grinned at each other the way parents do, mutually in love with the little life they'd created. He leaned forward to kiss her cheek, his hair falling across his eyes the way it had when he was a boy. His breath was hot and smelled of peppermint.

"Love you," she said.

"You'd better."

She felt the bed shift as he stood up, and heard the creak of the door as he eased it closed behind him. Left alone, she drifted into troubled dreams. Out there in the quicksilver, a woman waited.

"Mommy!" Gabriel shouted, barrelling through the door with enthusiasm. "I made you soup!"

"Did you?" She sat up and propped the pillows behind her back. "It smells delicious."

"It is," Gabriel said, as Leigh pushed through the door and lowered a tray over her lap. "It's chicken noodle. And crackers. And a card. Open the card, Mommy!"

"Did you make this for me? Thanks, buddy."

"Open it!" Gabriel bounced from one foot to the other.

"He wouldn't even let me see it," Leigh said. "Insisted it was a secret."

"You've used some beautiful colours here, Gabe." Eve ran a finger over the concentric circles her son had drawn on the front of the card. He'd used almost every colour in the crayon box, weaving them together.

"*Open it*, Mommy!"

She did.

"Well? Do you like it?"

"It's beautiful, Gabe," she said faintly.

"It's a silver garden," he told her proudly. "That's where you go to get better. Now I'll feed you."

Scooping a spoonful of steaming soup, he said, "Don't worry, I'll blow on it." He did, blowing spittle and spraying soup.

"Maybe I'll wait for it to cool down. Could you please get me a glass of water?"

Gabriel strutted off on his mission.

She didn't dare look at her husband. "It doesn't mean anything."

He didn't answer. Instead he turned and followed Gabriel out of the room, closing the door quietly behind him.

Eve awoke to the sound of Leigh snoring. Easing out of bed, she wrapped herself in an afghan. Leigh stirred and rolled over. Moonlight streaked through the blinds, making his bare shoulder look like it had been gilded. She shivered and turned away.

She decided to finish the last painting while the rest of the family slept. The paint needed time to dry before Hector came to pick it up. Trudging to the kitchen, she put on the kettle for tea. When it was ready, she filled a carafe and carried it across the damp lawn to her studio.

The last painting stood waiting on the easel, the paint still glossy in the thickest spots. She studied it critically and decided she was pleased with most of it. It was better than she remembered, actually. Just the hair needed more work, and the hands weren't right.

She set to work, choosing her brushes and mixing the paint. She hummed with contentment as her body warmed to the work, allowing her to tune in to the dance made between brush and canvas. She swirled strands of sunshine into dark curls, stroked shadows along the ridges of the fingers, defined the knuckles with slivers of pink and blue.

Eventually, she stood back and nodded with satisfaction. There were still imperfections, but one of Hector's most valuable lessons had been to lay the paintbrush down before she nitpicked her way into a mess. The beauty of life was found in imperfections, Hector had said, and so must it be in art.

The sky lightened toward dawn as Eve closed her studio. She felt drained, but satisfied. The house was still quiet, so she tiptoed down the hallway, taking an extra big step to avoid the squeaking floorboard near Gabriel's room.

Quietly, she eased through her bedroom door and dropped the afghan onto the end of the bed. As she crawled beneath the heavy covers, she saw that she hadn't needed to worry about waking Gabriel. He lay curled, thumb in mouth, against Leigh's side.

Sleep took her down on a black wave, and the next thing she knew Gabriel was bouncing on her head.

"Ow!"

"Sorry, Mommy." Gabriel hopped over to Leigh's pillow, shouting, "It's morning. It's morning, right?"

"It's *early* morning," Leigh said. "Come cuddle." He pulled Gabriel down between them and tickled him until Gabriel convulsed, squealing.

"Too. Loud." She rolled away, pressing her face into the pillow.

"Sorry, Mommy," Leigh and Gabriel said contritely, in unison.

"Were you painting?" Leigh asked. "It reeks of oils in here."

"Yes," she said with drowsy satisfaction. "I finished the last painting."

"That's great." Leigh patted his son's backside. "Hey, buddy, could you make us some pancakes?"

Gabriel giggled. "Daddy, I can't do that yet."

"But you made soup last night," Leigh said.

"*Daddy*." Gabriel shook his head. "I can't make pancakes until I'm *at least* five. And Mommy hates maple syrup."

"That's true," Leigh said.

"Mommy, your hands are dirty."

"Hmm?"

"He's right." Leigh pulled the covers down. "Holy cow, you're *covered*."

"I am?"

She was, indeed. Silver paint was crusted on her nails and dried into the whorls of her fingertips. It streaked up her arms, making her look like she was turning into the Tin Man.

"Mommy, you're so *messy*," Gabriel said with awe, and then his eyes widened with excitement. "Did you go to the garden I drawed? Do you feel better now?"

"Why don't you go take a shower?" Leigh said.

"Yes," she said faintly. "I suppose Hector will make do with nineteen paintings."

The corners of Leigh's mouth turned down with grief. "I suppose he'll have to."

And so began her second descent into cold confusion, and either two weeks or two years later, Leigh went out for a jog and didn't come home.

THIRTY

Sara's Thirteenth Birthday

"I'M THIRSTY," Eve said into her chest, when Detective Baird had finished with his seemingly endless list of questions.

Though some questions had seemed odd, none had been hard to answer: her name, date of birth, home address, favourite school subject, the name of her third grade teacher, and so on.

There was a notepad and pen beside him, but Baird didn't use them. Instead of sitting across the table from her, as she'd expected, he'd pulled a chair around so they sat almost knee-to-knee. He rested his hands, unmoving, on his lap.

She'd thrust her hands deep into the pockets of her sweatshirt to hide any shaking, and she did everything in her power not to swing her legs. This was a challenge since her feet didn't touch the ground. She wondered if they'd given her an extra-tall chair on purpose. She wondered why he'd sat close enough for her to kick.

Detective Baird gave her an easy smile. "Sorry about that. Detective Mathers, please get Ms. Gold a glass of water."

The other detective nodded and slipped through the door, closing it behind him with a definitive click.

"Eve," she said.

"Pardon?"

"It sounds weird when you call me Ms. Gold. Like you're talking about my mom."

Baird leaned forward in his chair. It squeaked beneath his weight, which was considerable. No matter how bad her current situation was, she thought his chair had it worse. Exhausted and overwrought, she almost giggled.

"Something funny?" he asked.

"Of course not."

"No," he said, with a sympathetic downturn of the lips. "When I was your age, the worst thing that had ever happened to me was wetting my sleeping bag on a school camping trip."

"That's pretty bad."

"I thought so at the time," he agreed. "Eve, I can see that you're scared, and that's natural. I'm here to help you get through this, okay?"

"Uh-huh."

"But I need you to promise me something, and it's very important."

"What?"

"Have you ever seen a movie where they hook some guy up to a machine to find out if he's telling the truth? He's got those bands around his chest, and wires attached to his fingers?"

"A lie detector?"

"That's right," Detective Baird said with a smile. He leaned closer, giving her an earnest look. "I'm like a human version of that lie detector test. I don't need to hook you up to a machine. I'll just know."

She shifted in her seat, her skin prickling with heat.

"I need you to promise me that you'll tell the truth. And in return, I promise that I'll do everything I can to help you." He watched her silently for a moment, and she did her best not to squirm. "Sound good?"

"Uh-huh."

"Great." He stood and patted her shoulder. His hand was heavy and warm. "Let me go see what happened to your water. Are you hungry? I could rustle up some crackers, or maybe a chocolate bar."

"No, thank you."

At the door, he paused and looked back at her. "Oh. When we brought you in, did you notice all the other rooms just like this one?"

She nodded.

He jabbed a thumb to the right. "Right next door is a woman who saw what happened at the river. Think I'll go have a chat with her. I'll be back soon."

It wasn't soon. By the time Detective Baird returned, Eve had sweated through her clothes and felt sick to her stomach.

He placed her bottle of water on the table, and settled into the chair across from her. For long minutes, neither spoke. He watched her, the only animation in his eyes. It made her feel hunted, like he'd pounce the moment her guard came down. If she were to draw a picture of the scene, she would make him a bear fattening up for winter, and make herself a rabbit so weary that being his dinner was starting to sound appealing — if only to put an end to the chase.

Tentatively, she asked, "What did that woman say?"

Detective Baird studied her, letting the silence stretch until she felt ready to scream. "Why don't *you* tell *me*?"

She shifted in her seat and shrugged.

"All right. Here's what I think happened. I think you and Sara had a big fight a couple weeks ago."

"How do you know that?"

"And while I don't know what this argument was about, *yet*, I can make some guesses."

She pinned her tongue between her teeth and stared resolutely at her lap.

"Girls your age … it often comes down to boys," he said. "Maybe you and Sara liked the same boy. Maybe he showed Sara more attention, and that made you angry."

"Not Sara."

"What's that?" He leaned forward and his chair groaned in protest.

"Sara's not — *wasn't* — interested in boys."

"Hmm."

She shut her mouth. Told herself to keep it shut.

"Well, you fought about something. And whatever it was, you two stopped talking after that, until your birthday. And then Sara, a girl her parents tell me wasn't a strong swimmer, decided to play on a log boom. Can you see why I'm having trouble?"

Eve shrugged.

"So I'm thinking, maybe you lured her there."

"No."

"Just to scare her, make her think about whatever it was she'd done. And you probably didn't realize how fast the current was, or how slippery the logs were."

"No."

"You didn't really want anything bad to happen to her. Am I on the right track?"

She shook her head.

"So correct me. What were you and Sara doing on that log boom?"

"We were playing a game."

"How did you get out there?" His voice rumbled like a dog chewing on a tasty bone.

"We climbed down from the pier."

"You dangled above the middle of the river, where the current is at its most swift."

"Yeah. No. There's a ladder."

"You climbed down the ladder."

"Right."

"Walk me through it."

She pushed her hands even deeper into her pockets and stared at the graffiti etched onto the table. "That's it."

"You're going to have to tell me more than that. Help me to understand. I know you want to help the Adlers. This poor family has lost their youngest, and they just want to know what happened to her. And today is her birthday, isn't it?" He shook his head, looking sorrowful.

Eve shifted in her seat. "We'd seen those guys walking on top of the logs, attaching them to the tugboats so they could be pulled down the river."

"Yes." He nodded understanding.

"Sara thought it looked like fun. She wanted to pretend to be like those guys, walking the logs and chaining them to the boats. She'd brought her camera, and she wanted us to take pictures of each other standing on the logs in the middle of the river. She thought it would make us look cool, maybe impress the kids at school."

"You're telling me that it was Sara's idea, and you just went along?"

"Yeah."

"That strikes me as odd."

"Why?"

"Because from what I've been told, you're the daredevil and Sara was the follower."

Eve was smart enough to know when to stick to the truth. "That's right. When we go to Playland, she only wants to do the little-kid rides." Her throat clogged with sudden emotion, and she coughed to clear it.

"But you're telling me that *Sara* was the one who decided to climb down to a log boom in the swiftest part of the river, and *you* were the one who followed."

"Yeah."

"How long have you two been friends?"

"Since she moved here when we were six."

"And had she ever gotten a hare-brained idea like this before?"

"No. I guess there's a first time for everything."

"Sara was known around the neighbourhood as not particularly athletic. A little chubby, a little clumsy."

"I guess."

"Did you think of her as clumsy?"

"I thought of her as smart and funny and really awesome. And I thought of her as my only real friend." Her throat threatened to close up again, and she coughed until it cleared.

He tapped her knee. "Hey, look at me. Talk to me."

"I am."

"It was your idea, wasn't it?"

"What? No!"

Detective Baird eyed her with interest.

"No," she said again, more calmly. "It was an accident. A *terrible accident*."

"An accident. That was my initial thought. Just two girls paying a very dear price for their stupidity."

"Uh-huh."

"But now that I'm talking to you, I'm not so sure," Detective Baird said.

"Why?"

"I'm thinking, maybe you *did* lead Sara onto that log boom. Maybe you even gave her a little push."

"Maybe I should talk to a lawyer."

"As I said before, that's your right. If you feel you need one."

"You think I did something wrong, so maybe I do. My mom's whole law firm is probably waiting in the lobby. I'd like to talk to them."

"There's no one out there."

"So they're on their way. I can wait."

"You've been here for three hours. How long do you think it takes to get here?"

For the first time since the interview started, she reached for a tissue.

"You are entitled to council," Detective Baird said. "Your mother gave permission for us to proceed without it, but if you'd like we can contact Legal Aid for you."

"She didn't get me a lawyer?"

"No." The worst part of all was the sympathy she heard in his voice. "Would you like us to get one for you?"

Eve wasn't sure what to do. She pulled her knees up and wrapped her arms around her shins, trying to think through the next step.

"Eve?" the detective said after several minutes had passed. "Would you like us to call you a lawyer?"

"No."

"All right. Let me give you a few minutes to calm down, and then we'll continue."

He left the room, closing the door behind him with a noticeable click. She pressed her face into her knees and tried to keep breathing.

THIRTY-ONE

"MRS. ADLER, I'm Detective Mathers. I understand you're concerned about your husband's whereabouts?"

Pushing his way behind the desk, he placed a cup of coffee near Eve's hand. It smelled like a damp mop, and there was an oil slick of fake cream making lazy circles on the surface. She shook her head no, so he lifted it to his lips instead.

The police station's reception area was a large glass atrium. Eve remembered it well from when she was thirteen. It had been raining then, too. Today, it sounded like they were inside a waterfall.

The building was bone-chillingly damp, and most of the officers in the surrounding warren of desks still wore their jackets. She was dressed in a down parka and thick boots, and she hadn't removed her wool cap. Nevertheless, every muscle and joint ached with cold.

"So." The detective put down the cup and pulled the keyboard toward his belly. He looked at her with kind eyes. "Let's start with some basic information about your husband."

He took her through a series of questions about Leigh's age, height, weight, and hair and eye colour. She answered as best she could.

"Do you have a picture of him?"

"I've got a bunch of pictures on my phone." She dug through her purse. Her cellphone wasn't in its usual spot in the interior pocket.

"Let me just …" She trailed off, searching a second time.

"Mrs. Adler."

"Just a minute, I know I have it." Her eyes started to burn with tears.

"If you can't find it —"

"I know it's in here somewhere!"

"Why don't we come back to this later?"

"Where the fuck is it?"

Officers nearby turned to look at her, and one placed a ready hand near his gun holster.

"Mrs. Adler, you seem …"

"Confused? Crazy? It's called brain damage, okay? Because ten or six or eight years ago — I can't keep it fucking straight — some asshole snorted coke and got behind the wheel of a car."

"I was going to say you seem distraught." He waved off the watching officers with a flick of his index finger.

"Yes, I *am* distraught!" She took a breath, trying to calm down. "My husband is missing. *Of course* I'm distraught."

"When did you last see him?" he asked, his fingers ready on the keyboard.

"Yesterday morning. He went for a run before breakfast."

"What time was this?"

"Just give me a second, let me think." She took a deep breath and closed her eyes. Before her, the scene began to unfold. "He was wearing navy blue Nike shorts with a reflective white strip along the side. A grey T-shirt. Umm … Asics. White ones, and he would have had the house key tied to his shoelace."

She opened her eyes. The detective watched her and tapped on the keyboard at the same time.

"It was about seven in the morning. He's been jogging every day. His blood pressure is creeping up, and he's trying to stay off medication. He's been under a lot of stress lately —"

"Why?" the detective asked, his fingers pausing on the keyboard.

She felt her mouth twist. "It's not easy being married to me."

"Did anyone else see him leave?"

"My son. My grandmother."

"How old is your son?"

Her mind stuttered, and she shook her head.

"You don't know?"

"I think he's eight."

"Did you have him before or after this car accident?"

"Oh, after. Leigh and I didn't get married until after. But I've known him forever. His sister was my best friend."

"Your son is how old again?"

"He's four."

"Uh-huh." His fingers clacked at the keyboard.

"What?"

"Let's get back to the last time you saw your husband. What day was it?"

"Don't you have this stuff typed into a form or something?"

He just continued to watch her. His eyes weren't as kind as she'd first thought.

"It was this morning," she said. "He left before breakfast. Gabriel was eating cereal. Button and I were drinking tea and talking about what needed doing in the garden."

"Button?"

"My grandmother. Her real name is Batya, but I had trouble saying that when I was little, so it came out as Button. Somehow the name stuck."

"Did your husband say goodbye before he left?"

"He asked what we had planned for the day. He didn't have to work, since it's Sunday. I told him that Button and I would take Gabriel to the library for storytime, and we'd be back before lunch. And we talked about going to see a movie this afternoon."

"Today is Thursday."

"What?"

"You said your husband didn't have to work today, because it's Sunday. But today is Thursday."

"I don't ... what?" She placed a shaking hand against her forehead. Her fingers were so numb she couldn't feel anything beneath them. It was like she wasn't there.

"Did your husband seem different lately? Upset? Or more distant?"

"No."

"Does he have any addictions? Alcohol? Prescription medications? Gambling?"

"No!"

"Any reason to believe he's having an affair?"

"What kind of question is that?"

"One I have to ask, Mrs. Adler."

"No way."

"All right, so when did you realize that he was missing?"

"When we came back from the movie."

"Movie?"

"I mean the library. I got lunch ready, but Leigh still wasn't there. I thought maybe he'd gone out to run some errands, or maybe he'd gotten a call about one of his patients."

"Did you try calling him?"

"Of course. But his cell is doing this thing where it only rings once and then an automated message says it's disconnected. That's when I really started to worry."

"What's his number?"

"I … don't remember it off the top of my head. I have it saved in my phone."

"All right, I'll get that from you later." Mathers continued to type, and Eve leaned back in the vinyl seat and took a few deep breaths, clutching tightly to the straps of her purse.

"Mrs. Adler, you look like you could use something warm to drink. We have tea, if you'd like?"

She didn't think she'd be able to hold a cup without sloshing it all over herself. "No, thank you."

The detective stood, his belly pressing the keyboard tray so it slid back under the desk. "Wait here, please."

"But —"

"It'll just be a few minutes."

* * *

She wasn't sure how long he was gone, but he eventually returned. "Mrs. Adler? Would you please follow me?"

"Why?"

"I think we'll be more comfortable in an interview room."

"*I* won't be."

"Please, just follow me." Assuming her cooperation, he turned and moved away. After a moment of indecision, Eve pushed to her feet and shuffled after him.

"Listen, Detective …" She'd forgotten his name. "Listen, I'd really rather stay out here."

"I'd imagine you would." He pushed open the door to Interview Room C.

"What's that supposed to mean?"

"Have a seat. We'll be right with you."

That's when it hit her. She clutched the front of his uniform shirt. "Oh my God. Have you found Leigh? Is he okay?"

She pictured a heart attack, Leigh sprawled face-up on someone's lawn. She pictured a car speeding through a stop sign, and his broken body flying through the air.

"I have no word on your husband. Please, just have a seat."

Shakily, Eve moved around the table and sat on a hard plastic chair. The door clicked closed behind him, and she stared at the mirror on the far wall. She wondered if anyone was on the other side, staring back. The colour was unnerving, and she remembered how Hector had always said that painting with silver was so difficult because it was more than a colour, it was a reflection.

The door swung open, and she turned away from the mirror.

Detective Baird pushed his considerable girth into the room. He looked exactly the same as he had the last time she saw him, more than a decade ago. Metal scraped linoleum as he pulled the chair around the desk and sat down across from her, knee-to-knee.

She shook her head. "No."

He flopped a folder — a thick one — onto the table beside him, and laid a notepad and pen on top. "Third time's the charm, Ms. Gold."

"It's Mrs. Adler. And I don't know what you mean."

"Detective Mathers tells me you married Sara's brother."

"That's right."

"The thick plottens."

"What in the world does that mean?"

"Well, *Mrs. Adler*, it seems like people pay a heavy price for being close to you."

"My husband is *missing*," she said through gritted teeth. "I'm here to file a missing person report, so you can look for him. I have nothing to hide."

"You never do."

"This is insulting!"

"You know what I find insulting? *Knowing* that someone has killed two people — maybe even three — and watching them walk around free and clear because I don't have enough evidence. *That's* insulting."

"I'm here to talk about my missing husband. Nothing else."

"All right. Let's talk about Leigh."

She sensed a looming trap, but didn't know where it might be. "Okay."

"When did you two marry?"

"Years ago."

"How many years?"

"Five or six."

"You seem uncertain."

She sighed. "I was in a car accident. I have brain damage. My memory isn't always good."

"I see." Rather than take notes, Baird let his hands rest on his lap.

"What does it matter, anyway? The important thing is that he's missing. And you don't seem to be doing anything about it."

"We've started the investigation. Officers are currently checking local hospitals and cruising your neighbourhood."

"Okay, good," she said, feeling only slightly mollified.

"A year ago," Detective Baird leaned forward in his chair, "a woman came forward to file a complaint. Annabeth O'Neill. Do you remember her?"

"She was the leader of this gang of mean girls that used to bully everyone else."

"Annabeth recommended we also talk to another girl from your neighbourhood, Myra Duborney. Her maiden name was Knottsworth. Do you remember her?"

"We used to call her Snottsworth. She was a friend of Annabeth's."

"In six hours of taped interviews, she gave similar testimony to what Annabeth gave. And we convinced her to join Annabeth in pressing charges. Before the statute of limitations runs out."

"Pressing charges. Against *me*?"

"No. Against your husband."

Her purse dropped from her lap and hit the ground. The contents scattered and rolled in all directions. "What?"

Detective Baird watched her, his expression bland.

"I can't believe this. What kind of charges?"

"Statutory rape."

"Annabeth's really pretty, isn't she?"

"No." Her mouth filled with the dry taste of pretzels, and she gagged.

"Her parents called the cops."

"Now, we believe that your husband is a sexual predator."

"Leigh denied it, of course, and I guess Annabeth was denying it, too."

Hot bile climbed her throat and she slammed her hands over her mouth, desperately swallowing it back.

"He groomed these girls over the course of at least six months, gained their trust, isolated them, and made them feel like he was the only one who understood them."

"No," Eve said through her hands. "No way. I don't believe it."

"And then he engaged in sexual contact with them. In Annabeth's case, it went on for years."

"He wouldn't do that to me."

"He did it to *them*, Mrs. Adler. And I suspect, as this gets closer to trial, we'll find many more victims. Predators like your husband keep on repeating the same patterns. Which got me thinking —"

"I'm going to be sick."

"Were *you* one of his victims? It would explain so much. Maybe even solve the mystery of what you and Sara argued about."

"The windows were all steamy. I knew then that I should walk away, but I didn't."

"Oh my God, I can't breathe."

"Mrs. Adler, either your husband took a powder to avoid going to trial, or —"

"I have to get out of here." She stood and pushed past the detective.

" — *or* you found out about these other girls, and took matters into your own hands. Either way, I'll find out."

Eve bolted, and to her surprise he didn't stop her. She was halfway through the maze of desks when Detective Baird called from behind her, "Mrs. Adler! Your purse!"

But she didn't stop.

THIRTY-TWO

Sara's Eleventh Birthday

"ARE YOU SURE you can't stay? There's cake."

Sara's mom didn't turn from the stove. Her arm moved in rhythmic circles as she stirred the pot of chili. It smelled like gassy heaven: fried meat and beans and tomatoes and onions.

Eve wished she could stay. Mrs. Adler was making her famous garlic knots, there was cake, and she could watch Leigh from across the table.

But she was saving up to replace the bicycle that had been stolen from the carport when she forgot to chain it. She hoped if she saved up half the money, Donna might chip in the rest. She needed to stay on her good side for that to happen, and Donna had told Eve to come home for dinner.

"I have to go," she said.

"Will you be all right? It's getting dark out there."

"I can walk her halfway," Sara said.

Mrs. Adler shook her head. "You have to practise your piano."

"It's my *birthday*!"

"Sara," Mrs. Adler said.

Sara wrinkled her nose. It was a long-standing battle between mother and daughter, and anybody could see who was going to win. They had spent a lot of money on that piano, Mrs. Adler was happy to point out, and they were bloody well going to use it. Since Sara was the only one of the four children who showed any musical talent, she ended up in the hot seat whether she liked it or not. And she didn't like it.

"I'll be fine. It's only six blocks."

"All right," Sara said.

"Can you come over tomorrow after school?" Eve asked as she followed Sara through the living room. "Button bought me some glitter nail polish. Want to try it out?"

"For sure! And we can look through your closet and figure out what you're going to wear to the dance."

"I'm not going to the dance."

"And I'm not going without you, so don't be a chicken."

"The boys in our class are stupid and immature. I don't want to dance with any of them." Eve said it extra loud, hoping that Leigh, who was doing homework at the dining room table, might hear.

"Jaime isn't stupid," Sara said, her eyes big with hurt.

"Well, I guess *he's* okay."

"Pretty soon you'll want to do all kinds of things with those dorks," Danielle said from where she was sprawled on the living room couch. She'd grown dangerously beautiful in the last year or so, with long legs and silky hair. Eve admired her a little, but hated her more.

"*Naked* things," Margie said, and both she and Danielle giggled.

"Gross!" Eve and Sara said in unison.

"Oh, don't worry. Nobody will touch you with that disgusting gut," Danielle said to Sara, slapping her own flat belly for emphasis. To Eve she said, "And you need to grow some tits." Danielle's were like ripe apples on full display.

"Yeah," Margie said. Hers still looked more like starving apricots, but, judging by the tight shirt she wore, she was pretty proud of them.

Eve wished she had a smart comeback, but they always came to her too late to do any good. Sara seemed to be in the same predicament. Her cheeks flaming, she opened the door and whispered goodbye, handing Eve her school bag.

"Hey." Eve reached out and took Sara's hand, running a finger across Sara's inner wrist. *Our hearts are joined together.*

Sara traced Eve's wrist with her finger, completing the ritual. *Always and forever.*

As Sara closed the door, Eve saw her suck in her tummy so it didn't roll over the top of her jeans.

She climbed down the stairs to the Adlers' walkway, sliding her arms through the straps of her bag and settling it on her back. At school she would let one strap dangle because it looked cooler that way, but there was no one here to see. She tucked her hands inside the sleeves of her hooded sweatshirt and started for home.

Dead leaves swirled around her feet. They crackled and scraped across the pavement, and her skin prickled with nervousness.

She reached back and pulled her cellphone out of the side pocket of her bag, turning it on and clutching it in her hand, a lifeline to safety. It was Donna's old phone, meant for emergencies only. She'd been hoping for a better one for her birthday last week, but that hadn't happened. Maybe she'd get one for her twelfth.

She wouldn't have noticed the car if it hadn't been for the noise it made, a high-pitched whine that sounded like the Chevy Monza Donna had traded for her current Buick. It passed her, an old behemoth that had been lowered to ride just inches from the ground, its windows tinted black. Slowing at the corner, it turned right.

Not long after, Eve heard it coming around for another pass. As it moved slowly past her, she cut away from the sidewalk, climbing the lawn toward a stucco house with dark windows and an empty carport. No help there. With a chirp of the tires, the car sped up and once again turned right at the intersection.

Belatedly, panic burned up her throat and threatened to turn her legs to Jell-O. She began moving as swiftly as she could, watching behind her and saying a silent prayer to whoever protected little girls from predators and psychopaths that she wouldn't see those square headlights coming at her again.

She heard the car before she saw it. It glided slowly around the corner, the street lamp highlighting its dark flank.

She lifted the phone and punched the button that pulled up her contact list. She hit *A* for Adler and lifted the phone to her ear, trying to quell the shaking in her hand. The phone began to ring, but she remembered Mrs.

Adler's rule about not answering the phone during dinnertime. Would they be eating yet?

The car slowed to a stop twenty feet behind her, and the engine revved. Eve broke into a run, her backpack swinging from side to side like a pendulous weight. She glanced behind her, and the car's high beams clicked on, blinding her. When she faced forward, all she could see was the ghost of the car's headlights. She stumbled and almost fell.

There was a click from the phone. "Hello?"

"Mr. Adler. Help!"

"It's Leigh. Eve? Are you all right?"

"There's a car," she gasped for breath, "following me!"

Behind her the engine roared, and the tires squealed as it sprang forward, closing the gap. It braked hard, and the engine revved with menace.

"Where are you?"

"Halfway home ... but I don't think ..."

The car roared forward again, and she screamed. It stopped half a block behind her, growling like a lion teasing its prey.

"I'm coming!" Leigh said, and the phone banged in her ear.

She could see the light from her porch, almost two blocks away. It seemed like another planet.

An eruption of whoops and jeers came from inside the car, growing louder in a way that suggested they were cranking down the car windows. It sounded like teenaged boys, and that was all it took to jog her memory. The car belonged to Steve Ryder. She'd seen him pull into the high school parking lot while she walked to school one morning. He and his buddies were still on the warpath after the stolen contraband incident, and she was clearly about to pay for it.

Another thought occurred to her: They knew where she lived. They were playing cat-and-mouse with her now, but if they were going to grab her they'd do it in the next block or so, before she got too close to her own front door. So she needed to give Leigh time to get there.

Going against every instinct, she slowed to a walk. Hobbling like she'd twisted her ankle, she tried to look as weak and pitiful as she could. How long would it take Leigh to reach her?

Though she couldn't possibly have heard his approach over the incessant roar of the car engine, she swore she heard the sound of feet slapping the pavement, and turned just in time to see Leigh fly from the shadows and land on the trunk of the car. He stormed up the roof and skated down the windshield. The juvenile delinquents inside let out satisfyingly girlish screams.

"Hey, boys!" Leigh said with deadly cheerfulness. "Does Coach know you're out harassing cherries instead of running your drills?"

He slid off the hood and leaned against the open passenger window. "No wonder you looked like a bunch of monkeys trying to fuck a football last Saturday."

"Bite me, Adler," Steve Ryder said.

Canton Forsythe said, "We're just messing with her, dude."

"Don't think she's enjoying it, *dude*," Leigh said with dangerous calm.

Silence greeted this.

"So, maybe you douchebags should just head on home. And let me make this clear. Eve Gold is under my protection."

"Oh, yeah? Her and how many others?" Canton said.

She caught a flash of Leigh's teeth, eerily green in the glow coming from the dashboard. "You even look at her wrong, and I'll fucking kill you. Got it?"

"You're lucky O'Neill isn't here, or he'd fucking kill *you*," Steve said.

Leigh laughed. "Oh, I'm shaking."

There was some angry grumbling from inside the car. Leigh reached through the window and switched off the engine. He stuffed the keys into his pocket.

"Hey!" Steve said.

"I think you need a little lesson before you go. Get out of the car."

Three of them piled out and stood around, hunched like apes with their hands stuffed in their pockets. Only the talking rooster was missing, probably because he was too scrawny to make the football team.

"One by one, you're going to get down on your hands and knees, and you're going to crawl across that pavement, and you're going to apologize and beg for her forgiveness." Leigh pulled his phone out of his pocket and held it up. "And I'm going to film it."

"No way, dude." Canton shook his head.

"Yes, way. Otherwise I'm going to call Coach and tell him what you've been doing. I mean, *everything* you've been doing. And I might just toss these keys in the sewer grate, as well." Leigh pulled them from his pocket and dangled them over the grate.

"That's my only set!" Steve said miserably.

"That's too bad. Bet they'll cost a fortune to replace."

"Don't film it," Slothboy said.

"The video is insurance that you'll leave her alone. As long as you do, I'll keep it to myself. One wrong move, and you know where it's going."

They grumbled and muttered some more, testosterone on downers.

"Get going." Leigh held up his phone.

Slothboy went first, crawling with his belly hanging almost to the ground. "I'm really sorry."

Leigh smirked. "Kiss her feet."

He hesitated a moment, and then planted a quick kiss on the canvas of her shoe. It tickled.

Steve went next, and then it was Canton's turn.

Eve stood still, feeling the burn of power deep inside her, relishing the flickers of heat that travelled down to her toes and up to her scalp. When Canton's lips touched the laces of her shoe, she laughed from the thrill of it. She looked at Leigh and saw the same flames dancing in his eyes.

When Canton moved away, Leigh turned off the camera and tossed the car keys at Steve. They dropped at his feet.

"You really need to practise your drills," Leigh said.

Silently, the boys climbed back into the car. The engine rumbled to life, and they pulled away.

"Well, that was fun," Leigh said, and Eve promptly burst into tears.

"Hey." He grabbed her arms. His hands were so big they wrapped all the way around them. "It's all right. They won't bother you again."

"I don't know what would have happened if you hadn't come." The truth of this brought on another torrent of tears.

He pulled her against him so that her head rested against his sternum. He held her there, stroking her hair and murmuring reassurances, until her tears abated. She could feel the solid thump of his heart against her wet cheek. Finally, she pulled back.

"Thank you." She snuffled and wiped an arm across her eyes.

"They won't bother you ever again. You're safe, okay?" Digging in his pocket, he came up with a crumpled tissue. "Go on. It's clean."

She took it, but the tissue did nothing to dam up the tears that continued to fall. It was as though, once unleashed, there was a tidal flood that had nowhere else to go. She sobbed and hiccupped, wiping futilely at the tears and snot that ran down her face and dripped onto the front of her sweatshirt.

If Donna saw her like this, she'd have a lot of explaining to do. And she'd probably have to come straight home from school for the rest of her life. "I can't go inside like this."

He looked her over, and nodded agreement. "Come on."

He took her hand and tugged her back the way they'd come. She matched him step for step, assuming he was taking her back to his house so she could get cleaned up. Where their hands joined, a fire burned. She wondered if he noticed, wondered if it confused him as much as it did her.

"Where are we going?" she asked when he ducked onto the trail leading to the Crook.

He didn't answer, and she didn't ask again. Wherever he led her, she would follow. She owed him her trust.

He sat her down on a log near the pond's edge and knelt before her, washing away her tears with handfuls of bitingly cold water.

"There. That's better."

"Thank you," she said.

"I'll always be here for you. You know that, right?"

"Yeah."

"For *whatever* you need."

"I know." She began to shake from the cold, or maybe it was shock.

"And will you be there for me, too?"

"Of course," she said immediately, thinking it was nice of him to make her feel like she had something of value to offer him. He was popular, athletic, and super cute. She was his dorky sister's even dorkier friend. He had it all, and she had no currency.

He gave her the smile that twisted her insides into knots. Pulling her to her feet, he led her toward the river. She matched him, step for step. When he asked her to, she took off her backpack and lay down in the matted reeds and prickling grass.

Bending over her, he said, "You have the eyes of a cat hunting in the moonlight."

His hands found the zipper of her sweatshirt.

"Leigh," she said.

"You said you'd be there for me."

The moon was low and red in the sky, a harvest moon, and it made the first of the night's stars look like they were bleeding.

She squirmed with discomfort, tried to move away.

"Do you love me?" There were tears in his eyes.

256

"Yes."

"Then trust me."

Through the fog of his breath she watched the moon rise, watched it get smaller and turn from red to silver. One by one stars pierced the sky, bearing witness to her silence.

THIRTY-THREE

BUTTON CAME FLYING at her as Eve unlocked the door and let herself into the kitchen.

"What happened? Is there any news?" Button asked.

Eve held a shaking finger to her lips in caution. She could hear the TV in the living room; it sounded like Gabriel was watching *Doc McStuffins*. She couldn't face her son, not until she had some grip on her own roiling emotions. Not until she managed to stuff the memories oozing to the surface back into the darkness below.

She slid down the wall and slipped sideways, until her cheek touched cold linoleum.

"Oy gevalt," Button said. "Did they find him? Is he ...?"

Eve shook her head, but when she opened her mouth to try to speak, nothing came out.

Easing down to sit on the floor by her granddaughter's head, Button asked, "Eve, what happened? Are they looking for him?"

"Uh-huh, but I don't think they're going to find him."

"Why not?"

"Mommy?" Gabriel bounced into the room. "Is Daddy home yet?"

"Not yet, buddy. Why don't you go back to Doc so I can talk to Button, okay?"

"Are you crying, Mommy? Are you hurt?" He wrapped his arms around her and patted her on the back.

She swallowed back her tears. "Thanks, Gabe."

"Don't worry, Mommy," Gabriel said reassuringly. "Soon you go to that garden I drawed you. Okay?"

"What garden?" Button asked.

"The one that's silver," he said matter-of-factly. "It's fun there. There are lots of toys to play with." He paused, looking at her thoughtfully. "And mommy-stuff to do, too. Don't worry."

They watched him bounce away, and then Eve said, "It's all falling apart."

"What is?" Button asked, stroking Eve's hair. If she noticed how cold Eve was, she didn't say.

"Everything. I'm remembering things. Things I'd rather not. And I can feel the woman growing like a cancer inside me. I can hear her calling to me. And this time I don't think the ECTs will help."

Gabriel's spoon was a submarine, and it searched for the remains of the *Titanic* in the bottom of the cereal bowl.

"I'm pretty sure submarines ease *gently* beneath the water, Gabe." Eve tried to keep her anger at bay as she mopped up the table once again.

"But this is a 'mergency." More cereal splattered on the table.

"Stop! You're making a mess!"

He looked up, amber-coloured eyes round and injured. "Are you mad at me, Mommy?"

"It's wasteful," she said, mopping up with such violence she knocked the bowl and sloshed half the contents onto the table. "Oh, hell!"

Gabriel burst into tears, his mouth opening to display the half-eaten contents of his breakfast.

"What is going *on*?" Button asked, hustling into the room. Gabriel wailed louder, reaching for his great-grandma.

Fear and fury unleashed, she said, "He's making a mess!"

Still wailing, Gabriel slid under the table, out of view and out of the line of fire.

"He's four! *Vos iz mit dir*, what's wrong with you?" Button gave her a hard, appraising look. "You should see some of the messes you made at that age. Gabriel, come out. It's okay, sweetheart."

After a moment, he eased out from beneath the table like a turtle testing the weather outside his shell. His obvious vulnerability made Eve shake, first with anger and then with shame.

"Oh for heaven's sake!" She threw the cloth on the table in defeat.

"Gabe," Button said. "The front of your shirt is wet with milk. Why don't you go get changed."

He didn't need any more incentive to leave the room than that.

She expected her grandmother to lay into her, but instead she gave her a sad look. "Day five."

Tears burned her throat and eyes. "Yes."

"Maybe we'll get word today."

"Maybe." Not only did she doubt it — she wasn't even sure she wanted to get word. So much had changed in less than a week.

Gabriel came flying back into the room, wearing a Spider-Man T-shirt. The incident with the cereal was clearly forgotten. "Can we go to the park? I want to run on the track like Daddy does."

"You do?" Button said.

"Yeah! I'm gonna train for a marapon!"

"A marathon," Eve said.

"Yeah! I need my runners!"

"They're in the hall closet," Button said, and Gabriel streaked off to find them.

"I suppose we're going to the park. Care to join us?"

"I'll meet you there in a bit."

"Of course." Button turned away, but not quickly enough to stop Eve from seeing the tears in her eyes.

"Just give me half an hour."

"You're not going to your studio, are you?"

"I'm just going to clean up the kitchen. Maybe have another cup of tea."

"All right." Button seemed relieved.

She listened to them leave while she mopped cereal and milk off the table. "Besides," she said to herself, to the empty house, to whoever was listening, "I think my painting days might be over."

She put the kettle on for tea, then put the rest of the breakfast dishes in the dishwasher and swept the floor. Drinking her tea by the kitchen sink, she looked out the window at the cherry blossom tree in the side yard. It was beginning to bloom. She hadn't realized it was spring. Grief sat like a lump in her chest. When she turned away from the window, it felt like goodbye.

She dumped the dregs of her tea in the sink, put on the dishwasher, and stuffed her feet into an old pair of running shoes. Despite the sunshine, she slipped on her winter coat.

She was halfway to the park when it occurred to her that she was walking in the wrong direction. She hurried back the way she'd come, passing the entrance to the Crook, where her childhood lay buried. She wondered if kids still played in there, or if they were now too tied to their electronics to venture into nature.

She had no desire to go into those shadowy depths, or to get anywhere near that field of quicksilver.

Trudging resolutely away, she hiked up her slipping pants. She was surprised to feel the jut of hipbones beneath the denim fabric; she was getting too thin.

Ahead, she saw the park. Gabriel swung across the monkey bars, his legs dangling, the shadow boy beneath him stretching across the grey sand for the next rung, and then the next. She stopped, holding her breath until he was safely across. He jumped down, landing firmly on the wooden plank at the other end, and Button cheered for him from her bench in the sun.

Leaving the sidewalk, she moved in their direction. She crossed the grass and stepped into the giant sand pit, making her way toward the playground equipment. She moved around toy dump trucks and diggers, around a little girl building a sandcastle, around a pile of shovels and rakes.

Halfway across, the sun disappeared behind a cloud, and everything turned grey and one-dimensional. Fog rolled in like ocean waves, cutting her off from the world around her. She heard the scrape and hiss of the wind kissing quicksilver.

"*Eve.*"

"No."

The fog rolled and reformed, and she caught a glimpse of playground and sunshine. Gabriel pushed a red Hot Wheels racing car up the slide, making engine noises. Button sat on the bench, her hair aglow and her face turned to her phone. They might as well have been on another planet. The fog closed in again, swallowing them whole.

The little girl who'd been building a sandcastle moved closer, a plastic shovel dangling from her hand. She had long blond curls and wide-set eyes. She couldn't have been much older than Gabriel.

"Are you okay?"

"The fog."

"Yeah, it's spooky," the girl said.

"You can see it?"

"Well, duh."

"Oh, I thought it was just me."

"I'm making a moat." The girl squatted and dug the tip of her shovel into the sand. In a conversational tone, she said, "One of the swings tried to strangle me. Spun me around and around and around until the chain was so tight against my neck I couldn't breathe. But it didn't really hurt."

"What?"

"My mommy says I just imagined it. She says I imagine lots of stuff since I bonked my head." She pulled her hair back from her face to reveal a crescent-shaped scar along her temple. It was puckered and painful-looking, and Eve winced in sympathy.

"But I don't go near the swings anymore," the girl said, letting her hair drop back into place. "They're weird."

"I know what you mean. I bonked my head once, too. Do you need help? Are your parents around?"

"They're just over there." The girl pointed her shovel in the direction of the sports field, where they could hear people playing touch football. "Want to help me build a castle?"

"Well, I came here to play with my son."

"Then why aren't you?" the girl asked.

Because she was afraid if she stepped into the fog she wouldn't come out on the other side. "I don't know."

The girl studied her appraisingly. "Don't worry, you'll get used to it."

"Get used to what?"

"Seeing stuff others can't. It's pretty cool, actually. We get to pick."

"Pick what?"

"What we can see," the girl said with a shrug. "Which is great if you're smart. But lots of people can't figure it out. They choose wrong, and then they're always trying to figure out why everything's so weird."

"You don't really talk like a kid."

"I've been choosing wrong for a long time." Her giggle, at least, was very childlike.

As though in reaction to the girl's tinkling laugh, the fog cleared. Steam rose from the ground and disappeared into an azure sky, and the sun beat warm against her shoulders and the top of her head.

"See? It's easy. Just tell the fog to go away, and it will. You get to choose." The girl nodded at Gabriel and Button, who were walking toward the swing set. "Go on. But watch out for the one on the end. That's the weird one."

Eve took a step in their direction and then paused to look back. The girl was very young. "Are you sure you're all right?"

"Totally," she said. "Look, there's my mom and dad. I have to go!"

The football game had ended, and people moved to the sidewalk and parking lot in small groups. The girl ran to a grey-haired couple and fell into step behind them as they left the park. When she reached the sidewalk she did a pirouette, her curls catching the sunlight as she twirled. She giggled and waved, and Eve waved in return.

Gabriel climbed onto the second swing in the row, and she breathed a sigh of relief. Not that she really believed a swing had tried to strangle anyone, but it was better to be safe than sorry.

"Hi, Mommy! Push me! Button never pushes me high enough."

"Where did you come from?" Button asked, blinking in surprise.

"I snuck up on you when you had your nose buried in your phone."

"*Ver volt dos gegleybt.* I'm like a millennial, aren't I?"

"We'll stop at Starbucks later for a soy latte," Eve said.

"I want one too!" Gabriel said. "Is it chocolate?"

"Not even close, buddy." She gave him a giant push that sent him soaring toward the treetops and squealing with delight.

"That's too high!" Button fretted.

"Higher!" Gabriel shouted.

She watched the swing's chains carefully, in case they wrapped around her son's neck. He sang the ABCs song at the top of his lungs, over and over, pumping his little legs vigorously back and forth.

Eve stepped out of the way to watch him, her throat thick with yearning. Though whether it was yearning to wrap him in her arms or to feel the wind on her face, she didn't know.

THIRTY-FOUR

Sara's Twelfth Birthday

"WHERE WERE YOU? I've been looking for you *everywhere*!" Sara's cheeks were red with indignation. She was so mad she actually stomped her foot.

"Sorry! I was skimming stones on the river."

Eve spread the blanket she'd had tucked under her arm on the ground. They'd met on the other side of the pond, far away from the Foil. Since she'd stumbled upon the man's bones two years before, she refused to go anywhere near that field of quicksilver. She'd begged and pleaded with Sara and, eventually, gotten her to promise that she'd stay away as well.

"Why were you skimming stones? We were supposed to meet an hour ago! I've been waiting and waiting, and I had to go hide in the forest for a while because Steve Ryder and Slothboy were riding their bikes along the trail."

Eve rolled her eyes as she settled on the blanket. "That was forever ago. I promise you don't need to worry about them anymore."

"How can you say that? They look like they're just waiting for the right moment, and then," Sara drew a finger across her throat, "dead."

"But have they ever even *tried* to hurt you?"

Sara straightened the corner of the blanket and sat down. "Well, no. But I'm not giving them any chances."

Eve pulled Sara's gift out of her pocket and held it out to her. The little box was wrapped in pink tissue with tiny silver bells. "Happy birthday."

Sara eyed the gift, but didn't reach for it. "I'm not done being mad at you."

"I know."

"Fine." Sara plucked the gift from her hand. With excruciating care, she pried off the strips of tape, laying them side by side on the edge of the blanket.

"Oh, come on." Eve would have ripped off the paper in half a second.

"Don't rush me."

Sara removed the paper, folded it into a neat square, and set it aside. She turned to the little white box and examined it from all angles, like there might be a secret message written somewhere.

"Hey, Gumdrop, are you *trying* to be irritating?"

Lip curling up in acknowledgement, Sara finally opened the box. "Oh, wow." She lifted the necklace, letting it dangle from her fingers. The letter *S* was crusted with tiny diamonds — not much more than diamond dust. "This must have cost you a lot of money."

She shrugged, smiling. "Do you like it?"

"It's beautiful, thank you." Sara sniffed, and tears fell from her eyes.

With a mixture of pleasure and discomfort, Eve said, "Hey. Come on now. Let me put it on you."

Sara handed her the necklace and lifted her hair out of the way so Eve could wrap it around her neck. The clasp took several tries. Once the necklace was secured, she took Sara's hand and traced a finger across Sara's wrist.

"Our hearts are joined together," she said, and waited for Sara to finish.

After a moment of hesitation, Sara completed the ritual. "Always and forever."

"It looks good on you." The *S* curled at the base of Sara's throat, diamond dust glittering in the sun.

"I love it," Sara said, cupping her hand over it. "Thank you."

"Hey. Did you bring the cards?"

Sara had used the early birthday money her grandma sent to buy a set of tarot cards at Secondhand Jane's, and Eve was eager to try them out.

"Yeah, and the guidebook." Sara pulled them out of her bag. As she handed Eve the book, she said, "I'm still kind of mad at you."

"I'm sorry. I just lost track of time."

"That's not like you. Or, well, it *wasn't* like you."

"What do you mean?"

"You've been getting really flaky. It's not the first time you've been late to meet me. Or not shown up at all."

"I'm really sorry." Eve felt horrible for keeping such a huge secret from her friend, but she knew Sara wouldn't understand. Even worse, Leigh had said she might tell the cops or something, and then they'd both be in really big trouble.

"Yeah, well," Sara said. "Sometimes it feels like you don't want to be friends with me anymore."

"What? Why would you think that?"

"You've changed a lot this year. You're getting boobs and walking around dressed like that." Sara nodded at Eve's cropped shorts and tight shirt. "Boys even follow you around, and I'm still just a … a boring kid. A big fat *gumdrop*."

"That's not true. You're the most amazing person *ever*."

"I'm so fat I'm invisible."

"You're *not* fat! And, you know, I can't help it if my body is changing faster than yours. I'm not doing anything to those boys, I'm not flirting with them or anything."

"Maybe not, but they can see the changes in you. Everyone can."

Eve flushed with fear. "I don't know what you're talking about."

Sara pulled the cards out of the box. "Whatever. Let's just do this."

"Sara …" She longed to tell Sara everything. It would be a relief in so many ways, no matter the fallout.

"Yeah?" Sara looked up from the cards, her eyes the same exact blue as her brother's. In that moment, she understood that she had to make a choice. It was either Sara or Leigh; she couldn't trust them both.

"Nothing," she said. "Do you want me to read you first?"

"I guess."

She opened the guidebook. "So, you have to shuffle the cards, and then cut the deck while you're thinking about a question you want to ask."

Sara did, and silently handed over the cards.

"Let's try a three-card spread. I think it'll be easiest," she said, reading from the book. "Pick three cards from the deck and lay them down on the blanket in whatever order seems right to you."

Sara did, and Eve turned them over to look.

"From left to right they're supposed to represent your past, present, and future. For your past you pulled a Four of Wands."

Eve flipped through the guidebook. "It represents teamwork and coming together with others to do positive things. It says it's a card about building foundations."

"I guess that makes sense," Sara said.

She looked at the middle card, and turned some pages. "Hmm. You pulled an Ace of Cups for your present. It's the element of water, and is related to fantasy and imagination. Ace is also the first card in the suit, so it represents beginnings. It also means you're thinking with your heart rather than your head."

Sara gave a short barking laugh.

"What?"

"Nothing. What's my future?"

"The Queen of Swords." Eve flipped through the book. "It represents the element of air, which deals with action, courage, and conflict. It can be constructive or destructive, and can even lead to violence."

"I don't like the sound of that," Sara said.

"It says it's considered the most powerful and dangerous suit, but the Queen card also means you've got lots of experience to draw from."

"Your turn." Sara gathered the cards into a pile, her mouth pulled down in a frown. She handed them over and Eve shuffled them, cut the deck, and then handed them back.

Sara held out the cards. "Pick three."

As she leaned forward, Sara said, "What's with the giant bruise on your leg?"

"What?" She looked down and saw a purple-and-green bruise high up on her inner thigh. "Oh, I fell off my new bike." She chose three cards and laid them out.

"All right." Sara turned over the cards and reached for the book. "Wow, you have two Major Arcana cards."

"Is that good or bad?"

"I don't know … let's see. Well, your past is the Five of Pentacles, which is the element of Earth. It's about losing relationships, or lacking faith during tough times. Seriously? That's your past?"

Eve shrugged.

Sara placed a finger on the next card, a naked couple on a bed of dirt. He strained between her thighs, his entire focus on the woman beneath him. Her nipples were dark like Eve's, and pointed with excitement — but her legs stuck out straight instead of curling around him, and one of her hands reached toward the sky as though asking for help. She bet the woman wouldn't get it.

"Your present is the The Lovers, which is a Major Arcana. And it's reversed, which means disharmony, imbalance, and," Sara turned the page, "a misalignment of values. Holy cow, have you been hanging out on a street corner somewhere?"

"Ha-ha." Eve's mouth had gone dry. "I'm more worried about that future one."

"Yeah, Death. But I read that it doesn't actually mean anything bad, not like you're really going to take a long walk off a short pier. Hang on." Sara flipped pages. "It means endings and beginnings. See? That's not so bad. It's about change, transformations, and transitions. Which makes sense. I mean, things *are* changing, right?"

Sara looked at the card again. "Oh, but wait, it's also reversed. So, it actually means the opposite. Like, resistance to changes, or an inability to move on."

"Huh," Eve said. "I don't think I resist changes."

"Maybe not now, but this is your future card, remember?"

"Yeah." She scooped the cards back into the pile. "I have apple slices. Did you bring any snacks? I'm starving." Sara always brought good snacks.

"There's stuff in my bag. Hey, there's Leigh!" She stood up and waved at her brother, who jogged along the trail. Leigh waved in return, and when Sara turned away he blew Eve a kiss.

"Did you hear that rumour about him and Annabeth?" Sara rolled her eyes. "As if. She's only thirteen."

"What about them?" She kept her eyes on the food in Sara's bag.

"The rumour mill in high school is out of hand, and it's so stupid! Don't they care that people can actually get *hurt*? Annabeth's parents called the cops, if you can believe it. Mom opened the door to two police officers on the porch, and she almost passed out. She thought one of us had died."

"What happened?" She gave up any pretense of disinterest.

Sara shrugged. "Not much. Leigh denied it, of course, and I guess Annabeth was denying it, too. But he's getting totally *harassed* at school. He says he can't wait to graduate and get the hell out of there."

"Has he decided where he's applying to college?" Eve asked, trying to sound only casually curious.

Sara shrugged. "He's got a good chance at a football scholarship, if he wants to go back east, or a baseball scholarship if he wants to stay here. I'm betting he heads east, even though he likes baseball better. Hey, are you okay?"

"Yeah, of course. Should we open the bag of pretzels or eat the apple slices first?"

"Pretzels."

The first pretzel turned to sawdust in her mouth, and she swallowed it with a grimace. She put the rest of her handful back in the bag.

"Annabeth's really pretty, isn't she?"

Sara shrugged. "I guess. You don't think he really did something with her, do you?"

"There's no way."

"Yeah," Sara said. "That would be gross."

THIRTY-FIVE

THE KNOCK ON THE DOOR came during dinner. Gabriel was wearing more spaghetti than he was eating, and Eve was trying to salvage his favourite dinosaur T-shirt by scrubbing it in the kitchen sink.

"I'll get it." Button slid out from behind the table.

"Why don't we ever remember to take off your shirt before we eat spaghetti?" Eve blew her hair out of her eyes in frustration, and then turned back to scrubbing.

"Show me how to twirl the noodles again?" Gabriel asked.

"Gabe, I'm trying to save a brontosaurus over here."

"Eve?" Button returned to the kitchen with Detective Baird on her heels. She clutched the collar of her bathrobe in both hands.

"Mrs. Adler." The detective looked dour.

Eve dropped Gabriel's shirt in the sink. "Did you find him? Is he okay?"

Detective Baird gave a pointed look at her son.

"Gabe, go wash your hands and face in the bathroom."

Wide-eyed, Gabriel slid off the bench seat and left the room, walking backward so he could keep an eye on the detective for as long as possible.

"Okay," she said once her son was gone. "What's going on? Have you found him?"

"Yes, we have," Detective Baird said, and then quickly added, "and he's alive."

"Baruch Hashem." Button plopped onto the seat as though her legs had given way.

"Is he okay? Was he in an accident or something?"

"He seems to be fine," Detective Baird said.

"Thank you. Seriously, thank you for finding him."

"Well, I can't say we had much to do with it, in the end," he said. "And I doubt you'll be thanking me in a minute."

"Why is that?"

"He walked into the station this morning and asked for a deal."

"What?"

"What does that mean?" Button asked.

"It means he's willing to testify against your grand-daughter for a lessening of his own sentence."

Button understandably looked flabbergasted. "What? What sentence? What have they done wrong?"

"He's willing to implicate you in all three, Mrs. Adler."

"In all three *what*?" Button asked.

"I need to bring you into the station. I'm willing to do it without the cuffs, for the sake of your family, if you agree to come peacefully."

Eve blinked at him. "You're arresting me?"

"Yes."

"You've filed charges against me?"

"Charges!" Button said. "What are you talking about?"

"It's okay, Button. It's just a mistake." Her voice sounded hollow and she doubted her words were any reassurance to her grandmother.

"I'm afraid it's not a mistake," Detective Baird said. "And yes, charges have been filed against you in two of the deaths, so far."

"Deaths!" Button said. "Whose deaths?"

"Mrs. Adler, I'd like you to come with me peacefully. But I do have officers waiting outside."

"No," she said faintly. "That won't be necessary."

"Good."

"Wait a minute! Just wait one darn minute. Could someone please explain what in the world is going on?" Button said.

She turned to her grandmother, trying to think of what to say to protect her. But she had no lies left to tell, and truthful words had failed her long ago. Button was wild-eyed, pale, and trembling from head to toe.

Detective Baird said, "Leigh is pleading down on two counts of statutory rape —"

"Rape!"

"In exchange for testifying against your granddaughter in the deaths of Thomas Mahoney, Sara Adler, and Donna Gold."

Button's eyes bugged out, and her skin turned an alarming shade of purple. *"Es vert mir finster in di oygn."*

"Button!" She grabbed her grandmother's arm. "Are you okay?"

Button wheezed, clinging to her like a drowning woman.

"Take some deep breaths." Eve went eye-to-eye with her grandmother, willing her to get through this moment. "It's going to be okay. I promise, I promise, I promise. It's going to be okay. Just breathe for me. Just breathe."

"The maple syrup."

"Don't try to talk. Just take some deep breaths, okay?"

Button managed a gasping, shaky breath.

"That's good. Just keep breathing. I need you to keep breathing."

"Mrs. Adler," Detective Baird said.

"Just give me a minute!"

"Would you like me to call an ambulance?" Baird asked.

"No," Button said weakly.

"Are you sure?" Eve asked. "Maybe —"

"No," Button said with more strength. "No ambulance." She took several deep breaths, and the colour in her cheeks dimmed to a less alarming shade.

The women clutched each other's hands, their fear travelling on electrical currents between them.

"Grandma, I promise …"

She wanted to tell Button that it would be okay, that she had nothing to do with their deaths, that it was just a mix-up — anything to make her grandmother feel better. But she couldn't form the words.

"You go and sort this out," Button said. "I'll take care of Gabriel until you get home."

Eve kissed her grandmother's cheek and followed Detective Baird out of the house. Three officers waited for them, and Baird said gruffly, "No cuffs." He led her to the cruiser parked at the curb and opened the rear door for her.

"Mommy!" Gabriel sprinted barefoot from the house and across the damp grass.

Detective Baird nodded. "Go ahead."

"Gabe." She caught him and lifted him into her arms.

"Where are you going, Mommy? Are they bringing you to see Daddy?"

"Kind of. Can you stay with Button while I get some stuff sorted out?"

"When will you come home?"

"I'm not quite sure." She buried her nose in his hair and breathed deeply. His head smelled like tomato sauce and baby shampoo.

"Will you read me a story tonight?"

Her tears disappeared into his mop of curls. "I think Button will have to."

"Mommy, you're not going to that garden I drawed you yet, are you?"

"No, buddy."

"That's good, 'cause I'm not ready."

"Me, neither."

And then Button carried Gabriel back to the house, and Detective Baird guided her into the backseat of the cruiser and closed the door, and she sobbed into the palms of her hands.

As they pulled away, she saw Gabriel standing in the living-room window, waving and blowing kisses. She placed a hand on the car window and imagined she touched her son's round cheek instead of the cold glass. She wondered if she'd ever touch him again.

THIRTY-SIX

Eve's Thirteenth Birthday

WHILE SHE WAITED for Sara to arrive, Eve sat on the bank of the river amid the weeds and prickling marsh grass, in the exact spot where her childhood had died, smoking one of Leigh's joints. It burned her throat and lungs, but she held it in like he'd taught her; she held it in until she had to exhale or explode.

She coughed, a dry and painful rattle, and then took another drag. She'd never smoked a whole one by herself, but today seemed like a good day to start. Her life had begun to spiral the week before, when Sara had confronted her before school. Now, as she watched the river flow steady and grey toward an ocean too far for her to see, she replayed their confrontation for the millionth time.

"I saw you," Sara had said with no preamble, approaching her on the sidewalk in front of her house. They fell into step together, their squat shadows leading the way.

"You saw me where?" On a different day she might have sensed the impending danger, or seen how dark and troubled Sara's eyes were, but that morning Eve was fuzzy-headed and focused on other things.

Both girls had their backpacks over one shoulder. Eve carried a banana for her breakfast. She'd slept late and with five minutes to spare before she had to leave for school, she'd thrown on clothes from the pile on her floor. She'd begged a ride from Donna, but her mother had told her that she needed to face the consequences of her lack of responsibility.

So, fine. A banana for breakfast on the walk to school, nothing packed for her lunch, and she would go through the day with her hair unbrushed and wearing yesterday's clothing. It wouldn't be the first time.

"I *saw* you," Sara repeated, and her tone of voice caught Eve's attention. Also, Sara never came to her house in the morning. They usually met in front of the Adlers' because it was on the way to school.

"What are you talking about?" Eve asked more cautiously.

"Last night."

"Last night?" She feigned confusion while her mind frantically searched for a story that would satisfy Sara's obvious suspicion.

"Yeah."

"What do you think you saw?"

Sara stopped walking, grabbed her hand, and turned to face her. "I saw you with my brother."

"What?" Despite the mental rehearsals she'd done just in case something like this ever happened, her tone and timing were all wrong.

"Stop treating me like I'm an idiot. I saw you together."

She decided to go on the offensive. "You watched us? That's *private*, Sara!" Pretending an anger she was too afraid to actually feel, Eve yanked her hand free and stormed off down the sidewalk, leaving Sara behind.

"Eve!" Sara called after her, but she kept going. Sara was bigger than Eve, but usually moved at a slower pace. She had to shift into a half-jog to catch up, but eventually she did, grabbing Eve by the hand as they reached the front of the school. At that point Sara was red from both exertion and anger.

"I'm not the one doing something wrong, so don't try this crap on me! I know you well enough to know when you're being manipulative."

"Shh." She looked around nervously. Kids turned to watch them.

"No, I won't be quiet! I want an explanation, and I want it *right now*."

She shook her head, feeling tears start to burn her eyes. "Please don't tell anyone, okay? We could get into big trouble."

"But what were you *doing* with him?" Sara asked, looking both disgusted and horrified.

"What did you see?" she asked miserably, deciding she wouldn't admit to anything that she didn't actually have to admit to. Maybe Sara hadn't seen very much, maybe she could still play it off.

"I saw you," Sara said, "around the corner from my house, when I was coming home from my piano lesson. I saw my dad's car parked against the overgrown lot, and I wondered why it was there, so I went over to check it out. It was dark, so I went up really close. And then I saw ..." Sara paused, swallowed hard, and looked at her with wide eyes.

"The windows were all steamy. I knew then that I should walk away, but I didn't. I moved closer instead, and I saw Leigh. I knew he was coming home this weekend, but I didn't know he was coming home so early. And then I remembered those rumours about him and Annabeth last fall. I wanted to see if they were true, so I moved around to the other side of the car to get a closer look."

"Oh." Eve's body was superheating with a toxic mixture of shame and terror, making her skin prickle and her throat burn, making her want to scream and cry and disappear into the sidewalk beneath her — into the pits of hell, where she surely belonged.

"But it wasn't Annabeth. It was *you*. And you ... and you were on top of him ..."

"Okay." She held up her hand for Sara to stop talking.

"Why?" Sara cried, and more kids turned to watch.

"Shh," Eve said again. "Please, Sara, *please* ..."

"Please, what?"

"Please don't tell."

"Are you serious? Are you actually *serious* right now?"

"*Shh.*" It seemed like half the school had stopped to watch them. From the corner of her eye, she could see them whispering and giggling from behind their hands.

"Someone needs to know. A grown-up, *someone*," Sara said.

"Oh no, Sara, *please*."

"This isn't kid stuff."

"I know, but it ... it's private. People won't understand."

"They won't understand because what you're doing is wrong!"

She shook her head. "It's not like that."

"Eve, it's *wrong*."

"But we love each other."

Sara looked horrified. "He's *eighteen*."

"He's going to marry me when I'm old enough. He promised! And then you and I will be *real* sisters."

Sara's mouth dropped open. "Oh, Eve …"

"You can't tell anyone, okay? *Please*?"

Sara shook her head, watching Eve like she didn't know who she was anymore.

"Please."

Sara turned and walked away.

"Sara! *Please!*"

Her friend didn't answer. And she didn't speak to her again until the night before Eve's birthday, when she called to ask her to meet the following morning.

Now she sat like a convicted felon, waiting to see if she'd be given the death penalty or merely life in prison. Neither option was good; one was just faster than the other. During that awful confrontation in front of the school, she'd been too terrified, too ashamed, and too shocked to feel any other emotion. But everything had had a week to fester, and now she was angry. She was furious, in fact. How dare Sara threaten her the way she had?

Eve shook her head, trying to give her friend the benefit of the doubt. She was sure that, given some thought, Sara would realize that telling an adult would ruin not just Eve's and Leigh's lives, but both their families' lives as well. It was too high a price to pay.

284

Taking a final drag on the joint, she flicked it toward the river, where it hissed out against the damp mud. Sara would be there any minute. She was as reliable as death and taxes, as Donna would say.

THIRTY-SEVEN

DETECTIVE BAIRD KEPT YAWNING.

Eve watched him dispassionately, wondering whether there was any point in asking for a lawyer. She knew it was the smart thing to do, but she wasn't sure there was much point. If Leigh had truly thrown her under the bus, and she didn't have much trouble believing that he had, then she was in a big steaming pile of trouble. She didn't have the will to do anything about it at the moment. And really, it was no more than she deserved.

"Is Leigh here? I mean, somewhere in the station?"

Detective Baird gave a small nod, arranging his usual blank notepad and pen on the table beside a large folder that she had to assume was all about her.

"Can I see him?"

"Why would you want to do that?"

"I want to see for myself that he's all right."

He blinked at her curiously. "I would think you'd want to scratch his eyes out."

She sighed. "He's protecting himself. That's what he does best."

Baird yawned widely, his jaw cracking, and then shook his head. "Long day."

"Why don't we get this over with, then?"

"All right. Let's start with Thomas Mahoney." Baird shifted forward in his seat, his knees a foot away from hers. "Mr. Adler says he came upon you in the forest, and saw you clubbing Thomas Mahoney over the head with a tree branch."

Eve stared at him blankly. "What?"

"He says that you told him that Mr. Mahoney had exposed himself to you and his sister, Sara, and that you chased him until he tripped over a tree root. At which point you hit him several times over the head."

"No."

"He says you begged him to get rid of the body. So he did, in a field of quicksilver plants not far from your home. Which is, of course, where Mr. Mahoney's remains were found some years ago."

"I don't understand. Why would he lie like that?"

"What part of Mr. Adler's testimony do you disagree with?"

"Well, it's just … I don't think that's what happened."

"Then why don't you enlighten me?"

She shook her head. "I don't remember."

"Oh, but I think you do." He leaned close enough that he could have shared her oxygen if she'd still been breathing. "I think you remember everything. Everything you've done wrong, everything that's been done to you." He reached over and tapped her on the forehead. "It's all right in there, just waiting to be freed."

The skin he'd touched burned as though seared by a hot poker.

"Look at me," he said.

"Please, no." But she looked.

His eyes. She'd thought his eyes were blue, but she was wrong. They were a deep golden brown. Like amber.

"I can't do this," she said, but it was too late to stop.

Remember. See the truth behind your lies.

The bedrock on which she'd rebuilt her life shifted. A chunk of dirt broke loose and fell away, and then another. Small stones followed, and then larger ones, until giant chunks of her foundation joined the landslide. One fragment at a time, bones and memories were exposed.

"Tell me what happened," Baird said.

Sara grabbed her arm. Her jaw worked in a funny, nervous kind of way. "Keep packing! Pretend everything's normal."

"Sara saw the man, um, Mr. Mahoney, watching us from the forest. It scared her. But I thought it was someone else. Annabeth, actually."

"Annabeth O'Neill? The woman who pressed charges against your husband?"

"Right. She ... we didn't get along with her very well."

"Why did you think it was her?"

"She threw your scooter into the yard of Groaning House last week. Don't you want revenge?"

"She and her friends used to sneak around, following us. And they'd grab our stuff if we left it lying around.

288

Sara and I were having a picnic on the edge of that field of quicksilver plants. Everyone calls it the Foil, because of the colour of the leaves."

The detective made a rolling motion with his hand, encouraging her to continue. He didn't take any notes; he just stared.

With a warrior-like whoop, Eve flew over rocks and tree roots without feeling the ground beneath her feet.

Her foundation kept shifting beneath her, faster and faster. "I chased him. I mean, I thought I was chasing Annabeth and her cronies."

Except it wasn't them. It was a man. His jeans sagged around his hips, and he held them up as he stumbled forward.

She shifted in her seat, wrapping her coat more tightly around herself in a futile effort to get warm. "He tripped and flew through the air, like they do in cartoons. And he hit his head on the trunk of a tree."

"What part of his head?"

"Around here." She touched the left side of her head near the temple.

Blood trickled from a cut on his forehead. His pants gaped open, revealing a tangle of black curls and a flesh-coloured tube that shrank back like a snake retreating.

"Leigh showed up, and Sara was coming, and he didn't want her to see what had happened. He told me to go get his sister and bring her home, and that he'd take care of it."

"Did you check Mr. Mahoney's vitals?"

"I was nine."

"I'll take that as a no," the detective said. "What happened then?"

Wiping rain out of her eyes, she took another look at the man on the ground. Did he blink? Turn his head a little?

"What happened then, Mrs. Adler?"

She scrubbed a trembling hand across her face. "Nothing happened. I left."

"Well." Detective Baird shifted in his seat and the chair gave a squeal of protest. "The problem with your story, Mrs. Adler, is that the evidence aligns better with your husband's description of events."

"What do you mean?"

He pulled a paper out of the file, and held it up for her to see. It was part of an autopsy report. There was a diagram of a skull, with several areas circled in red, and a lot of medical jargon that she didn't understand.

"Mr. Mahoney died of multiple blunt-force trauma wounds to the head."

"Multiple?"

"There *was* an injury consistent with the one you describe, on the left side of the head. But the front part of his skull was also crushed. The medical examiner estimated that he was hit at least three times with a blunt object. Considering the location of the body and the nature of the wounds, the guess was a large branch or stick."

Hunching against the rain, he lifted a thick tree branch from the ground near his feet. His eyes were bloodshot, but dead sober.

"Did you hit Thomas Mahoney in the head?"

"Go now, Eve."

Unable to speak, she shook her head *no*.

"And here I thought we were getting somewhere. Any idea where those wounds came from?"

"I … I swear, I never touched him."

He tucked the medical report back into the folder. "Not very convincing, Mrs. Adler."

She lowered her head to the table and closed her eyes. Her mind raced, and the memories came at her faster than she could process them.

"Let's talk about Sara Adler."

"Oh, please. I can't …"

"You've lived with this guilt for a long time, haven't you? Tell me what happened."

"This wasn't how I expected us to celebrate your thirteenth birthday."

"What were you two arguing about the week before her death?"

"About Leigh," she said. "She saw us in their dad's car, and she confronted me about it."

"Saw you doing what?"

"You know."

"You and Leigh were having sexual relations?"

"Uh-huh."

His chair squeaked. "When did that start?"

"I was eleven."

"And he would have been …" The detective shuffled papers.

"Sixteen."

"Did you ever tell anyone?"

"I saw you. I saw you with my brother."

She sat up, but kept her eyes closed. It was easier that way. "Sara was the only one who knew, but not because I told her."

"Mrs. Adler, you know you could press charges against your husband for statutory rape?"

Eve gave a bitter laugh. "I'll keep that in mind."

"Tell me about the day Sara died."

"She called me the night before and asked if we could meet to talk about things. I'd been waiting all week for the cops to show up on my doorstep."

"You thought you'd be in trouble?"

"Of course," she said.

"Where did you and Sara meet?"

"Near the river, just west of the pier."

"And what did you discuss?"

"She tried to tell me that what was going on with Leigh wasn't my fault."

"She was right."

"I drew pictures of him, dreamed about him being my boyfriend."

"Why am I in so many of your paintings?"

"A childhood crush —"

"He said I led him on."

"You were *eleven*."

"Yeah, but I followed him around like a puppy —"

He leaned forward, hands gripping his knees. "You could have ripped off your clothes and jumped on top of him, and it would have been *his* responsibility to stop you."

Grief welled in her chest, a giant lump that threatened to choke her.

"Many victims feel guilty because they couldn't stop the abuse, or they feel like they somehow caused it to happen. And they feel especially ashamed if they experienced physical pleasure. But that doesn't make it the victim's fault."

"But, I ..."

Her eyes were drawn to the mirror on the far wall of the interrogation room. She wondered if someone watched her from the other side. And if they did, what did they see? A woman or a beast?

"But, what?"

She understood the logic of what he said, but the idea was terrifying. If Leigh was her abuser, then who was she? She'd hurt too many people to be an innocent victim. And what about Gabriel, who was knitted from their cloth? Did that make him an abomination? A sick mistake?

She shook her head. "Sometimes you go too far down a path to be able to change direction."

He watched her for a moment, and then nodded. "All right. Tell me about Sara. You were arguing about this relationship with her brother. And then what?"

THIRTY-EIGHT

Eve's Thirteenth Birthday

THE JOINT WAS HAVING an effect on Eve's head, making everything seem slow and fuzzy, but it hadn't calmed her nerves one bit. There was a ball of fire in the pit of her stomach, a burning pain that nothing could extinguish.

"Hey, Doodlebug." Sara approached unexpectedly from the right instead of the left.

The nickname hurt. She squinted at the river, feeling for a moment like a cowboy in one of those old movies Button watched on late night TV — she was Clint Eastwood, hardened by hard days and even harder nights. "Sara."

After a moment of awkward silence, Sara eased down in the weeds beside her.

"This wasn't how I expected us to celebrate your thirteenth birthday," she said softly.

"No."

Sara sighed. "You're mad."

Eve didn't respond, but her jaw clenched in acknowledgement.

"Well, I'm mad, too. I'm mad at you for getting yourself into this situation, even though …" She choked up and swallowed hard. They sat in silence for several minutes, only a foot apart physically but so much farther by measurements of the heart.

"I've done some reading this week," Sara said.

Eve stole a glance at her friend, feeling her chest tighten with nostalgia. *Of course* Sara had done some reading this week; what else would she do?

"I wanted to tell you that it's not your fault," Sara said. "This book I read, it talks about predators and how they groom their victims by making them feel like they're the only ones who understand them, and that … that you're too young to be able to make a legal decision like this …"

"Legal decision."

"I'm trying to say that Leigh," she stopped and swallowed hard again, "that Leigh … that *you're* the victim. And he's twisted things so much, you don't even know it."

She shook her head, unable to find the words to explain how Sara had gotten it all wrong. But every argument kept floating away into the fog of her brain. She probably shouldn't have smoked that joint.

"So, I wanted to tell you that I'm going to go to the police station this afternoon. To tell them what I saw."

Groaning, Eve slumped forward until her head hit her knees.

"You're not going to get in trouble. I promise! This book says you've done nothing wrong. But Leigh …" Every time Sara said her brother's name, there was a crack of heartbreak in her voice. "Leigh needs help."

"He won't get help, he'll get jail."

"If you know that, then you must know he's doing something wrong," Sara said.

"I know *they'll* think it's wrong."

It hit her then, how badly she'd failed him. She'd promised to protect him no matter what, and now look at the mess they were in. He would feel so hurt, so betrayed. It would ruin everything. And Donna would find out. And Button! She imagined the look of sadness and disappointment on her grandmother's face, and it was all suddenly too much. She let out a huge, wracking, full-body sob.

"Oh, Eve." Sara laid a hand on her back.

She sprang to her feet as though Sara's touch had electrified her, and backed away.

"Where are you going?"

"To take a long walk off a short pier." A joke of their childhood, but she wasn't joking. In fact, it seemed like the best idea she'd had in a long time. She pushed through the tangle of weeds and marsh grass, and once she hit the trail she began to run.

"Wait!" Sara screamed after her. "Eve, what are you *doing*?" She could hear Sara running behind her, but Eve was faster. She always had been.

The pier wasn't far, but she gasped for breath by the time she reached it, her lungs burning from grief and dope. Her feet thundered across the wooden planks, the pier rocking beneath her. Blinded by tears, Eve plowed through a flock of crows — or was it a murder of crows?

Sara would have known — and they took off before her in a feathered exodus of squawking displeasure.

She leaned over the railing at the edge of the pier, wiping at her eyes and trying to judge the drop. The wood smelled of sunbaked resin, a ghost of summer. A log boom floated just beyond where she stood and the water lapped peacefully against the logs.

Eve took one deep breath and then hoisted herself up, leaning on the railing. She lifted her right leg over, straddled the railing for a breathless moment, and then pulled her left leg over to join it. She slid down until her feet hit the ledge that ran along the outside of the pier. It was maybe a foot wide. She wrapped her arms around the vertical slat in front of her and held on for dear life. She was starting to think this was a bad idea.

"Eve!" Sara's footsteps thundered along the wooden pier. "Oh my God, what are you *doing*?"

She was blind with tears, but she was too scared to let go and wipe her eyes. She rubbed her face against her shoulder instead.

"Climb back over! You're going to get yourself killed!"

She looked up at Sara, her only friend. "That's the whole point."

"No!" Above her, Sara's eyes were round blue marbles of horror. "Don't you dare!"

"He's never going to forgive me for this!"

"What? What are you talking about?" Sara sobbed now, too. Her tears fell on Eve's upturned face, landed on her cheeks and lips, salt mixing with salt.

"How can he go on once this comes out? It's going to ruin him!"

"Him?" Sara cried. "What about *you*?"

"I'm nothing! Everybody knows that. Even my own mom knows that!"

"Oh, Eve, that's not true! Please, climb back over." Sara reached down.

"If I'm gone, then Leigh can't be charged with anything. He can't go to jail."

"No!"

"I'm sorry I hurt you. I never wanted you to get hurt."

"No, Eve," Sara sobbed. "Please don't do this."

She looked down at the river. It seemed like a much bigger drop than it had before she climbed over the railing. She could see the rush of the current, and wondered how long it would take to get to the ocean. Would she still be alive when fresh water mixed with salt?

A shadow moved above her, and she craned her neck to look. Sara swung awkwardly over the railing.

"Are you crazy? What are you doing?"

"Coming to get you!"

"No! Get back up there."

"Only if you do." Sara swung her second leg over.

"Damn it, Sara." Eve shifted left, moving slowly along the narrow ledge toward the corner pylon. Sara's feet found the ledge, and she wheezed in terror. Heights were not Sara's thing.

The corner pylon had a metal ladder along its outer edge. Without thought, she climbed onto it and started to descend. She expected Sara to lose her nerve and climb back over the railing, but to her surprise Sara kept going, moving slowly along the ledge and easing onto the ladder ten rungs above her.

"Stop following me!"

"Stop running away!"

"You're going to get hurt."

"Then climb back up if you're so worried about me."

It was like some weird game of chicken. But Eve wasn't going to be the one to back down. She descended to the bottom rung, eight or ten feet above the river. She now had two choices: She could climb back up the ladder and follow Sara back to safety and a miserable existence, or she could jump onto the logs below.

She jumped.

Her left foot hit first, sliding between two logs and twisting painfully. She fell backward and landed hard on rough, wet wood. Splinters pierced the skin of her legs and backside like a million jagged needles. She screamed, and above her Sara reacted by screaming, as well. But she kept climbing down the ladder. She reached the bottom rung and hesitated, peering under her arm at the drop.

"Don't do it!"

Now that Eve was on the boom, she could feel how it rocked and swayed back and forth in the current. It was pure luck that she'd jumped at the right moment. If Sara picked wrong, she'd land in the water instead of on the logs.

Apparently Sara had no intention of listening to Eve. She closed her eyes and let go of the ladder's rung. She neither landed in the water nor on the logs, but managed to do something in between. Her shoulder hit the edge of the log boom and Eve heard the crack of a bone breaking even above Sara's blood-curdling scream. Sara catapulted sideways and sank beneath the water.

S.M. FREEDMAN

"Sara!" Eve rolled onto her hands and knees.

Sara's head popped up, hair and water streaming into her eyes. "My arm!"

"Sara, hang on!" Eve scrambled up and over splintery, slippery logs, moving frantically to the edge.

"My arm! My arm!"

By the time she reached the edge of the boom, Sara was twenty feet downstream.

"Sara!" On her belly, she slid over the end log and eased into the water. It was bitingly, numbingly cold. The current pushed her legs out from under her, trying to sweep her away. Clinging to the log, she looked back over her shoulder. Sara was maybe thirty feet downstream. If she was going to reach her, she needed to get moving.

Sara was still screaming, wasting all the energy she should have used to try to swim to shore. She seemed really far away.

Could Eve reach her? And if she did, would she have the strength to fight the current and pull Sara to shore? Or would they both drown?

Gasping in fear, she tried to ignore the slippery part of her mind that had recognized the opportunity being presented to her — on a silver platter, so to speak. The part that said that all she needed to do to keep Leigh safe was to stay put.

Eve pressed her face against the log, tasting the salt of Sara's tears. She heard her screams for a long time after they stopped.

THIRTY-NINE

"YOU DIDN'T WANT HER TO TELL THE POLICE."

Eve ran a finger over the graffiti on the table. "I know that looks like motive."

"It's mighty convenient."

"I never wanted her to die. She was my dearest friend. My *only* friend."

"I'm not convinced you're as innocent as you say you are when it comes to Sara's death."

All she needed to do to keep Leigh safe was to stay put. She shook her head, trying to break loose of the memories.

"But I don't yet have enough evidence to lay charges. You *are* being charged with second-degree murder in the death of Thomas Mahoney. We know there'd been complaints about him from other kids in the neighbourhood, so I'm inclined to believe your husband on this one. I'm thinking Mahoney exposed himself to you, as Leigh said. Then maybe you came upon him sometime later. Maybe he was asleep. Defenceless. You saw an opportunity."

"Opportunity."

"To crush his skull with a stick."

"I didn't. I swear."

"Leigh saw you do it."

Eve shook her head.

"And you're being charged with first-degree murder in the death of your mother, Donna Gold. That means premeditated."

She'd been expecting it, but nevertheless felt a cold wave of shock wash over her.

"Let's talk about your mom," Detective Baird said.

"My client spent years being molested by her own father. You think you've had such a terrible life? You should be grateful for everything I've given you."

"I'd like a lawyer."

He sighed and pushed away from the table. Reaching into his pocket, he came out with a rusting tin of maple syrup sealed in an evidence bag.

"Your husband gave us this. We're having the contents tested for about a billion different types of poison."

He moved to the door, then paused and turned back to Eve.

"I believe you are the victim of long-term abuse, and I have sympathy for you in that regard. No child deserves to have their innocence stolen from them."

Tears burned her eyes, but she didn't let them fall.

"I also think you're capable of love, at least when it comes to your grandmother and your son. And maybe you even cared about Sara, in your own way."

She shifted in her chair but kept her gaze on the table in front of her.

"But you also showed your true nature before the interview even started. Do you know one of the surest signs that someone's a sociopath?"

She didn't answer.

"They don't yawn when someone else does, because they aren't capable of feeling empathy."

She looked up and met his gaze. She'd been right the first time. His eyes were blue.

"Detective Baird?" The officer poked his head into the interrogation room. "Oh, sorry. I thought he was in here."

"He's gone to charge up my electric chair."

The officer blinked at her, showing no sign of a sense of humour. "We don't have the death penalty here, ma'am."

"Officer Smith, what can I do for you?" Detective Baird came up behind him carrying another Styrofoam cup of coffee.

"We were just notified that Mrs. Adler's grandmother has been taken to St. Vincent's."

"What?" Eve jumped up, causing the chair to fall with a clatter behind her. "What happened? Is she all right?"

"I'm not sure, ma'am," the officer said. "They seem to think it was a stroke."

"Oh my God! I need to go see her."

"You're under arrest, Mrs. Adler. And no bail has been set."

"Oh, no." She turned to plead with Detective Baird. "Can't you take me there in handcuffs? Please, I need to see her. What if she ..." She choked up, unable to finish the sentence.

"I simply can't —"

"Gabriel! Where's my son? Is he okay?"

The officer shook his head. "I'm sorry, ma'am. I didn't hear anything about a boy."

"The paramedics probably brought him to the hospital in the ambulance," Detective Baird said. "They'll have called Child Services to take care of him."

"He'll be terrified. Please let me go see him."

Detective Baird shook his head, but she could see he was wavering.

"Please. Can you imagine what he's going through right now?"

Sighing, Detective Baird said, "All right. Let's go."

They went in through Emergency, the only hospital doors that were open in the middle of the night.

Detective Baird hadn't put her in handcuffs, but he'd brought Officer Smith with them and the officer kept a hand on her arm to prevent her from running. She thought it was ridiculous. Even if she'd been physically able to outrun them, where on earth would she go? The most important people in her life were somewhere within the sterile walls of this hospital.

They passed a woman clutching a croupy child to her chest, a family holding hands with their heads bent in prayer, and a man talking to a police officer while holding an ice pack to the side of his face.

"Wait over there," Detective Baird said as he went to the reception desk.

Officer Smith led her to a row of hard plastic chairs, giving a nod of solidarity to the officer interviewing the man with the ice pack. The officer returned the nod, and then continued his questioning.

"Mr. Gauthier. We're running tests on the blood sample you've provided, so you might as well tell me now what we're going to find."

The man holding the ice pack sighed and looked away. "Do you think that girl's all right?"

The officer's lips pursed, and he seemed to be reining in his anger. "Not in the slightest, sir. Were you using drugs this evening?"

"Is someone going to look at my head? What if I die of a brain bleed or something while you're sitting here harassing me? That won't look very good, will it?"

"You've had a CAT scan. You'll get the results soon."

"What about my Lexus?"

"What about it?"

"Are they towing it? I want it towed to my mechanic, not some overpriced scam artist."

"Your car is currently being processed as evidence in a crime scene," the officer said. "I'm not sure when you'll be getting it back."

"A crime scene! That's ridiculous."

Detective Baird moved away from the reception desk and nodded his head for them to come over. Eve jumped up and moved toward him.

"Well? What's going on?"

"Your grandmother's had a stroke. They're admitting her into the ICU."

"Oh, no!"

Officer Smith grabbed her arm to prevent her from falling over.

"It will be a while before they know the severity of the stroke, or what the prognosis is for her recovery."

"Poor Button."

"I spoke to one of the paramedics who brought her in, and he said she showed signs of full paralysis along one side of her body, but she tried to speak to them, which is possibly a good sign. Also, they attended the scene within minutes of her calling 911, so she received medical attention very quickly. This is good news."

"Okay," Eve tried to say, but it came out as a sob.

"There's one other thing." Detective Baird's tone was strange.

She looked up at him. "What?"

"Neither the nurse at the reception desk, nor the paramedic who brought in your grandmother, know anything about your son."

"What?"

"I've radioed for patrol officers to go to your house. I suspect he was asleep in his bedroom when your grandmother had the stroke, and by the time the paramedics arrived she wasn't able to tell them that he was in the house."

She cupped a hand over her mouth. "Oh, no!"

"He's probably still asleep," the detective said.

"Oh, I hope so."

"Officers will confirm that he's safe, and wait there until someone from Child Services arrives."

Eve erupted in wracking sobs. Through the blur of tears, she saw the man with the ice pack watching her. Officer Smith handed her a clump of tissues with which she tried to mop her face and blow her nose. Detective Baird produced a blanket from somewhere and wrapped it around her shoulders. They led her over to a bank of plastic chairs on the far side of the waiting area.

Eventually, she calmed down enough to ask, "May I go in to see her?"

"Once they've got her admitted and stabilized, they'll let you have a few minutes with her."

"Okay." She pulled the blanket up around her chin.

"Ma'am, can I get you some water?" Officer Smith asked. "Or something hot to drink?"

"Some tea would be nice, thank you."

Detective Baird eased into the seat beside her and picked up a magazine.

"They'll let you know how Gabriel is doing when they get to my house?"

"As soon as they get there."

"Okay."

The man with the ice pack still watched her, like she was a car wreck on the side of the road or a natural disaster that was impossible to look away from. She did her best not to meet his eyes.

Officer Smith returned with her tea, and Eve held it with both hands and sipped, relishing the flicker of warmth it provided. Her teeth chattered, and the cold had sunk so deep into her bones that she wasn't sure if she'd be able to stand up when the time came.

"Shouldn't they be at my house by now?" she asked at some point, but Officer Smith had left and Detective Baird stared dopey-eyed at his magazine.

The praying family moved along, and the mom with the croupy child was shown into an examination room and then ushered out minutes later with instructions to let the child breathe the damp outside air. The man with the ice pack kept watching her.

"Mrs. Adler?" A doctor stood before her, her pale hair slicked back into a ponytail, her expression grim.

Eve found she could stand up after all. "Is she okay? What's happening?"

"You may come see her now," the doctor told her. "She's stable, but unresponsive. It was a major stroke, and we'll get a better idea about her potential for recovery in the next twenty-four hours. But as you know, she's elderly, and I think it's best if you prepare yourself for the possibility that she may not wake up from this."

"Poor Button!" Eve said, hands over her mouth. "This is all my fault."

"A stroke can happen at any time. It's nobody's fault."

She didn't bother explaining to the doctor that she was wrong. "Where is she?"

"Follow me."

She turned to get Detective Baird's permission, but he was gone.

"Did you see where the man who was sitting beside me went?"

"No," the doctor said. "Would you like to wait for him?"

She hesitated, and then shook her head. "No, I'd like to see my grandma."

She followed the doctor through a set of double-doors marked *ICU* and past a central nursing station. As they passed, one of the nurses waved a clipboard, clearly requesting a consultation. The doctor raised a hand to the nurse in acknowledgement and said, "She's in Room 201. It's at the end of the hall and around the corner. I'll come by in a bit to answer any questions."

"Thank you."

The ICU was quiet save the beep of machinery and the squeak of wheels on linoleum as a janitor rolled a mop bucket down the hall. The light in the hallway was dim, greyed-out, and strangely one-dimensional. Eve moved silently, her muscles stiff with cold and tension.

She passed the janitor, turned the corner, and stopped dead. Button sat on a plastic chair outside the door to Room 201. She wore her grey wool coat, the one with the red buttons, and her hair tangled around her head as though she'd been running her fingers through it repeatedly. Her head hung down, chin to chest.

"Button?" She sprinted down the hall to her grandmother. "What are you doing out of bed?"

Button didn't look up as she approached. Her eyes were closed, her makeup long gone, her tears like rivers on her cheeks. Her nose was red and raw, her face swollen with emotion, and her frail body shook with such violence it was a wonder she didn't fall off her chair.

"Button?" She squatted down in front of her grandmother. "You shouldn't be out of bed, it's not safe for you to be walking around."

Button didn't respond.

Eve reached out to her. "Hey, it's okay. You've had a stroke, but considering you're already up and about, I'm betting you're going —"

Her hand passed right through Button's leg, and through the chair below it. She screamed in shock and fell backward, landing in a sprawl on the linoleum floor. It didn't hurt a bit.

"Button?" she asked, and then more faintly, *"Grandma?"*

Button didn't look up, didn't respond, didn't seem to hear her at all. But from inside Room 201, she did get a response.

"Eve," the woman called.

"No. I don't want to talk to you." But, even as she said it, she stood and walked past her sobbing grandmother, moving inexorably toward Room 201. It reminded her of the recurring dream she'd had as a child, the one where she was locked on a chairlift as it descended into the pits of hell. She was as powerless to turn around now as she had been in those dreams.

The room was lit by the dim glow of the street lamps in the parking lot two stories below. She could see the expanse of dark pavement and empty parking stalls pock-marked by pools of light. A curtain was drawn most of the way around the bed, and she moved through the gap.

The figure on the bed lay unmoving, covered in wires and tubes and bandages. Eve edged around the foot of the bed, around the medical equipment stacked beside it, and up toward the head.

She saw the curls first, dark tendrils on a white pillow. One side of the head was crushed like a melon dropped on the sidewalk, leaving the other side swollen and deformed.

The mouth was a mess of broken teeth and dried blood. The eyes were open and aware.

In that moment, her consciousness split in two. One part stood beside the bed, staring down at her own broken face, feeling the cold and nothing more. The other part of her lay on the bed, seeing nothing but feeling everything — she felt every fracture, every bruise, and every laceration. She felt every body part that was broken beyond repair.

"What's happening?" she asked.

From the bed, the other Eve replied, *"We're dying, of course,"* and her voice was the same voice she'd heard in every dream and every tangled memory and every broken moment since the accident. It was the voice of Eve, haunting her with all the truths she didn't want to know.

"Why … how can we be dying?" she asked.

"The accident. With the silver Lexus."

"What?"

Eve recalled the main in the waiting room. *"I want it towed to my mechanic, not some overpriced scam artist."*

"But that was years ago. I survived. I *recovered*."

"No, Eve." A man stepped from the shadows and moved into the light cast by the lamp above the bed. His fedora was tipped at a jaunty angle across his forehead, dripping rain onto the shoulders of his overcoat. His eyes were just like hers, like Button's, like Donna's. "Time is fluid in the silver. But the accident happened today, and today your body will die."

As he'd done in front of the coffee shop, he held out his hand. His ring finger was missing from knuckle to tip. "It's time to come with me."

"I can't do that. I have a child —"

"You don't."

"Gabriel —"

"Is a boy who might have been," the man said.

The woman on the bed let out a mournful moan. Eve looked down at her broken body, watched a tear roll down the swollen cheek, and looked back up at the man in the fedora. "No, my son —"

"Your son is a dream you painted on a dying canvas. But it's time to put down the brush."

"That's not true. I married Leigh. We have a child!"

His eyes were soft with sympathy, but the hand he extended to her remained firm. "You haven't seen Leigh since the day of your mother's funeral. The marriage, the art shows, even your grandmother's stroke, they're all part of this story you created to shield yourself from the truth."

"I need to see my baby. Please tell me where he is."

"Eve, your son's not real."

The compassion she saw in his eyes was unbearable, and she buckled under the weight of it. "Oh, please, don't say that. He's … he's just the sweetest little guy … and he's so smart …"

"This life is over, Eve. You must come with me."

Her legs gave way, and she crumpled to the floor. "My baby. I don't want to lose my baby."

The man sat down beside her and placed his hand over hers. He held on while she fell apart.

Eventually, she was able to speak. "Please help me, I don't want to die."

Surely the kindness she saw in his eyes was a lie. She didn't deserve kindness any more than she deserved forgiveness.

She sat up straight. "The girl in the playground. She said we get to choose."

"No, my dear. That's how you get stuck. Your soul needs to face its reflection, to be cleansed."

"I'm too scared," she said, acknowledging the bitter heart of her even more bitter truth. Though she'd lived with her guilt every day, she couldn't see a way to die with it.

"Just let me go back. *Please.* I'll do better. I'll be a good mom. I'll stay away from Leigh."

"You need to face what you've done," he said.

She shook her head. "I can't. Oh, please, I can't do that."

"It's the only way."

"But then … will I go to hell?"

He didn't answer, just watched her with those kind amber eyes. Maybe if she'd seen that kind of love in Donna's eyes even once, she would have had the strength not to make such a horrid mess of her life.

"No. I can't."

"Eve," he said.

With enormous effort, she pulled away from him.

"Don't do this," he said.

She hauled herself off the floor and looked down at the broken body on the hospital bed. The eyes had glazed, and the skin was grey. It was no more than a useless husk.

The girl in the playground had said she could choose.

"Eve, don't," he said.

"I'm sorry."

With the swiftness of a dream, she flew back through the gap in the curtain, and out the door of Room 201, and past her weeping grandmother. She hurried down the hall, and by the nurses' station, and out of the ICU, and through the waiting room, and out the sliding doors of the hospital.

Outside, she found morning light that was cool and lemony — her favourite light in which to paint. She was a talented artist; she could turn a blank canvas into anything she wanted.

She needed to get home, where Button waited with arms wide open to receive her. She'd bury her grief and fear in her grandmother's embrace, and when Gabriel awoke from his nap, they'd take him to the park. No, not the park. Maybe they'd go to a movie, or to get ice cream. Yes, ice cream sounded good. She could get a chocolate sundae with extra whipped cream.

Eve ran so hard she felt the wind on her face. And when the man in the fedora called her name, she ran faster. Seconds or centuries later, she passed the entrance to the Crook. A woman waited for her in the quicksilver, eager to tell her all the things she didn't want to know.

She didn't stop. Her home was just ahead. She pounded up the sidewalk, across the wet dew on the front lawn, and around the side of the house. She leapt up the stairs to the kitchen door, turned the handle, and yanked the door open.

"Button," she said as she entered the kitchen. "I'm home!"

The door closed behind her, and she was back in the interrogation room at the police station. Detective Baird sat in his accustomed spot, his hands on his legs. A large folder, a notepad, and a pen lay on the table beside him.

"Come join me, Mrs. Adler."

"Oh, please, *no*."

"Have a seat."

"Where's my family?" she said, even as she took the seat across from him. It seemed she had no choice, after all.

"Look at me," Baird said.

She didn't want to, but she looked. "Please don't make me do this. I'm so *scared*."

"It's time to face your reflection," Baird said.

As she watched, amber bled into the blue of his eyes. His face thinned, and his hair became a gossamer cloud around his head.

"Let's talk about your mother," said the man in the fedora.

FORTY

Eve's Seventeenth Birthday

"I KNOW YOU THINK you've got some talent, but I'm not willing to fund this starving artist lifestyle you're setting yourself up for."

It was three in the morning, but Donna was still drinking coffee. The kitchen table in front of her was heaped with papers, and she scribbled notes on a yellow legal pad. She didn't look up, so Eve spoke to the top of her head. Grey strands mixed with black at the part in her hair.

"I'm not planning to be a *starving* artist."

"There's no other kind."

"But I'm good. *Really* good. You must know that!"

"Art's not my thing." Donna half-stood to reach across the table. She unearthed a thick folder from the bottom of a pile, sat back down, and flipped through it.

"Did you bounce the cheque on purpose?"

"Why would I do that?"

"Because you don't want to waste your money on art school."

"Well, you make a good point. It is *my* money." She ran a highlighter over a paragraph of text and then made a note on her legal pad.

"When I did the program to graduate early, you promised you'd pay for my first two years of college."

"Emily Carr is not college. Eve, are you done? I have closing arguments in the morning, and I'm exhausted."

"I'm going to reapply for next year."

Donna sighed and closed the folder. She opened her giant wheeled briefcase and stuffed papers and folders into it. "I won't stop you."

"No. You won't."

She finally looked at her daughter, her amber-coloured eyes cool and appraising. "But I also won't pay for it. And you'll have to find somewhere else to live, too."

"What?"

"Quiet, or you'll wake your grandmother. I was going to tell you this soon, anyway. There's a real estate agent stopping by this weekend. We're going to sell the house."

"What are you talking about? This is Button's house. It's not yours to sell!"

Donna gave a tight smile. "Your grandmother is needing more and more care. I've got her name on the waiting lists of several assisted-living facilities. Selling the house will help pay for that."

"I don't … what the hell are you talking about? Button doesn't need to live in some old folks home. She's *fine*."

"I'm not having this argument with you," Donna said. "I'm sure you mean well, but these are adult decisions."

"And where am I supposed to go?"

Donna shrugged as though she couldn't have cared less.

"Wait. No, this isn't right."

"At the end of the day it's not your decision to make, Eve."

She practically jumped up and down with fury. "It's not your decision to make, either! This isn't *your* house!"

"It's my responsibility to make these tough choices. I have power of attorney."

"But —"

"And don't go running to Button for financial help, either. Between funding your trip to Paris and paying for the courses you're taking this year, she's scraping the bottom of the barrel."

"What am I supposed to do? I can't save that much money in a year. Especially if I have to pay rent somewhere, too."

"If it's important to you, I suspect you'll find a way."

Donna closed her briefcase and carried her coffee mug to the sink. She rinsed it and placed it in the dishwasher.

"I'm going to take a shower and get a few hours of sleep. You should sleep, too. You're getting bags under your eyes."

"I'm not tired."

"Then put on the dishwasher once I'm done with my shower. And make a pot of oatmeal for the morning."

After her mother left the kitchen, Eve stood frozen for a moment. Then she stormed after her.

Catching up to Donna in the hall, she hissed, "Why are you such a bitch?"

Donna turned in her bedroom doorway. There was something shiny and dangerous in her eyes, something that looked a lot like tears.

Hissing back, Donna said, "Yes. You have the worst mother in the world. Little do you know how much I've protected you."

"Protected me from *what*?"

"From knowing the pain I felt raising a child of rape." Her mother's voice was so quiet, so matter-of-fact, that it took several heartbeats for her words to sink in.

"What?"

"Shh."

"But you said —"

"I said I used a sperm donor, but that was a lie. I was raped. By someone I trusted a great deal. Someone I really cared about. And every time I look at you, I see his face. I feel him hurting me."

Eve reached for the wall to keep herself upright. At that moment, everything she'd ever believed about her life flipped upside down, so she could see the dark underbelly. The things she'd always felt from her mother but never understood — the contempt, the alienation, the anger — it all suddenly made sense.

"And you hate me for it."

Tears fell down the marble of Donna's cheeks. "You're a part of him."

"But I'm a part of *you*, too. Can't you love me for that?"

"I've given you a good life. I've done everything I can for you."

"You really think so?"

"My client spent years being molested by her own father. You think you've had such a terrible life? You should be *grateful* for everything I've done for you."

Without another word Donna left Eve in the hallway, staring blankly at the closed bedroom door. A storm brewed inside her, electric and deadly, and it felt so good.

"What you've done for me," she said, tasting the words on her tongue. They burned like acid. "Is teach me to hate myself."

She looked at the paintings Button had proudly hung, like a timeline, along the hallway. Her whole life spread across the walls before her, and it was all a lie. Near the kitchen were a couple of Paris scenes, their paint still slightly wet. Farther along were paintings of the river on New Year's Day, and the Foil in springtime with its yellow flowers in bloom.

She approached the one of the Adlers' backyard. It was one of her earliest paintings, done in the backyard before she even had her art studio. She barely looked at it anymore. The grass needed some work. It was too one-dimensional, too green. The flowers looked like daisies, but they had blood in their roots. She wondered if they were still there.

She moved back into the kitchen, seeing the room with the eyes of a stranger. Her mother's briefcase stood near the door. The kitchen cart was wedged beside the stove. It was stacked with cooking utensils, a large bottle of olive oil, salt, pepper, and other frequently used spices. Donna banged a hip into the corner of the cart at least once a week, but Button refused to let her move it.

The Formica counter was chipped and cracking in several places. The kitchen table was pale and scratched from years of use, empty except for Donna's tin of maple syrup.

As though in a dream, she placed water and oats into a heavy lidded pot and set it on the stove at a low simmer. When she heard Donna's shower start with a rumble of pipes, she turned on the dishwasher. Then she grabbed a Ziploc bag and a pair of rubber gloves from under the sink, stuffed her feet into a pair of old running shoes, and slipped out the kitchen door into darkness.

FORTY-ONE

Eve's Twenty-Seventh Birthday

THE RAIN HIT as she left the bakery, and it meant business. It pummelled her blind and deaf, and by the time she ducked under the Starbucks awning to wait for the southbound bus, she was soaked to the skin. Her feet squished inside her boots and her hair dripped into her eyes. Even worse, the cake box sagged from her fingers by a twist of string, waterlogged and threatening collapse. Button would be ticked.

Lightning cracked, and across the street the courthouse's glass atrium mirrored the blinding flash. Eve wondered if Donna still haunted those darkened courtrooms, unable to sleep until justice had been served.

A man approached, wearing a long overcoat and a fedora. He stepped through the sheets of rain pouring from the awning, and paused at the door to the coffee shop. He reached for her hand, and she saw that his ring finger was gone from knuckle to tip.

"Eve, it's time."

She heard the screech of tires in the distance and the pounding of rain on the awning, like a drumbeat calling her home.

His eyes were the colour of dark amber, what Donna had called fool's gold. She saw herself in their reflection, both the beast and the broken woman, and remembered everything.

"Don't worry, I'll be with you," he said.

"But where am I going?"

She didn't really expect an answer, and he didn't give one. He just smiled his kind smile.

"I'm sorry," she said. "I really am sorry for what I did."

"Then take my hand."

She thought of Gabriel, the boy who should have been; and Sara, who'd died before her first kiss; and Donna, who'd seen a rapist in her daughter's eyes. She thought of Leigh, who'd stolen her childhood; and Button, who'd loved her with blind certainty.

And she thought of Eve, the girl who'd smeared make-up on the blank wall in their hallway, creating a universe of unicorns and fairies and rainbows.

She'd spent too many years trying to paint a better life, and she'd grown weary. So, she took his hand.

Acknowledgements

THANK YOU TO the amazing team at Dundurn Press. To acquisitions editor Rachel Spence for loving this story and being its champion; to project editor Jenny McWha for her expert guidance; to Shannon Whibbs for her thorough and thoughtful editing; to art director Laura Boyle and the rest of her team for designing a cover so gorgeous I gasped when I first saw it; and to Stephanie Ellis and the rest of the team for their brilliant marketing.

To Kim Lionetti for being the most amazing agent. Thank you for continuing to push, uplift, and guide me. You are the stuff of legends.

To Hannah for being the first (and second and third) editor of this book. I never feel confident in my words until you've run your eagle eyes over them. But more than that, thank you for your friendship. I love you forevermuch.

My eternal gratitude to my family. To my husband, Jon, for being the coffee in my cream. Thank you for supporting this crazy dream of mine. Thank you for eagerly reading each of my first drafts, no matter how much sleep you lose in the process. To my mom, Sheryl, for being the smartest mystery reader I'll ever know. I haven't managed to slip one past you yet, but I'll keep trying. Thank you also for being my art advisor on this project. To my children, Asher and Ivy, for breaking my every notion of what parenting would be. You two are my greatest teachers and my greatest loves. Thank you for choosing me.

About the Author

 **S.M. FREEDMAN** studied at the American Academy of Dramatic Arts in New York and spent years working as a private investigator on the not-so-mean streets of Vancouver before returning to her first love: writing. Her debut novel, *The Faithful*, is an international #1 Amazon bestseller. It reached the quarterfinals in the Amazon Breakthrough Novel Award, and was selected by *Suspense Magazine* as a "Best Debut of 2015." The sequel, *Impact Winter*, was published in 2016 and also became an international Amazon bestseller. S.M. is a proud member of Sisters in Crime, Crime Writers of Canada, International Thriller Writers, and Mystery Writers of America.